THE HUNGER WAS RISING WITHIN HER . . .

From her throat a low growl emerged, almost like a cat's purring. The boy's face went momentarily slack.

She reached out to him, placing her hands on his chest. Then she dragged her nails down his stomach. His skin sliced easily and hung off him in strips. A torrent of blood sluiced down beneath his legs and jeans.

He roared in agony, leaping convulsively from the log. She grabbed him beneath the chin and lowered him. She reached into a pocket on her vest and retrieved the small, glittering blade.

"You said you had some time," she growled, leaning toward him.

He shook his head, trying to scramble away from her. "No, please, I'm sorry . . ."

She leaned over him, gripping his hair and pinning him down.

"So let's have some fun with this," she said, trying to smile around her teeth.

With the blade she sliced a clown's smile in his throat. And as he gurgled, struggling ever more feebly, she began to use her teeth.

BEASTS

STEPHEN R. GEORGE

ZEBRA BOOKS
KENSINGTON PUBLISHING CORP.

To my mother and father.

ZEBRA BOOKS

are published by

Kensington Publishing Corp.
475 Park Avenue South
New York, NY 10016

First printing: June, 1989

Printed in the United States of America

PROLOGUE

Jesus Murphy listened patiently as the footsteps drew closer. The fingers of his right hand caressed the cool metal of the knife in his pocket. He had been waiting here in the dark alley by Kroeger's Foods on Fillmore Street for almost an hour, melting into the shadows, becoming part of the scenery. This was a good spot. A rich neighborhood, but dark. Rich usually meant bright lights and clean pavements. He felt lucky.

He had taken the train from the west side just after noon and had spent most of the day walking around, thinking. It was nice to be away from the leaning buildings, the stink of Hispanic cooking, the dirty faces on the corners who knew him by name.

"Jesus Murphy!" They pronounced his name like the white men did, like their fucking god. Not *Heysoo*, as was intended. And they always added an exclamation mark. He hated his name almost as much as he hated the man who had given it to him.

His mother was a non-English-speaking immigrant who had married a swarthy Irish cop at least twice her age named Shaun Murphy. She had given her only son a first name she admired, Jesus, not realizing the cruel joke she was playing on him. His father must have laughed when she chose the name, laughed inside and never said anything. Let the kid grow up and find out for himself. Jesus Murphy! But the fat, stinking Irish son of a bitch had died before his son ever got to thank him, something Jesus had regretted ever since. He had longed to slit his father's throat, but a bad heart had let the bastard go easily. Jesus Murphy hoped there was a hell.

At fifteen he was just over five feet tall, gaunt-faced and bright-eyed. He had taken the lives of two human beings since he turned fifteen, both times in the process of relieving his victims of their money. The second time he had realized that he enjoyed the killing as much as he did spending the money afterward. There was something seriously erotic about watching another man's soul slip away. For weeks he felt himself infused with a power he could hardly comprehend, as if the soul he had taken had somehow come into him. Strengthened him.

Tonight he was driven more by his need for cash than by the other. Money had a power of its own, a power that was tangible on the street. He listened to the approaching footsteps with anticipation, and when the silhouette appeared in the mouth of the alley he darted out, knife glittering in the darkness.

His victim tonight was of a type that Jesus truly hated. About thirty years old, well-dressed, neatly groomed. From the television he had gleaned the word *Yuppie*, and it was a term he applied to anybody who wore a tie. This guy was a Yuppie. His face, pale

6

and clean-shaven, was slack with surprise. Jesus grinned.

"Hey, man, how much money you got? Gimme your wallet."

The Yuppie stood still, mouth hanging open in astonishment, staring at Jesus in open confusion. "I said, gimme your wallet!" Jesus repeated, this time swinging the knife in an arc that should have sliced the Yuppie's right arm nicely. But the Yuppie stepped back effortlessly, as if the knife had been moving in slow motion. For a very brief moment Jesus Murphy experienced a sense of indecision, of something not quite right. But his mind was set, following a plan as rigorous as a concrete path, and there was no turning back.

"Your wallet, or I cut you!"

"Okay, okay," the Yuppie said at last, reaching into his jacket pocket and pulling out the dark leather wallet. He flipped through it and pulled out what looked like a couple of twenties. "Listen, just take these and we'll forget all about any of this."

Jesus laughed. "Fuck you, man. Just gimme that thing!" He reached out and took the wallet from the Yuppie's trembling fingers. The cold that had been eating at him all day was dissipating like fog in a wind. Adrenaline heat coursed through him.

"Please, just take the money. But I need my wallet."

"Yeah?" Jesus said, smiling. "How about this? You need this?" He slashed out with the knife, and this time the razor point snicked into the fabric above the Yuppie's left elbow. A line of blood dribbled across the fabric of the dark coat.

The Yuppie stumbled backwards, eyes wide with

fear. "Please, don't . . ."

"Hey, man, okay. I won't do that." Jesus's tone turned apologetic. "You want your wallet. Okay, man, here, you can have it. I'm sorry I cut you. I didn't mean it. Here, take your wallet." Jesus smiled, holding out the wallet. He had edged further into the shadows. The Yuppie looked at him quietly for a few seconds, then came to a decision. He took a step forward. Jesus took a step back. The Yuppie frowned, then took another step, moving into the shadow.

"Here, man, you can have it," Jesus said softly. He stepped forward, smiling, and brought the knife up in a glittering arc intended to slit the Yuppie from gut to rib. But Jesus's hand slammed into a bar of steel. That's what it felt like, anyway. One moment his arm was swinging, the next moment it stopped in midair. He tried to pull back but he was caught. Glancing down he saw that the Yuppie was holding onto his wrist, bending the knife away from him.

"What . . ."

"Give . . . me . . . my . . . wallet. . . ." The words were mere grunts.

Jesus Murphy froze, a sudden chill spreading across his neck and shoulders. The voice that had come from the darkness was not human. It was guttural, coarse, forced from lips not meant to speak. In the darkness he could not make out the Yuppie's features, only the silhouette against the brighter light of the street. But there was something wrong with the silhouette, something not quite right. It was stooped, almost bent over double. Jesus tried to pull back his arm, but the Yuppie's grip was incredibly tight. He felt that his skin would tear before he would get free.

This was not the way it was supposed to be at all.

"Okay, man, here, take your wallet." With his free hand Jesus tossed the wallet onto the ground.

The Yuppie did not move. His breathing was shallow, loud. Jesus felt as if the eyes, hidden in darkness, were burning into him, that they could see him clearly, and worse, that they could sense his fear. A small whimper escaped from his lips.

The Yuppie's grip suddenly lessened, and Jesus found himself free. As the Yuppie bent to pick up the wallet, Jesus kicked with all his might. His black leather army surplus boot connected with the Yuppie's ribs. It felt as if he had kicked a tree. He yelped in pain, then turned and ran deeper into the alley, not waiting to see the effect of his kick on the quarry that had so quickly turned on him.

The darkness unfolded before him. In the distance he could see the square of light that was Hempill Street. Less than fifty yards away, but looking more like a million miles. Behind him Jesus Murphy could hear something else, something that made his blood freeze. It was a low growl, wet and deep, closer than possible. He must have had a twenty-yard start on the Yuppie. How could the guy be so close? Jesus glanced over his shoulder. It was a mistake.

What he saw made him gasp in terror, and his feet tripped over one another. He skidded to the cement, cutting his palm on a sliver of glass, tearing his leather jacket. He rolled on his back. The Yuppie was standing over him. This was still the same Yuppie he had accosted, but something was different. The face, so smooth and clean only a few moments ago, was now twisted in a rage that brought taut tendons pok-

9

ing out through the skin. The dull grey eyes he had seen earlier were now wide, gleaming, ferocious, pinning him to the ground. The formerly tight-set lips were hanging open, revealing gleaming white teeth, dripping saliva. Jesus moaned and tried to scrabble away, but the Yuppie reached down, grabbed him by the jacket, and hauled him effortlessly to his feet.

The Yuppie smelled of aftershave and clean linen and . . . something else. Something primal. Something that reminded Jesus of the butcher shop next to his mother's apartment building. A thick, cloying odor. Like some kind of animal. The Yuppie's mouth snapped reflexively, the teeth clicking loudly together, as he brought his face closer to Jesus's neck. Jesus felt the hot breath below his ear, and suddenly the cold hardness of teeth on his skin. The Yuppie growled.

Jesus screamed, a loud eruption that exploded from his center, a sound filled with terror and pain and shame. It slowly dwindled to a whimper as he waited for the ripping pain in his neck. But the pain did not come. Jesus Murphy gasped for breath and started to cry.

The Yuppie stepped back and let him go, but Jesus could not move, could not bear to be pursued again. He bowed his head and wept.

"Go." The word was a bark, hardly intelligible.

Jesus looked up. The Yuppie was staring at him, eyes huge and hungry. "Go!"

Jesus nodded once. Then he turned and ran toward the square of light. When he reached Hempill Street he did not pause, but ran, and continued to run.

* * *

From the darkness of a doorway across the street, she had watched as Michael Smith turned on the boy.

At first she had been worried that he might submit completely to the mugger, that he might somehow maintain control of himself long enough to extricate himself from the situation without feeling the effects of the virus, but her fear had been unfounded. When his shoulders had hunched, hands reaching out like claws, she knew he had stepped over. Even from across the street she could detect the change in his breathing, the sudden transition from frightened gasps of air to deep throaty inhalations. And the boy had sensed it too.

His fear had filled the air like a pungent perfume, and she had hardly been able to stop herself from growling her pleasure.

But something had gone wrong. Michael had pursued, his long legs carrying him swiftly, smoothly, after his prey. In the total darkness of the alley she saw the scene as if illuminated from the inside, in the eerie phosphorescent glow of her night vision. She watched the two shapes, shifting outlines amid the blue glow of the alley walls, and her own hunger grew within her. When Michael reached out to grab the boy, she held her breath, waiting for the strike, waiting for the blood mist to erupt. The boy's fear was a physical presence, flooding the night. She wished she was closer to it. Wished she was causing it. But Michael paused, and slowly, as if reluctantly, he lowered the boy to the ground.

"No!" The word emerged from her mouth as a grunt, filled with disappointment. She leaned back into the darkness of the doorway and watched, a mixture of anger and loss filling her.

In the alley, Michael released the boy, who scampered fearfully into the bright lights of the next street and ran, ran, a tiny rabbit. Immediately the wonderful stench of fear dissipated. Regaining his full posture, Michael stumbled from the alley.

"You pitiful creature," she said softly. He did not hear. He walked, head hung low, toward his apartment building.

She watched him for a few moments then left her hiding place. It was not to be. Not tonight.

Now her own hunger began to rise within her, prodded by the lingering traces of the boy's fear. She raised her eyes, looking up at the glowing sky, brighter to her eyes than the aurora borealis had ever been in her previous life, and growled. The sound, alien in this environment of steel and concrete and glass, slid into the night like a knife. She allowed the hunger to rise, allowed it to change her. In a moment, crouched low, she loped into the darkness of the alley across the street.

The boy had evaded Michael's grasp. But he would not escape hers.

She moved in the darkness, a shadow amongst shadows, a whisper of sound and movement along deserted streets. Twice, unnoticed, she passed others walking. Her stealth was complete, utterly effective. Soon she began to pick up the boy's scent. Still a trace of fear, but fading quickly, replaced by the false bravado she sensed in so many young ones. Such an easy veneer to destroy.

She followed the scent, allowing it to permeate her mind until it was all she knew. It led her to the station, and at the entrance to the stairwell she paused and allowed the virus to ebb within her. She straightened, purchased a token from a disinterested man in the booth, and began to descend.

The platform was nearly deserted. There was an old woman standing beneath a poster of a black policeman, staring straight ahead, oblivious to everything. And there, at the end of the platform, leaning against the dirty green wall, was the prey.

She walked slowly along the platform, face impassive. He saw her coming, and stood upright, swelling his chest. *Peacock,* she thought, smiling. His eyes regarded her body with open interest, and she invited it. She eyed him, smiled at him. She was not dressed for winter and much of her body was exposed. But the cold had no effect on her. None at all.

When the train came, she was pleased to note that it was nearly empty. Traffic into downtown was negligible at this hour. She entered an empty car and turned to face him. He stood on the platform, undecided. She smiled at him, inviting him, and he followed. He took the seat next to her. She ignored him for a moment, studying a Budweiser ad above the opposite window. She would drink afterward, she decided. She turned to him.

He was small, wiry, and handsome. Glossy black hair flowed off his head like liquid coal. His eyes, deep and dark, studied her openly. The fear was gone completely now, replaced by something she liked almost as much. He was *hungry* for her, but not in the same way as she was hungry for him.

The doors closed and the train began to move. As it did so, he slid closer to her on the seat.

"I'm gonna make you happy," he said, his voice low, almost threatening.

He had recovered quickly from his close call with death, she decided.

She smiled, baring her teeth. Something in her expression must have returned him, for a moment, to the alley. His eyes narrowed. She reached out a pale hand and touched her blood red nails to his cheek, then leaned closer so her lips were almost touching his. His lust leaked from his body like a vapor, exciting her. She pushed her tongue out and ran it along her lips, and his eyes followed the movement eagerly. But when he leaned in to kiss her she stopped him with her hand. He frowned, surprised at her strength.

"You've lived ten minutes longer than you should have," she said softly, smiling at him again.

Now the acrid smell of fear again exuded from his pores. "What you talkin' about, bitch?" He stood, hand disappearing into his pocket. But the knife, she knew, had been left in the alley.

Her hunger rose again, pushing warmly at her innards. She opened her mouth and a soft growl emerged. Watching her, the boy's face became slack, his eyes widened. His fear flooded the car.

"Oh, shit," he muttered.

She reached for him. He tried to back away, but she grabbed his jacket and tugged him closer, lifting his feet off the floor. He felt fragile within her grasp, a baby. She brought her mouth close to his neck, pressing her teeth into his warm skin.

"Oh, God, please." His voice was like a little girl's. She smiled at his terror. "I promise, man, I'll never come to that neighborhood again. I promise."

"I know you won't," she said, but the words were unintelligible, mere barks.

Panic provided him with a surge of strength, and he managed to loosen her grip with a hard blow to her elbow. She grunted, pulling her hand back reflexively, and he dropped to the floor. He scrambled quickly away from her, pushing himself along the dirty steel floor of the car until he hit a handrail. She smiled at him. She liked it when they struggled.

"Keep the fuck away from me . . ." He was pushing himself to his feet, getting ready to retreat further.

But there was nowhere to go. The train passed through a short tunnel, and the lights embedded in the tunnel wall produced a bright strobe effect within the car. He froze, trying to focus on her, and she pounced.

He ducked to avoid her, but her hand caught his hair. She twisted her fingers into the oily strands and lifted him from the floor. He squealed like a baby, eyes shut tight, mouth open in an expression of protest and pain. His legs flailed uselessly against her thighs.

With her right hand curled into a claw she reached inside his jacket and gutted him in two quick motions. She turned him away so that his entrails spilled to the floor. A thick moan came from his mouth. She placed him carefully on the seat, holding his arms so he could not struggle. His face was pale, eyes wide in predeath shock, not seeing her at all. She held her mouth next to his ear and bit off the lobe.

"Dying is no fun, is it darling?" she said.

He moaned again, mostly an exhalation of air. His breath smelled of cigarettes and bubble gum.

From the pocket of her leather skirt she retrieved the familiar small blade. In a quick, delicate motion, she cut a deep incision in the flesh below his ear.

Then she tore into the soft meat of his throat and fed.

CHAPTER ONE

Sunday morning, 8:00 A.M., Michael Smith packed two suitcases into the back of the blue Chevrolet Corsica, unfolded a Minnesota state map on the passenger seat, and guided himself northwest out of the city. Chicago's sky was its typical mottled grey, dropping foul snow to the ground. Michael found himself driving in a semiblind stupor, not paying attention to the scenery around him. He followed I-94 northwest through Wisconsin, stopping at Madison for gasoline and a cheeseburger, then on into Minnesota, where he bypassed Minneapolis and St. Paul. It was dusk when he arrived in St. Cloud, around 6:00 P.M., and booked himself a room in the Holiday Inn. He ordered a meal of scrambled eggs and toast in his room, then slept like a baby straight through until six the next morning. It was the best night's sleep he had had in years. It must have been the fresh air, he thought. The memory of Chicago seemed to simmer in an acrid stench of exhaust and human sweat.

After a quick breakfast of two cups of coffee and an apple cinnamon danish, he continued northwest on I-94, finally turning off at Fergus Falls, two hours later. For the first time since leaving Chicago he seemed to wake up. The blacktop of Route 210 east from Fergus Falls was a thin ribbon of reality winding through a glittering frozen landscape. Thick snow hung from trees at either side of the road, winter postcard views, and occasionally the pure white expanse of a frozen lake would come into view, crisscrossed by cross-country ski and snowmobile trails. Michael began to feel at home. He remembered traveling this same road with his parents, at this same time of year, so long ago. Small town exits whipped by in eyeblinks. Underwood. Battle Lake. Vinning. And finally, twenty miles beyond Vinning, the exit he had been waiting for. He slowed the Corsica to a stop, studying the sign with a mixture of sentimentality and honest elation.

NEW YORK, MINNESOTA
POP. 2321

He wondered at the identity of the odd, single person.

At one corner of the sign somebody had neatly painted a shiny green crab apple. Michael smiled. New York, Minnesota, the little crab apple. From his position at the sign he could see a slice of Great Lake (another intentional misnomer) glittering in the morning sun, and the beginning of the line of cabins that wound its way into the town proper.

He felt his smile turn into a grin and was powerless

18

to stop it. He put the Chevy in gear and turned onto the exit.

New York took the form of an elongated horseshoe curled around the south bay of Great Lake, a pear-shaped body of water four miles across at its widest. Downtown New York, the arch of the horseshoe, consisted of a motley collection of small businesses, most of them geared to the summer tourist population: a cinema that ran a different movie every week during the summer but that, on a good year, might run only three different shows in the winter; two motels, one on either end of town, whose main winter business came from their restaurants and bars, and that only meager. Between the two motels ran a string of small storefronts: Lake Country Real Estate, Horn's Books, Anderson Hardware, Fine Foods, a few others dealing in the needs of everyday life. The ends of the horseshoe were rows of houses and cabins, most small, some extravagant, all squeezed down toward the lake. Their number thinned in direct proportion to their distance from town, although a string of out-of-county-owned cabins circumnavigated the entire lake.

Michael drove slowly from one end of town to the other, feeling as if he were fifteen years old and riding in the back of his parent's car. New York hadn't changed at all, not in any appreciable way. Some of the buildings had received face-lifts, and there were one or two structures he didn't remember, but otherwise it was like stepping back into a dream. The police station was a squat concrete bunker next to Granger's

19

Inn, at the north end of town, and was one of the new buildings. He parked the Corsica at the curb and walked slowly up the wide concrete pathway, careful to avoid the few icy patches that had been sprinkled with sand. Inside, the station reflected the efficient simplicity of most small town police stations. To the left were a row of three barred cells, though Michael could not imagine any need for them, and to the right was a small reception area, two desks, and a closed office. Bright rows of fluorescent lights split the ceiling.

A dark-complected young woman, hair combed tightly into a bun, looked up from the reception desk as he entered. Michael leaned on the counter and smiled.

"Hello," she said, but did not return the smile. If her hair had been down, Michael thought, she would have been pretty. As it was, she radiated an aura of severe efficiency. "Can I help you?"

"I think so," Michael said, continuing to smile. "I just wanted to let you people know that I'll be opening up my parents' cabin today. Lot sixty-three North. In case you see any lights or anything like that."

"Sixty-three North?"

"Henry and Barbara Smith's cabin. They died a year ago. Cabin's been closed up ever since."

Her right eyebrow rose slightly. "Do you have identification?"

"Sure." Michael dug out his wallet and began to open it. As he did so the closed office behind the reception desk opened, and a short, but trim and athletic looking man emerged. The police uniform did little to hide his well-muscled torso. If it had not

20

been for his short stature he would have been very imposing.

Michael blinked, recognition finally clicking. "Bob Brisk?"

Bob Brisk's wide face split into a smile that revealed a set of teeth that might have been chiseled from porcelain. "You'll have to excuse me. I wasn't eavesdropping, really. But I thought I heard the name Smith, and . . ." He came over to the reception desk, grinning widely, and held out his hand. "Michael Smith, I never thought I'd see you back in New York."

Michael chuckled. He reached out and pumped the offered hand and returned the grin. "Never thought I'd come back," Michael said, and realized the moment he said it that it wasn't the truth. He'd *always* intended on coming back. "I was just telling the officer," he nodded at the woman behind the desk, "that I wanted to let you people know I'll be opening up my parents' cabin."

Bob Brisk nodded, the smile fading. "Sorry to hear about your Mum and Dad. It was an accident that should never have happened."

Michael shrugged. "They're gone. No need to go over it all again."

Brisk nodded again. "Anyway, I think you'll find the place in good shape. Normally there'd be some vandalism in an empty cabin like that, I mean, that's what we spend most of our winter taking care of around here. But your parents' place was so close to town it never got touched. You'll have a year of dust to clean up, that's all."

"I expected that," Michael said. He put his wallet back in his pocket. "Is there anything I have to do before I open up, any forms to fill out?"

"You didn't even have to tell us you were coming. Glad you did, though. Save us a run out there when we see the lights." He grinned. "If you wouldn't mind, though, just give Sally your home address and other particulars in case of trouble."

Michael nodded, digging out the wallet again. Sally smiled, and her dark face suddenly looked quite pretty. Michael handed her the wallet and she copied his Chicago address, then handed it back.

"Listen, Mike, if you feel like it, maybe we can get together for drinks sometime. Mull over old times."

"Sure," Michael said. But old times were something he didn't really want to mull over, he thought.

"How long will you be staying?" Brisk asked.

Michael shrugged. "Depends, I guess. It's sort of a holiday. Maybe a month. Maybe longer."

Brisk raised his eyebrows and whistled. "Nice job."

"A benefit of being the boss," Michael said.

Once outside again, he leaned against the front fender of the Corsica and regarded the small stretch of town with something close to affection. Chicago felt a million miles away. It seemed impossible that the huge city could exist in the same world as this small, idyllic place. But it does, he thought. It does. His mind turned to Bob Brisk. It had been almost twelve years since he had seen Brisk, the shortest kid in class. They had never been friends, had never even talked much. The conversation today might qualify as the longest, Michael thought. Yet, he wasn't surprised to find Brisk still in New York. He had never attended college, as far as Michael knew, and had never entertained ambitions of leaving. But he could not have

22

imagined the small-statured kid of twelve years ago running the police force, even if it did only consist of two people. He stayed and I came back, Michael thought. Who was smarter?

He smiled to himself, then climbed back in the car. He looped around and drove slowly past Granger's Inn toward the north lots. As he drove, the sun glinting through the trees and off the frozen lake made him wince. Needles of pain stabbed into his eyes.

Michael groaned softly. Hypersensitivity to light was one of the earliest symptoms in the viral cycle. He smiled grimly, keeping his attention on the road. New York, Minnesota, was a world away from Chicago. But there were some things he hadn't been able to leave behind.

The cabin was not nearly as bad as Michael had anticipated. He had not returned to New York at all after the funeral but had left the chore of cleaning up the belongings and paraphernalia of a lifetime to his aunt from Minneapolis, who had spent three days here sorting things out. The lawyers had phoned him in Chicago, wanting to know his wishes in the disposition of the property. His first thought had been to sell, to get rid of everything. But a smaller voice rose within him and rebelled. He'd ordered them to donate all his parents' personal effects to the Salvation Army for sale, but to keep the cabin and the furniture. He'd known, even then, that he'd be coming back.

Plywood shutters had been hung over the front screen door and all the windows, and his first job was to remove these, a job that took nearly an hour with the few tools he'd had the foresight to bring along. The interior of the cabin was relatively clean, though barren. He spent an additional hour opening all the windows, allowing the clean air to sweep away the musty odor of a year of neglect, and generally tidying up. None of the utilities was hooked up, and he found it necessary to wear his coat the whole time. By noon he had done all that he could do.

Michael dropped onto the sofa facing the large front window and allowed himself to relax. His breath formed small clouds of condensation in the air. Less than fifty yards away, the frozen expanse of Great Lake stretched to the horizon. He allowed his eyes to follow the curve of the far shore, trying to remember what it was like. He used to swim across the lake at least once every summer, accompanied by Dad in a small boat. They would spend the afternoon on the other shore, sitting on the big rock at the north point, fishing and drinking Cokes.

He sighed at the memory and cleared his mind. There was too much to do to get caught up in memories. Not yet. He forced himself to concentrate on his body. The initial pang of sensitivity to light had subsided, and no other symptoms seemed apparent. He focused his attention on his left hip, another telltale indicator, but could detect no pain. He was becoming paranoid, that's all. Anybody's eyes would have stung at the glare of sun off ice.

He took a deep breath, letting it out in a hiss. Safe for now, he thought.

He closed up the cabin without locking it and returned to the car. With the motor running he made a small list of his needs. Food, drink, utilities. That

24

would do for a start. He started the car, swung back out onto the access road, and drove back into town.

"You're old Henry Smith's kid, ain't 'cha?" The clerk behind the desk at the New York Utilities Board building was a grizzled old man in a ragged sweater. His gaze held open suspicion and not a hint of friendliness. Michael did not recognize him.

Michael nodded. "Just opening up the cabin. How soon can the utilities be turned on?"

The old man shrugged without taking his small eyes off Michael's face. "Tomorrow, maybe. Gotta kid I can send out, but he's over in Vinning for the day. What'cha got out there? Gas? Water? Electrical?"

"All three."

"Phone?"

Michael paused. How badly did he want a phone? The thought of being isolated was appealing. Yet there was always the chance he might need to call out in an emergency. He thought of John Muir in Chicago and nodded. "Yes, phone too."

"Well, like I said, tomorrow. Around noon."

"Okay, that'll be fine."

"And I need a deposit."

"How much?"

"Fifty each. Two hundred."

"Two hundred dollars? Is that normal?"

"You're new. I don't know you. You want them utilities hooked up, you pay the deposit. You'll get it back when you move out."

Michael sighed and wrote a check. "I should be there all day, but if I'm not the door will be open.

Your man can get inside to do what he needs."

"Against regulations to enter a house without the owner being there. Breakin' an' enterin'."

"Just in case," Michael said.

Outside, he took a deep breath of the clean, cold air. Small town red tape was as hard to cut through as big city red tape, the only difference being that here they knew your name. It certainly wasn't any easier.

He left the Corsica at the Utilities Board building and walked through the downtown area. At Fine Foods he picked up a loaf of bread, a slab of cheddar cheese, a two-quart carton of milk, and a half pound of shaved roast beef. The clerk was a spotty-faced young man who smiled constantly and did not say a word. Michael was grateful.

Carrying the small bag of groceries under one arm he continued his stroll through town, peering in each store window, letting the place soak into him. The sun passed overhead at a low angle, sinking toward the west. Night came quickly to these parts, he knew. There was a small liquor store at the south end of the street, and he dropped in and picked up a six-pack of Coors Light, and on impulse a bottle of a California Burgundy. The wine might help keep him warm later.

On the way back to the car, he stopped at Horn's Books and peered in the window. One thing he wanted to do while he was here was to read. As a child and teenager he had been a big reader, but it was a habit he had somehow fallen out of since moving to Chicago. Words seemed too slow for that city. He pushed open the door and entered the store.

A small bell above the door tinkled, announcing his entry. The smell of books, both old and new, assailed him, along with the fainter smell of cigarette smoke. His mother had been a voracious reader, and he remembered coming in here with her some mornings. She would come in with a bag of books and sometimes leave with an even bigger bag. He smiled at the memory. Four tall rows of shelves stretched to the back of the shop, books on both sides. A row of flickering fluorescent bulbs cast equally flickering shadows across the green linoleum. Michael placed his groceries on the counter by the cash register and stepped further into the store.

"Hello?" His voice was swallowed by the rows of books.

There was a noise at the back, and suddenly a shape emerged from the dark frame of an open doorway. A young woman stepped from the darkness of the small back room and smiled at him. She stood only a few inches short of Michael's six feet, wearing a pair of faded jeans and a pink sweatshirt, rolled up sleeves revealing sweat-sheened forearms. She had obviously been lifting things in the back room. Her light brown hair was pulled back into a loose pony tail that fell across her left shoulder. Her face, smooth and oval, was pale, features accented by light touches of makeup. Her brown eyes seemed very deep in the dimness of the store.

"Hello," she said. "Can I help you?"

Michael could not stop himself from staring. He was used to the streamlined, almost plastic good looks of Chicago women, and this young woman's easy, natural, almost causal beauty surprised him.

"I . . . uh . . . you must be the Horn of Horn's books?" He found himself at a loss for words.

27

The woman laughed, coming completely into the store, and Michael decided that he liked that laugh a lot. Its light sound, honest and clean, was infectious, and he found himself smiling sympathetically.

"No. Mrs. Horn is the owner. I'm Elizabeth. I run the place," she came behind the counter and studied him openly. "Is there anything in particular you're looking for?"

"I . . . uh . . ." The second stuttering start since entering the store made him blush, and he shook his head. "Actually, I'm here on holiday. I haven't done any reading in a long time. Since I was a teenager, really. I'm going to have some time, so . . ."

"What type of books do you like to read?" She looked honestly interested, and was leaning on the counter.

Michael glanced down and saw, with a sudden sinking feeling, the wedding ring on her left hand. Now why, he thought, does that bother me? "I used to read some science fiction. You know, Isaac Asimov. I read *Rosemary's Baby* one summer, I enjoyed that."

"Science fiction and horror, huh? My son would like you," she smiled brightly, revealing even, white teeth. "But we really don't have much of a selection."

Disappointed as much by her admission of parenthood, as by the lack of reading material, he shrugged. "It was just a thought. I guess I could try a run into Fergus Falls for something." He smiled, and reached to pick up his bag of groceries.

"No. Wait just a minute." She touched her chin thoughtfully, eyes scanning the shelves. "There was a young man who traded in a bag of books a month ago, and I haven't even got round to sorting them out

28

yet. I'm sure there was some Stephen King in there, maybe even a couple of space stories. Would you be interested?"

Michael smiled. "Sure. Anything to get me started."

She pulled a pad of paper from beneath the counter. "I'll dig them out for tomorrow. If you'll give me your name, I'll have them ready for you if you want to drop by tomorrow."

"That sounds fine. Michael Smith is the name. I . . ."

She stopped writing and looked up at him with a shocked expression on her face. "Michael Smith?"

Michael frowned. "Yes, I'm staying at my parents' cabin, in the north allotments, and . . ."

"You're Barbara's son?"

Michael took a deep breath, prepared for an attack of false sympathy or grief. "Yes."

Elizabeth shook her head, smiling again. "I really liked your mother. She used to come here a lot, before the accident. I miss her." She said this with such a lack of self-consciousness that Michael could not help but be touched.

"She bought a lot of books, did she?"

"Oh, yes. Your father too, though only recently before he died." Her eyes had taken on a faraway, glazed look. Suddenly she snapped back. "I'll tell you what. I'll dig those books out this afternoon and I'll drop them by your cabin on my way home."

"You really don't have to go to all that trouble, tomorrow will be fine."

Elizabeth smiled. "No, please. I'd like to. It's on the way. Our cabin is Eighty-seven North, just a little past yours."

Michael shrugged. "Okay. If you don't mind. That would be nice."

She held out her hand. "By the way, since I know your full name, mine is Elizabeth Turner."

Michael held her hand and shook it lightly. Her skin was warm and smooth beneath his touch, and he felt something catch in his throat. He forced a smile. "Nice to meet you," he said.

When he was outside he breathed deeply to calm himself. What was wrong with him that his first meeting with an attractive woman outside of Chicago should send him into a nosedive like that? He had spent the last three years steering clear of any emotional involvement, and this was no time to seek it out.

He returned to the car and drove quickly back to the cabin.

CHAPTER TWO

The cabin became colder as the daylight waned, and Michael found himself walking through a haze of his own breath. He drank two beers before discovering that the remainder had partially frozen. The milk was a heavy brick of ice. Only the wine remained liquid, but he had neglected to purchase a corkscrew and so it was effectively lost to him. He sat on the ancient sofa, staring out the living room window at the lake.

After this morning's initial pang of sensitivity to light he had not detected any of the virus's other prodromal symptoms. But now, sinking into the too-soft cushions of his parents' sofa, his hip was heavy with the promise of pain.

He stood in one quick motion and swore angrily.

At one time he could have predicted the viral cycle with an accuracy that left no room for mistakes. Every twenty-eight days, give or take a few hours, the fever would rise and he would consume the compound prepared for him by John Muir. For three years, since contracting the virus, his life had followed a rigid schedule of crest and trough, never once straying from its established pattern. It had been eminently livable, a satisfactory arrangement.

Until two months ago.

Suddenly the symptoms had begun to appear almost randomly. Sudden stress, or even a few hours of depression, would end in the sharp prodding of hip pain that heralded a rise in viral activity. John Muir, who had been Michael's only confidant over the past years, had been at a loss to explain it.

"It baffles me," he had said. "The twenty-eight day cycle seems to have gone by the wayside. Why, I don't know. And you don't seem to have a clue either. As a wild guess, I'd say we're seeing the emergence of a new, longer term cycle, one that's remained hidden so far. Perhaps all you've been experiencing up to now is the incubation period."

Those words had sent a pang of terror through Michael.

"You don't really have a choice now, my friend," Muir had said. "You must submit yourself to research. It's the only way to find out exactly what this thing is, and how to fight it."

And again, his words had terrified Michael.

Any effective research program would mean going public. There would be, John Muir had warned, attention from a large portion of the medical community, very likely from the anthropological community, and of course from the media. The good and the bad. The sympathetic and the damning.

Michael had run possible headlines through his mind a million times. If not prepared for them, he was a least expecting them.

The incident with the mugger had been the deciding factor. He had come *that* close to killing the kid. Closer to going over the edge than he had ever come before. One step away from becoming just like Sondra.

The sudden thought of Sondra caused him to straighten up, and he forced his mind away from the thought of her.

After the mugger he had visited John Muir and they had come to an agreement. After a holiday of indeterminate length, Michael would return to Chicago and allow John to pursue a research program in any manner he saw fit. It was the only way Michael was ever going to get his life back to normal. If that meant destroying the life he had now in order to procure even a chance at a new one, then so be it.

Now, pacing about the icy living room of his parents' cabin, Michael wondered if he had made a mistake. Perhaps there was no time for a holiday. Perhaps he should have handed himself over to John Muir right then, without delay, before this thing got the better of him.

The pain in his hip seemed to second that motion.

Stifling a groan, he limped through to the bathroom and removed one of the three bottles of John Muir's compound crushed into the top shelf. In a serving spoon he poured enough of the viscous black liquid so that it quivered on the verge of spilling. He raised the spoon to his mouth and tipped the contents over his tongue. It was very cold. The sharp, coppery taste filled him with revulsion yet at the same time almost instantly sated the quivering hunger that tortured his body, a hunger he had not been aware of

33

until the moment the liquid passed his lips. He poured another spoonful and gulped it, almost gagging on the taste, sickened by his knowledge of what it was.

Then he went back through to the living room, lowered himself carefully into the sofa, and tried not to think about anything.

She parked the rented Pontiac Sunbird on an access road to an empty cabin just north of the town, hidden from the highway by a windbreak of closely packed pine. With the engine shut off the interior of the car quickly became cold, and the windows fogged up with her breath. But she did not care. She did not feel the cold, and with the driver's window partially open she saw all that she needed to see. It was late afternoon, but already the sun was sinking. Soon it would be dusk. She waited.

It seemed that all her life had been spent following Michael Smith. But that wasn't true. Not entirely. There had been almost three glorious years when she had stood alone, isolate, perfect, needing no other. It was only recently, only after the sudden change in the viral cycle, that she had begun to seek him out.

For three years the virus had been predictable, exact, almost menstrual in its regularity. But two months ago there had been changes. Inexplicable, frightening changes. She had prided herself on the control she had developed, her ability to keep the hunger keen-edged so that the symptoms never completely disappeared. It was a matter of controlling the appetite. Too deep a gorging and the virus would ebb, and she might sink into the obscurity of normality.

Starve the virus, however, and it stayed active.

But then the new hunger had arrived, and she had been at a loss to explain it.

Despite frequent feedings, the viral cycle remained in peak activity, making her life almost unbearable. And soon, against her wishes, her thoughts became preoccupied with the past, dredging up images of Michael Smith. It did not take long to ascertain that Michael was the object of her desires, the food this new hunger required. And from there it was a short leap of logic to reason why.

She had been in Los Angeles at the time, a city where her strange needs and hungers could pass almost unnoticed amidst the usual nocturnal activity. She had left without qualms, stealing the car of her latest victim. She remembered Michael's words the last time they had been together, his admonishment to come with him to Chicago, to fight the virus. Perhaps the dark, brooding, glass and cement sprawl of Chicago would provide as good a cover for her needs as Los Angeles had done.

After arriving in Chicago, it had taken her a week to locate Michael, and only a few hours after that to determine that he was still fighting the virus. For three weeks she watched him from a distance, studied him surreptitiously. The change in the viral cycle was affecting him too, but he did not understand it. How could he? He had spent all his time fighting the thing, separating himself from it. It was an alien to him, and he to it. Enemies within the same skin, neither one capable of understanding the other.

Michael was frightened, she could see that. Trapped in his clean, well-organized, urban life, denying the very thing that might set him free, not knowing how to fight its sudden new attack. She had almost felt sorry for him.

But she needed Michael. And although he didn't know it yet, he needed her. It was the incident with the mugger that showed her how it might be accomplished.

Michael was close to coming over. The mugger had brought him right to the brink, had actually managed to drag one of his feet over the line. Somehow Michael had fought back, recovered his poise.

But what if the impetus was greater? What if he found himself in a situation where crossing over that line, giving over completely to the virus, was the only path available?

Then, perhaps, there would be no going back. Then they might be together. Then, and only then, this new hunger might be satisfied.

When he had suddenly packed his things and left Chicago she had worried. But when she realized where he was going she understood the opportunity presented to her. He was isolating himself. Removing all that was familiar to him. In such a state he would be vulnerable to any attack she chose to mount.

Even now, she could sense his proximity. Less than half a mile away he was resting in his cabin, waiting. Perhaps he could even sense her. But even if he did, he would not understand the signs. Not yet.

Outside, a few flakes of snow were drifting down from a partially cloudy sky. A soft wind pushed through the open window, tugging her hair. The thoughts of Michael Smith were stoking her hunger. Both hungers.

She started the car and waited a few minutes until the windows cleared, then turned onto the blacktop and drove north. In a minute she passed Michael Smith's cabin, but she could not catch a glimpse of him. Disappointed, she continued on. She was just coming round a sharp curve in the road when she saw the boy ahead.

He was walking on the blacktop, hands stuffed into the pockets of his blue and black checkered plaid jacket, facing away from her. She slowed the car as she approached, stopping it beside him. Snow and ice crunched loudly beneath the tires. He was young, perhaps sixteen or seventeen. Spots of acne peppered his face and faint whisps of blond hair clouded his chin. His eyes widened when he saw her, and she smiled, lowering the passenger side window.

"Need a ride?"

He opened his mouth to respond, then gave an embarrassed shrug. "Just going up the road a little bit. Not far."

She opened her mouth slightly so that he could see tongue. "I could use the company," she said.

She could almost see the wheels and cogs turning in his mind, already planning the story he would relate to his friends. She moved her legs so that he caught a glimpse of the exposed white flesh extending into the glossy blackness of the leather skirt. His eyes blinked once, almost audibly. He grinned, then shrugged, then reached for the door handle.

"Are you in a hurry?"

Again his eyes widened at this question, and he could not quite find the words to answer.

She smiled, reached out a pale hand to touch his

leg. Her red nails glittered against the washed-out blue of his jeans. "I have some time," she said softly.

She pulled the car out onto the road and drove another hundred yards, then turned left into a small clearing, partially hidden from the road by a number of trees. She put the transmission in park, but left the engine running. Beside her, the boy was fidgeting nervously, not believing he was here, almost wishing he was away from here so he could talk about it.

She leaned over, and with one hand behind his neck pulled him to her. She surrounded his mouth in a kiss, pushing her tongue past his teeth, caressing the inside of his mouth. When she pulled back he was gasping for air, his mouth smeared with her lipstick. "Oh, wow," he managed to say at last.

She pulled a tissue from the box on the seat and wiped his mouth clean, smiling apologetically. She made herself sound breathless. "Let's do it outside."

He blinked. "But it's *cold*."

"There's no room in here for what I want to do with you."

His lips trembled in a smile, then he nodded.

There was a fallen tree at the edge of the clearing, and together they brushed the loose snow from it. She made him lean back against the huge trunk, then began to unbutton his coat. Despite the cold, he did not shiver. She ran her fingers over his smooth chest, down his flat stomach, probing beneath the elastic of his shorts. He groaned, eyes wide with disbelief.

She unbuckled his belt, then pulled his pants down around his ankles. He was hard, jutting out into the cold air. She stepped back, then lifted the hem of her skirt and exposed herself to him. She had thought his eyes could get no wider.

But now the hunger was rising within her, sharp and demanding. From her throat a low growl emerged, almost like a cat's purring. The boy's face went momentarily slack.

"You okay?" A faint tang of glorious fear poked into the air.

She smiled, but already her lips were pulled so far back from her teeth that it must have appeared to him like a grimace.

She reached out to him, placing her hands on his chest. Then she dragged her nails down his stomach. His skin sliced easily and hung off him in strips. A torrent of blood sluiced down between his legs and over his jeans.

He roared in agony, leaping convulsively from the log. She grabbed him beneath the chin and lowered him again. His breathing was ragged, emerging as an agonized whimper. He had softened instantly, and now goose bumps were rising on the skin of his thighs.

She reached into a pocket on her vest and retrieved the small, glittering blade.

"You said you had some time," she growled, leaning toward him.

He shook his head, trying to scramble away from her. "No, please, I'm sorry . . ."

She leaned over him, gripping his hair and pinning him down.

"So let's have some fun with this," she said, trying to smile around her teeth.

With the blade she sliced a clown's smile in his throat. And as he gurgled, struggling ever more feebly, she began to use her teeth.

By dusk Michael felt much better. He had located two small candles, and their feeble light provided enough illumination for him to skim through the magazines he had brought from Chicago. At one point he heard a siren on the main road, and through the maze of trees he saw the flashing red lights speed by. Either a car accident or somebody was vandalizing a cabin, he thought.

Less than half an hour later the sound of a car's engine drew closer to the cabin, and two brilliant arcs of light passed across the living room, casting everything into brilliant illumination. Michael jumped to his feet and went to the front door. He opened it, shielding his eyes against the brightness of the car's headlights. After his eyes adjusted he saw that it was a small orange Volkswagen Beetle, battered and rusted. The door opened and Elizabeth Turner emerged, a small bag tucked under one arm. She stepped lightly up to the front of the cabin, smiling. Michael found himself smiling back.

"I'd invite you in, but I've got no power, no heat, and no water."

Elizabeth blinked. "You're kidding."

Michael chuckled. "I'll have it all by tomorrow."

"Yes, but what about tonight? Do you have any idea how cold it's going to get?"

Michael shrugged. "I've got two suitcases of clothes to keep me warm."

Elizabeth shook her head, her soft brown hair swaying against her shoulder. "Forget it. You're not staying here tonight. Come on, get in the car." She walked away from the cabin.

Her words caught him off guard and he could do nothing but stare, mouth hanging open. She paused and glanced back. "Well, come on. I won't let you stay here like this. Your mother would kill me. We've got an extra room, you'll stay with us until you get set up, now come on."

Still at a loss for words, Michael stepped back into the cabin and snuffed out the candles. How could he refuse? To do so would be extremely ill-mannered and perhaps fatally stupid. Her invitation was obviously nothing more than an effort to help. Nothing more.

So why was his heart beating faster?

On impulse he picked up the bottle of Burgundy and stuffed it into his coat, then closed the cabin and went to the car. He opened the passenger door and slid in. There was somebody else in the back.

"Michael Smith, this is my son, Tommy," Elizabeth said. "Tommy, say hello to Michael."

The young boy in the back smiled shyly. "Hi." He had his mother's brown eyes and firm mouth, Michael noticed.

"Hi, Tommy," Michael said.

Elizabeth put the car in reverse and backed out onto the access road, then roared up to the main road. Without pausing she darted onto the blacktop and continued northward around the bay. Her concentration was fully on the dark road, so Michael did not interrupt her with conversation. The silence in the car was uncomfortable, but he was not sure how to break it. Ahead, to the left of the road, a number of red lights were flashing.

"Must have been the siren I heard earlier," Elizabeth said, slowing the car.

"I heard it too," Michael said.

Tommy pressed his face up to the glass, peering out at the police car parked beside the road. Elizabeth brought the car to a stop and rolled down her window. A dark shape silhouetted in the police car's headlights separated itself from the trees and came toward them, and as it stepped into the Volkswagen's lights Michael saw that it was Bob Brisk. He bent over to peer into the car.

"Evening, Elizabeth. Tommy." His eyes rested on Michael for a moment. "Michael."

Michael nodded, but did not say anything. Brisk's eyes left him at last, focusing on Elizabeth.

"What's going on, Bob."

"Got a body," Brisk said.

Accident?"

Brisk shrugged. "Don't know. Looks like the Jaeger kid, the seventeen-year-old. Looks like he's been chewed up. Animal of some kind."

Elizabeth drew in a sharp breath. "Oh, God."

"You head on home now, Elizabeth, and don't be venturing outside tonight."

Elizabeth nodded. "Thanks, Bob." She put the car in gear and drove away. Michael swung his head to focus on the scene behind them, and for a brief instant caught sight of the small, crumpled form on the ground, the almost black splatter around it. He cringed.

"Gross," Tommy said from the back.

"Tommy, you turn away from that right now!" Elizabeth said sharply, glancing in the rear view mirror.

"Awww, Mom!"

Elizabeth turned to Michael, smiling faintly. "You mustn't think this happens all the time, Michael. This is the first nasty thing I've seen in years."

Michael nodded. "I believe you. Like he said, it must have been an animal. I'm sure they'll catch it."

Elizabeth nodded, guiding the car carefully along the almost invisible blacktop.

Michael frowned, staring out the passenger window. The crumpled body in the snow, surrounded in blood, had brought back another memory. A memory from three years earlier. For an instant Sondra's face flashed through his mind, but he blotted it out immediately.

"Here we are. Home sweet home," Elizabeth said, slowing the car.

Michael forced his mind back to the present. Don't even think about those things, he warned himself. Don't go near them.

But the scene of the crumpled body in the snow hung immobile behind his eyes, like the afterimage of a camera's flash.

CHAPTER THREE

Elizabeth parked the Volkswagen at the side of the small cabin. She plugged the block heater into an outlet on the front corner. Michael watched this operation with some amusement. Seeing his reaction, Elizabeth shrugged and smiled.

"I know, it's not *that* cold. But this baby needs all the help she can get."

Michael smiled. "It's just been a long time since I've seen cars plugged in like toasters. Chicago is tropical compared to this."

Elizabeth laughed lightly, and again Michael found himself enjoying the sound of it. But the humor quickly faded from Elizabeth's face as she followed Tommy up the path to the cabin. Michael followed her gaze as she looked back down the highway, where the flashing lights of the police car were still visible as a dull red throb amidst the darkness of the trees. Like the beating of some monstrous heart, he thought uneasily.

Inside the cabin, Michael peeled off his coat with

relief and handed Elizabeth the bottle of wine. Her eyes widened.

"Oh, Michael, you didn't have to do that."

"I thought it would keep me warm tonight. It's the least I can do for your offer of hospitality," he said. As a very calculated afterthought, he added: "I hope your husband doesn't mind."

"My husband died five years ago," Elizabeth said, her eyes holding his very steadily. She placed the bottle of wine on a small table by the door and unbuttoned her coat.

Michael opened his mouth to say something, but no words came. He felt an instant of admiration for this woman who talked of death in such a simple way. Her mention of his parents' accident earlier had been so natural he had not even felt a twinge of the guilt or suppressed grief that had risen on every other mention. And now, talking of her husband, the same *the dead are dead* tone was in her voice. He was strongly aware of the slight flutter in his stomach.

She smiled slightly at the stunned expression on his face, and Michael felt himself begin to blush.

"No, don't be embarrassed," she said. "I saw you glance at my ring earlier."

But this only intensified his blush.

"It was a natural question. Bobby died when Tommy was five. He had cancer, but he went quickly." She took Michael's coat from him and hung it on the rack beside her own. "I wear the ring, well, for sentimental reasons, really. I guess I still feel married." Her smile widened, and Michael found himself responding.

Tommy came barreling through from one of the bedrooms, arms supporting a small refracting telescope and wooden tripod. "How long till supper, Mom?"

"Tommy, not tonight," Elizabeth said.

"But, Mom, it's a perfect night!"

"You heard Chief Brisk. He said to stay inside."

"But Mom!"

"No arguments. Besides, we're got a guest. I'm sure he'd like your company as much as I would."

Tommy sighed and glanced up at Michael with a shy look. Michael smiled. "Sure. You can tell me what you were going to look at. I used to have a telescope myself."

"You did? What kind?"

"Sort of like yours," Michael said, remembering the two-inch-Acme refractor he'd received from his father on his eighth birthday. "I never got much beyond the moon, but once I saw Jupiter's moons, and even Saturn's rings."

"Yeah? Me too." His forlorn expression began to fade. He turned and marched back to his bedroom, the body of the telescope hung carefully over one arm. The legs of the tripod clattered against the doorframe as he pushed through.

"He's going to be an astronomer when he grows up," Elizabeth said softly. "Please, come on in to the living room. Can I get you a drink? Not much of a selection, I'm afraid. Your wine or my beer."

"Your beer will be fine," Michael said, following her through to the cozy living room.

This cabin was much smaller than his parent's, his

own, but it had the comfortable lived-in atmosphere that his would likely never regain. He settled into the sofa facing the TV, savoring the warmth that was slowly beginning to permeate his body. He had not realized how cold he was. Elizabeth's invitation was beginning to assume the proportions of a godsend. A brief image of himself, frozen to the frame of his parent's bed, icicles dripping from a rock-hard nose, flashed through his mind, and he smiled.

Elizabeth appeared with a bottle of imported Molson Canadian beer and handed it to him. "What's so funny?"

He accepted the bottle. "Just congratulating myself on being invited to spend the night in a warm house." He offered her a smile.

"Please, it's the least I could do for Barbara's son. Besides, she talked so much about you," she said, grinning. "Now I'll get to find out the truth." She walked back to the kitchen, then called through: "Listen, just relax. I'll get supper ready."

"Sure." He sipped the beer.

Tommy came through to the living room, turned on the television, and took a corner of the sofa opposite Michael. "They've got Star Trek reruns on Four. Is that okay?"

"Sure." Michael said.

Tommy smiled briefly, then focused on the TV, where Captain Kirk was slowly fading out as the transporter beam dissolved him. Michael found himself quickly absorbed in the show and realized how long it had been since he'd settled back and relaxed. When was the last time his television in Chicago had been tuned to anything but the weather channel? He was also aware of Tommy's periodic intense scrutiny, but he did not respond in any way. It was the boy's right to study strangers in his household.

Supper was a simple, tasty offering of baked chicken breast, fried rice, salad, and hot buns. Michael savored every bite of the home-cooked meal, again aware of how different this world was from his own. His menu in Chicago consisted entirely of packaged dinners, spaghetti, or restaurant fare. At one point he noticed Elizabeth's amused expression as she watched him eat, and again he blushed.

"S'good," he explained through a mouthful of chicken.

She nodded her acceptance of the compliment, unable to hide the faint smile that tugged at her lips. Tommy spent the meal looking back and forth between Michael and his mother, as if he were at a tennis match, and Michael found his attention constantly on Elizabeth. He felt powerless to look elsewhere. On the occasions when their eyes connected he quickly averted his gaze. She must think him a fool, he thought.

After dinner, while Tommy entertained himself at the television, their conversation in the living room was easy and relaxed. He found himself telling her of his childhood in Minneapolis, the big move to New York when he was fifteen, his education in fine arts, his business. He was delighted at Elizabeth's own life story. A Fergus Falls girl, she had married Bobby Turner at eighteen, he only two years older, giving birth during their first year together. Bobby's cancer had shattered her life at first; but his death had pulled her together. There was Tommy to take care of. She could not afford to be a grieving widow. The job at Thorn's Books had been offered in sympathy, she suspected, but nonetheless she had accepted it. It provided enough to get by on, and she really did enjoy the books.

"Ever been married, Michael?" Her look was level, careful.

"No," he said simply.

"No lines of eager women at your door?" Her playful grin only marginally concealed a real interest.

Michael smiled. "Never. I've never seemed to have the time to . . . get involved," he said. It was an outright lie, but the truth was not something he cared to reveal. He had longed, every night of the past years, for someone to be with, to share with. But that, then as now, was an impossibility. His smile became grim. The conversation had turned intimate far too quickly for his liking, but he relished it. It was so nice to be talking with someone on this level. He knew, consciously, that he should stop, but on a deeper level he could not. "How about you?"

For the first time since he had met her, Elizabeth blushed. The blush, like her laugh, appealed to Michael in a way he could not fathom. It was something intimate, something honest, something unadulterated by . . . by self-consciousness. She reached to the coffee table for a pack of Carltons, lit one, and exhaled a pale cloud of smoke. "Never wanted to, really," she said softly, and took another puff on the cigarette.

"You dated, Mom," Tommy said, turning from the

television.

"Tommy!"

"Well, you did," Tommy said, obviously enjoying putting his mother on the spot.

Elizabeth turned to Michael again, smiling through another blush. We're getting even on that score, Michael thought.

"Okay, I did," she said. "But none of them developed." She turned her attention to Tommy again. "I thought you were watching TV, fella," she said.

"I can listen too," Tommy said, smiling out of one side of his mouth. "I didn't know it was top secret."

Elizabeth harumphed. "Precocious monster." She mouthed at Michael silently.

He smiled.

When the knock sounded at the front door Tommy bounded from the sofa to answer it. A familiar voice drifted through to the living room. Michael rose, along with Elizabeth, and went through.

"Evening, Elizabeth." Bob Brisk's eyes focused on Michael again. There was very little boyhood comraderie there. "Michael."

Michael nodded. "Any luck finding the animal you were looking for?"

Bob Brisk was silent for a moment, eyes still locked on Michael's. "That's what I came about," he said slowly. "I've got Sally working the south allotments, letting people know. Not sure it was an animal that actually killed the boy. Pretty strange. It was Syd Jaeger alright, and he *had* been chewed up. But there were . . . indications that there might also have been foul play involved." He turned to Elizabeth, "Just wanted to let you know. Like you to keep a lookout for anything strange, if you would. Anybody you don't know, anything like that." Again he turned to Michael, and the small smile that turned his lips was cold and humorless.

"Haven't seen anything, Bob," Elizabeth said, and took another puff on her cigarette.

Brisk nodded, and Michael began to feel very uncomfortable under his gaze, as if he were a laboratory specimen. "Well, I guess I'll be heading back to town," he said. "If you want I can give you a ride back to your cabin, Michael."

"Uh . . ." Michael suddenly found himself short of words.

"He'll be staying here tonight, Bob," Elizabeth broke in. "Nothing hooked up at his cabin yet. He'd freeze to death."

Brisk stopped and glanced quickly at Elizabeth before turning to Michael again. "I could drop you off at Granger's Inn, if you want. Might be a bit crowded here."

"You'll do no such thing, Bob Brisk!" Elizabeth said, hands on her hips. "This is Henry and Barbara's son, and I think that he deserves a little northern hospitality."

Bob Brisk opened his mouth to say something else, then snapped it shut. He turned a cold gaze on Michael. "Sorry to bother you folks. Have a good evening." He turned and walked back down the path.

Tommy closed the door, sealing out the cold.

Michael sighed. "I get the impression Bob Brisk might have been one of your dates," he said, raising an eyebrow.

Elizabeth's eyes widened, then her lips turned into a smile and finally she laughed. "I guess that didn't take super powers of observation to see." She went back to the living room and Michael followed. "Bob's okay. He'll find a nice girl sometime."

Michael sank back into the sofa. Tommy stuck his head into the room. "I'm going to bed."

"Okay, kiddo," Elizabeth said, and held out her arms. "Kiss."

"Mom!" Tommy shook his head and disappeared from view.

Elizabeth offered Michael a mock pout. "Jeez, they grow up so fast."

Michael chuckled. "I stopped kissing my Mom when I was six. I didn't kiss her again until my graduation from high school, and only because I had no choice."

"Boys," Elizabeth said in disgust, and then her face assumed a serious cast. She turned to Michael, frowning. "It scares me that there's some sort of animal running around. What do you think it could be?"

Michael shrugged. "No idea. I didn't realize there were any dangerous animals around here at all. A bear, maybe?"

"Maybe," Elizabeth said. "Or a big cat. They get them sometimes. But Bob said there might be foul play involved."

Michael nodded. "I don't think you should worry. We'll keep our eyes open for anything strange."

"Guess you're right," Elizabeth said. She stretched and yawned. "I hope you don't mind, Michael, but

I'm going to sack out myself. I'll get you blankets and a pillow. I hope the sofa's okay." She took a final puff on her cigarette, then crushed it out in the ashtray by the table lamp.

"Perfect," Michael said.

Elizabeth lay awake in bed, staring at the ceiling. It was too early to be in bed, far too early, but she had been frightened about what might happen if she stayed alone in the living room with Michael Smith.

"Michael Smith." She mouthed his name silently, smiling to herself.

What was it about the man that had attracted her so suddenly, so forcefully? She had met him less than twelve hours ago, yet felt she had known him much, much longer than that. Their after-dinner conversation had explored personal realms she had not touched in a long time. Too long, perhaps.

She lit a cigarette and blew a wraith of smoke into the air. She watched the grey animal coil, expand, and dissipate.

Perhaps it was the faint, but unmistakable aura of vulnerability he exuded. Something had hurt Michael Smith, was *still* hurting him, something he had not mentioned yet. She could sense it in his eyes, in his manners. He was withholding something. A relationship gone sour, or . . . or something worse.

She shook her head. Damn it! The first guy who comes along since Bobby died who shows the slightest hint that he might not be mister perfect macho lover and you're falling for him!

She stabbed the cigarette out with three violent motions and turned over to face the wall. He's on vacation, for God's sake! He'll be leaving before you could possibly get to know him properly. That means somebody gets hurt, probably you. Did she really want that to happen? Was she ready for a relationship doomed from the start?

No. No, she was not ready.

And she would not allow it to happen.

Tomorrow she would establish an air of formality between them that he could not mistake. She would not be his backwoods fling. She tried to bring a supportive anger to a boil, but was unable.

When she closed her eyes, an image of Michael's pale, narrow face appeared in her head. She felt her lips curl into a smile. And something else.

Elizabeth opened her eyes, blinked, and muffled a small gasp.

"No," she whispered. Please, not with this man, not in a relationship that can't possibly have time to develop!

But her protestations were to no avail. Her body would not listen to reason.

And for the first time in five years she felt the tremulous, delicious stirring in her loins.

Tommy pushed his head as close to his bed's headrest as possible, giving himself a narrow view of the sky through his bedroom window. The handle of the Big Dipper—Ursa Major, he corrected himself—was slowly swinging into view. Already he had a good view of Mizar and its visual companion Alcor.

In his star atlas it said that Mizar itself should show a double, but the optics of his telescope had so far been unable to split the pair. The double was very faint. Every night he tried. Some night the visual conditions would be good enough, or his own eyesight would condition itself, and he'd see Mizar and its faint little friend as clear as if they were a billion miles apart. Mizar was supposed to be an easy target for splitting. But it hadn't happened yet.

He looked away from the window, studying instead the Iron Maiden poster on the wall. The ax-wielding demon seemed to look out of the paper toward him. He did not like the poster. And neither did Mom, which was a good enough reason for having it. He smiled to himself.

Mom had been funny tonight. It was obvious she had the hots for Michael Smith, the guy from down the road, and it was obvious that he had the hots for her. Didn't they see it?

"Stupid adults," he whispered.

When he grew up, if he ever met a girl he liked he was going to come right out and say it. None of this stupid small talk stuff. No "Have you ever dated before?" or "Any women lined up at your door?"

Jeez. How sickening. Just come right out with it and get to the good stuff. Sometimes he wondered if adults even *knew* about the "good stuff," or if they forgot about it as they got older. He wondered about that a lot. If it were true, it meant you had maybe ten years to get things going before you didn't want to do it anymore.

Jeez, again.

He rolled over again, and faced the window.

Anyway, Mom liked Michael, and that was fine. Michael was okay. Not like some of the other jerks she'd dated after Dad died. Like Bob "Bait Bucket" Brisk. Christ, why did she even talk to that half-pint slimeball anyway?

There was something about Michael Smith that he liked. He didn't know what it was, not yet, but there was something. He was kind of quiet. He wasn't pushy, not like Bob Brisk.

Tommy remembered, a year ago, when Brisk had been over for supper, and he had said to Mom: "I've got the same name as your husband. Shouldn't be that hard a transition."

Mom had sort of laughed, but Tommy had fumed. *Asshole.* Bob Brisk could never be like Dad, nobody could be like Dad. It was soon after that that Mom had stopped dating Bob, and Tommy had been glad.

But Michael was different. It was like he was holding back. And Mom was holding back too.

The thought suddenly occurred to him that if both Mom and Michael held back, then they would never get together.

He frowned. That would be stupid. Really stupid. Just like adults.

He rolled over again, yawning.

He'd see what he could do about it.

An hour after Elizabeth and Tommy had gone to bed, Michael lay awake on the sofa, blankets stuffed beneath his chin, eyes open. Starlight reflected off the snow cast a pale, ghostly illumination across the walls. At first, his presleep thoughts had revolved around Elizabeth Turner. Her face danced in his mind. The vague, elusive smell of her perfume haunted him.

He imagined running his fingers through her soft, shoulder-length hair. And he cursed himself.

It was stupid, really stupid, to think that he could possibly allow himself to become involved with somebody. Things don't change that easily.

Chicago was eight hundred miles away, but the virus had come with him. It could destroy him here, in New York, Minnesota, as easily as it could in Chicago, Illinois.

Things don't change at all.

But still, he saw the humorous curl of her lips, the glint of her eyes, and he imagined his lips touching hers, his tongue probing . . .

Christ, no!

Michael groaned, rolling over to face the back of the sofa. Don't. *Don't.* Think about something else. Why torture himself like this?

Soon his thoughts began to wander down another path, one he found equally as unwelcome.

On the screen of his mind he saw the flashing red lights of Bob Brisk's police cruiser, his dark shape silhouetted in the glare of headlights. And on the ground, the crumpled form of a young boy, torn and mutilated, surrounded in blood that looked black in the harsh light.

No!

But it was no use. It was too late. The connection had been made.

The other memory came back, full force, and he found himself examining it. Comparing the old images with this new one.

The flashing red lights were the same. The same everywhere.

And the crumpled body on the ground was similar enough. Do all bodies, folded in death, look alike?

Coincidence, that's all.

But still, he could not help himself. And Sondra's face flashed across his mind, her gleaming grey eyes piercing him.

And he remembered, three years ago, the flashing red lights, and the torn and mutilated body of the young man, and what Sondra had done.

CHAPTER FOUR

The following morning Elizabeth dropped Michael at his cabin on her way to Horn's Books. The sun had just risen over the eastern tree line by 8:00 A.M., and the snow of the lake glittered in the low-angled light. The sky was pure, clear, expansive blue, and Michael regarded it with an ill-disguised look of wonder. Summer sky above but arctic cold below. The seemingly incongruous pairing cheered him up. Anything was better than the mottled grey sludge that passed for Chicago's winter sky, Windy City or not.

Although he had retired early the night before, Michael still felt tired. His thoughts and dreams had not been conducive to deep sleep. Elizabeth too, he noticed, did not seem completely rested. When they passed the small clearing where the body of Syd Jaeger had been found, Michael turned away, forcing himself not to look. Tommy pressed his face to the glass. "Nothing there," the boy said, disappointed, then settled back in the seat.

Elizabeth slowed the car to a halt at the gravel road leading to his cabin. She turned to him, and a very small smile turned up the corners of her lips. "If you need anything, please let me know," she said.

Michael nodded. "You've been a great help already," he said. Her words had sounded formal, as if she hoped he would *not* ask for any more help. But he smiled gratefully. "Nice to meet you, Tommy," he said, nodding at Tommy in the back seat.

"Bye," Tommy said, regarding him thoughtfully.

Michael turned back to Elizabeth. "Listen, I . . . ," he heard the words coming out, hardly believing what he was saying. "I'd like to see you again."

For a long moment Elizabeth locked eyes with him, and it seemed to Michael that she was wrestling with her emotions. Finally her mouth seemed to set into a tight line, and she looked away from him. "I'll be at the bookstore," she said softly.

Michael closed the Volkswagen's door firmly and waved as the orange car roared away toward town.

He shook his head slowly and began walking down the gravel road to his cabin. The morning sun glinted through the naked, crippled branches of the trees, stinging his eyes but providing no warmth for his face. He found himself regarding an image of Elizabeth in his mind, focusing on the gentle fall of hair across her left shoulder. Both of us feel attracted, he thought, but neither of us wants it. We're fighting it. The thought made him smile faintly, and then grin. Mixed-up world.

The cold austerity of his cabin was depressing, and it was not until near 2:00 P.M. that the blue Ford Econoline with the words NEW YORK UTILITIES stenciled on the sides rolled up outside. Michael watched the slow revival of his cabin with little interest, remaining in the living room while the young man in tattered overalls did his work. The entire operation took less than half an hour.

"Y'know," the kid said, "that furnace of yours has got a backup system. You could pick yourself up a tank of propane in case the line goes down someday. I'd recommend it myself."

"You mean I could have had the furnace running yesterday?"

"Sure. Just needed a tank. Could'a picked one up in town."

Michael shook his head, subduing the sudden surge of anger that welled inside him. "Well, thanks anyway."

After the van had gone he set the thermostat to sixty-five degrees, put the meager supply of groceries in the fridge, and then drove into town. He parked the Corsica outside Horn's Books. When he entered the store the bell above the door tinkled loudly, and Elizabeth stepped immediately from the room at the back. When she saw him her face stiffened slightly, but then she smiled.

Michael let the door swing shut. "Hi," he said.

Elizabeth walked up to the front of the store. Again, she was wearing faded Levis, and a pink pastel sweat top. A half-smoked cigarette dangled from the fingers of her right hand, filling the small store with a delicate tracery of smoke, an underodor that did little to quell the smell of books. "Didn't expect to see you today," she said, leaning across the counter.

Michael shrugged. "Everything's hooked up at my cabin." He smiled.

Elizabeth smiled back, but he could sense the strain behind her eyes. Again, the thought occurred to him: *neither of us wants this.*

"You'll feel more at home now," she said.

"Guess so," he ran a hand through his hair. "I was thinking, maybe you and Tommy could come over for dinner tonight?"

The suggestion caught her completely off guard. She blinked. "I don't . . ."

Michael produced his best winning smile. "Please. You were so kind to me last night. You can't leave a man in debt, not when he's willing to repay your generosity." His smile widened.

Finally the force of his suggestion penetrated her outer layer of armor and her face softened. This time her smile was genuine. "Sure. Why not. Tommy likes you, anyway."

Michael stared at her, his eyes slightly widened, and she blushed furiously. She held out a hand to touch his wrist. "Oh, Michael, that came out wrong. Tommy likes you, but I didn't mean to imply that I *didn't* like you. I . . ."

Michael laughed softly. "I know what you meant."

Elizabeth sighed, face still flushed with embarrassment. "What time should we come over?"

"When you finish here? That should give me enough time to run into Fergus Falls."

"If you're running all that way for groceries . . ." Her hands were on her hips.

"No, nothing like that. Art supplies."

"You're an artist?" The look of genuine surprise on her face was almost comical.

"In my own estimation, perhaps," Michael said, and grinned. "Haven't done any painting in years. I thought I'd try again."

She seemed impressed by his admission, as if she

had not expected him to exhibit any artistic tendencies at all. Once outside, Michael leaned against the Corsica and took a few deep lungfulls of air. The small store had seemed almost claustrophobic. He could see Elizabeth, still leaning on the counter, looking out at him, and he smiled. As he followed 210 into Fergus Falls he allowed his mind to dwell upon her.

There was no way he could spend two months in New York without making a friend. Elizabeth had naturally fallen into that role, and there was nothing else to it. Friends. Neighbors. That's all.

Then what, he thought, was this fluttering feeling in his stomach? A feeling he had not experienced since high school: precursory date-night nervousness.

But this was different. He felt sure he could keep this relationship on the level of friendship, and certainly there was no danger yet of it going beyond that stage. Even in New York, Minnesota, things didn't move that fast!

But he smiled most of the way to Fergus Falls.

The evening followed the general pattern of the previous evening, though both he and Elizabeth seemed slightly more relaxed, Michael thought. It was as if they had both decided that "friendship," without any further complications, might be a possibility. The decision on both their parts seemed to drain away some of the tension that had been present earlier. Michael had picked up a number of groceries in Fergus Falls, including three good sized T-bone steaks, and with Elizabeth's help managed to prepare a moderately impressive meal.

The other factor that kept things from getting beyond their control was the presence of Tommy. The boy seemed to assume the role of a human pressure control valve. While he was present there was absolutely no possibility of the relationship developing unintentionally.

Whenever their conversation seemed to move towards the intimate, Michael noticed that both he and Elizabeth resorted to involving Tommy in one way or another. Though crude, the move was effective. Unfortunately, as the night wore on, this well-used escape route brought to light a fact that neither of them could deny. Whether they wanted it or not, the *tendency* was there to become more intimate. *But we're not allowing it to happen.*

The realization frightened him.

But not enough to stop seeing Elizabeth.

Every night that first week back in New York he saw Elizabeth and Tommy, a ritual that involved alternating cabins. During the days Michael painted. He found himself eager to get lost in his canvases; as soon as he finished his first he became instantly involved in the second. The tensions of three uninterrupted years of Chicago living slipped away, dirty bath water swirling down a drain. The dimension of time assumed new, exciting proportions. One week in Chicago had been like any other, an eyeblink in an eternity of work weeks, each identical to its predecessor. That first week in New York seemed much longer, as if it had elongated to encompass a month. Or maybe more.

One thing Michael could not deny: this was the best he had felt in years. Apart from a few expected twinges, the midmonth low-level throbs, there were no serious bouts of the viral symptoms. In Chicago, though he could easily discern the twenty-eight day regularity of the viral cycle, the periods of ebb were also bothersome. Anxiety and stress were, as John Muir had said from the first, contributing factors. And Chicago, if nothing else, was a stress factory. Perhaps that was why the virus had been acting so crazy lately. Living in New York, Minnesota, was the equivalent of receiving a week-long massage.

She was angry.

And she was hungry.

Together, the combination was a fuel that sent her stalking. For the first time since coming here, she left her car parked at the outskirts of New York and moved on foot. She stuck to the south allotments, moving in the shadows of trees, pale flesh camouflaged perfectly by snow. She moved barefoot, wearing only the leather skirt. Her breasts welcomed the rush of unhindered air. Her skin tingled in the subzero temperatures, comfortable counterpoint to the rising heat within her.

The anger was a result of Michael Smith's actions over the past week. She had thought he had come here to this little pit of a town in order to isolate himself, to gather his senses, but the first thing he had done was to get involved with the bitch from the bookstore. He had seen her almost every day, her and her little boy. Even the thought of the liaison caused her to growl, and once she let loose a long, wavering howl. It cut through the trees like a knife, echoing across the frozen lake, returning as the sound of a haunted wind. Michael, the fool, was directing his desire toward the wrong thing. Even now he did not understand what his body was trying to tell him.

The hunger, of course, was the result of the virus. It's ebb and flow were becoming unpredictable, its sudden risings almost violent. Once or twice she had felt herself on the verge of being swept away by it, engulfed completely. That had never happened before. Always she rode the crest of the wave; always she retained control. This threat of complete possession was not entirely pleasant, and yet it was undeniable. To begin fighting the virus now, after three years of submission, would not be wise. Its symptoms were as much a part of her life as anything she had ever known. Besides, who knew what beneficial changes might be wrought in this new phase? Who could foresee what kind of wondrous creature she might now become? In the meantime, there was the hunger.

She hungered as she had never hungered before. Insatiable.

She moved quickly, silently, through the trees, passing invisibly across clearings. Light snow covered her tracks immediately. She gloried in the power, the simple grace of movement. And she denied the hunger as long as possible, relishing the wave she rode. The stalk was pure fun, a game that took all her attention.

Soon, however, the hunger's voice grew strident, and the stalk became earnest.

Crouched low, stomach almost brushing the snow, she moved now with purpose. Her senses took in everything, cataloging every detail. She was not aware of this process as such, only of the sudden knowledge

66

that *this* was the right way to turn, that *now* was the right time to stop, that *there* the prey was hiding. She moved instinctively, enjoying the heightened awareness the virus afforded, but hardly conscious of what motivated her. Tempered by intelligence, animal instinct turned her into the most dangerous predator the world had ever seen.

Soon, the light began to fade, and darkness seemed to flow from the trees themselves. But the lack of light did not affect her. Her night vision revealed outlines in startling color. Trees pulsated with their own light, and the snow was a softly glowing carpet surrounding her feet. Even the clouds above seemed lit from within, as if a flash of sheet lightning had somehow been caught and tamed.

It was the sound that stopped her.

Thud. Thud. Thud.

She lifted her face, sniffing, and caught the scent. Then, using both pieces of information, she angled across a small clearing, careful now to keep herself hidden.

The cabin was close to the lake, the only one in a row of five or six that showed light. A boy, perhaps seventeen years old, was standing near a leaning shack at the back, whacking at a log with an ax. Sweat glistened on his forehead and the man-smell filled the night. She crouched in darkness, growling. But he did not hear.

She studied the scene before her, searching for danger. The door to the cabin was less than a yard from the boy, and beside the door was a window. A swath of light cast a brilliant square in the snow, sending an arch of illumination out across the frozen lake. Inside she could see two others. Moving. Talking.

The boy's parents?

Yes.

But no danger. They would hear nothing. She would be finished before they had even an inkling that something was wrong.

From her skirt pocket she pulled the small blade, holding it tightly between the thumb and forefinger of her right hand. She disliked using it, but had discovered, long ago, that human flesh was easier to tear if an incision had already been made.

She bolted from her hiding place, silent, hands outstretched. The boy raised his ax, brought it down on the log. The log split, and he began to lower the ax to the snow. She saw all these things as if in slow motion, watching from a distance, an impartial observer. And then she was upon him.

His sudden gasp of breath was a prelude to a scream, she knew that. She planted her hand across his mouth to smother the sound. Her momentum carried him backward, toppling him to the ground. The ax fell from his hand with a clatter, and a small pile of logs, already split, scattered across the snow. Beneath her, he struggled, eyes wide with terror above her silencing hand. She smiled at him, growling, and jabbed the blade into the soft flesh beneath his left ear. He stiffened and convulsed beneath her, a scream vibrating against her hand.

"Shhhh," she said, holding him still. "Enjoy it."

She tugged the knife forward, a smooth movement through skin and muscle and artery. Blood spewed out into the snow like rainwater from a culvert. Again he convulsed, almost throwing her from him.

But she held him tightly, twisted his neck, and ripped his throat out with her teeth.

She ate none of the meat, spitting the chunks into the snow beside the body, but gorged herself only on his blood. He continued to struggle feebly as she fed, but his arms were drained of strength and he was like a child beneath her.

Afterward she stood. Her breasts dripped with his blood. She reached down for some snow and cleaned herself quickly, wiping her face as much as possible. Still the virus worked within her, though not as strongly as before. She debated carrying the body away, dumping it, but decided against it. There was too much blood to hide what had happened. Better to leave it here. Something to attract Michael.

She crouched, and lunged into the snow, moving quickly away from the cabin. The night surrounded her like a blanket and she welcomed it. The smell of blood surrounded her, followed her into the trees. Hunger partially sated, her thoughts again began to work in their accustomed patterns. Michael filled her mind.

For now, one part of her hunger was satisfied. But the other still ached within her, and only Michael could fill that need. How long would she be capable of denying it? She did not know. But she must force him to cross over before that point was reached. He must be ready for her.

Next time, she would hunt closer to him.

Incriminate him fully.

Perhaps the woman from the store. Perhaps her boy.

She smiled at this thought.

But perhaps not.

Continuing to smile as she moved, she began to plan.

On Saturday, Elizabeth and Tommy came over in the early afternoon, intending to take Michael cross-country skiing. But by the time they had waxed their skis the midafternoon snowfall showed signs of intensifying, and the weather reports from Fergus Falls warned of an approaching storm. They remained in the cabin all afternoon, Tommy engrossed in a science fiction novel titled *Ringworld,* by Larry Niven, while Michael and Elizabeth sat at the kitchen table and played crazy eights. By six, after darkness had fully fallen, the snow began to let up. The storm had missed them. By eight, patches of clear starry sky were showing through the slowly moving clouds.

"I'm feeling a bit of cabin fever," Michael said. "Anybody for a short walk?"

"Good idea," Elizabeth seconded.

Tommy looked up at the two of them with disgust. "I'm almost finished. You two go for a walk. I'm staying here."

Michael looked at Elizabeth. She winked, and shrugged back. Michael felt a slight flutter in his stomach.

Outside, the crisp night air was instantly refreshing. The new-fallen snow was a pristine, virgin blanket across the land. Only the blacktop, kept mostly clear by the wind, was suitable for walking on. They walked slowly back toward Elizabeth's cabin.

Earlier in the day Elizabeth had asked to see his

paintings. Reluctantly, Michael had agreed. She had studied one and then the other, her face impassive. Finally she turned to him and said: "You painted this one first and then this one." She had been right. How had she known? "Look at it," she had said. "This first one, it's so strange. The lake is a bowl of light. . . ."

"Snow," Michael had said in defense.

"Yes, but look at the tree line. It's a wall of darkness. Almost a living wall of darkness. It looks almost like a conglomeration of bodies, demons or something, watching. Like the lake is an arena. Look how the trees melt into the sky. You can hardly tell which is which. It's spooky."

He studied the picture again and was forced to agree.

"But this other one is different. It's the same scene. . . ."

"I wanted to get it right."

Elizabeth had laughed. "Yes, but it's a *lot* different. Like somebody else painted it. See, you can even see glimmers of light through the trees in this one. And the sky, it's bright and clean, trying to reach through and touch the lake. It's a much happier painting."

Michael studied them, one after the other.

"It's how you've changed since you got here, Michael," Elizabeth said. "The dark one is earlier; the light one is later." She smiled at him, but he had not smiled back.

Her analysis had been far too close for comfort. "I paint what I see and feel."

Now, walking along the road, the newly fallen snow a glowing carpet through the trees, echoing the light of a gibbous moon, he brought up the subject of his

71

paintings again. "You liked my paintings?"

Elizabeth nodded. "Yes. Very much." She lit a cigarette and exhaled a cloud of smoke. They were walking close but not touching.

"I never really saw what you saw in them until you said it," Michael said. "About the dark and the light."

Elizabeth chuckled. "You're not supposed to, are you? Artists are too close to their work. They paint their souls and don't recognize themselves." She smiled at him and took another puff on the cigarette.

Michael frowned. "But you were right. You were right on the money. I've changed since I came . . . home. I can feel it. I feel like I'm washing away years of dirt and grime."

Elizabeth looked at him thoughtfully. "Is there a lot to wash away?"

Michael glanced at her, then away again, troubled by the compassion in her eyes. "Who knows. City life is dirty, I guess."

"Nothing more than that?"

"Elizabeth, I . . ." He turned to face her fully, both of them stopping in the middle of the road. Her eyes were unreadable. "This is a therapeutic holiday for me," he said softly. "You, and Tommy, are really making it work."

For a long moment they stood, staring at each other. Michael found himself getting lost in her deep brown eyes. And then, before he could stop himself, he stepped closer, brought his face down, and kissed her softly on the lips. When he stepped back her eyes were wide in undisguised shock. Michael felt a stab of shame at what he had done.

"I'm sorry. I shouldn't have done that." The apol-

72

ogy sounded lame and scarcely adequate.

But the shocked look quickly left Elizabeth's eyes, and she smiled up at him. "Don't be sorry. I just wasn't ready."

"It should never have happened," Michael insisted.

Elizabeth laughed softly. "Michael, we've been *stopping* it from happening since the day we met."

He gazed steadily into her eyes, and after a moment's hesitation leaned forward and kissed her again. This time he felt her lips move beneath his own. It was as if a wave of electricity had passed through them. His whole body began to thrum to some impossibly high frequency. Elizabeth's lips were soft, warm, and pliable beneath his own. He brought his arms up and drew her body closer to him and felt her arms grip him. When he probed gently with his tongue at her lips, she opened eagerly to him. Michael pushed himself away and heaved in a deep breath.

"Jesus . . ."

"Whew," Elizabeth said softly. She smiled nervously at him. "I don't know what just happened, my friend, but I think we should talk about it."

Michael nodded numbly. In a brief span of seconds he had stepped across a boundary carefully guarded over the past three years. Stepped over, and destroyed his defenses. For a moment he was gripped in such terrible, cold anger that he could hardly breathe. But Elizabeth reached out and touched his mitted hand with her own.

"Michael what's wrong?"

And the anger was gone, replaced instead with incredulity. A grin spread across his face and he could not get it off. Nothing was wrong, he realized. Absolutely nothing. He clasped his hand around hers and began to walk again. But they did not talk. There seemed nothing to say. The moonlight-dappled darkness had assumed an aura of romance, something Michael found himself incapable of defending himself against. His thoughts were in turmoil.

Upon reaching Elizabeth's cabin they turned around and began walking back toward his own. Michael was intensely aware, right down to the tips of his toes, of Elizabeth's proximity. It was if there were an electrical field around her, stimulating him fully. She, too, seemed lost in her own thoughts.

About a hundred yards from the turnoff to Michael's cabin, Elizabeth stopped dead in her tracks, staring ahead. Michael followed her gaze.

"What is it?"

"There's another car at your cabin," Elizabeth said softly.

Michael squinted his eyes. "Damn. That's Bob Brisk's car."

"Oh, Jesus," Elizabeth said, a tremor in her voice. "Tommy . . ."

"Come on." Holding her hand, Michael began to walk faster, finally pulling her into a trot as they turned into the snow-covered gravel turnoff.

The front screen door of the porch swung open as they approached, and a dark figure emerged. Michael and Elizabeth slowed to a halt.

"Evening, Elizabeth," Bob Brisk said. "Michael."

"Bob, what's wrong. Is Tommy . . ." Elizabeth's voice trembled uncontrollably.

"No, no, nothing like that," Brisk said. "I came by to see Michael. Tommy said you were out for a while.

But he wouldn't let me in." He smiled without humor.

Michael chuckled. "You'd disturb his reading," he said.

Brisk stopped smiling. He stared steadily at Michael. "Been for a walk, have you?"

"Yes," Michael said carefully. "It's a nice night."

Brisk nodded, glancing quickly at Elizabeth, then back to Michael. "Been together all day?"

Michael did not immediately answer. The anger he had felt earlier suddenly returned in a rush. "I'm sorry if you're not able to deal with my seeing Elizabeth. I really am. But I don't think it's any of your business what Elizabeth and I have been doing."

Brisk's face turned noticeably whiter. "Oh, but it is my business, Mr. Big City Fella." He took a step closer to Michael, and although a good six inches shorter, he radiated a definitely menacing aura.

"Bob," Elizabeth said sharply, "stop acting like a child!"

Brisk turned to Elizabeth, and grinned. His teeth gleamed white in the darkness. He chuckled. "You don't understand. I don't care what you've been doing together. I just want to know where you've been." He turned back to Michael, and the smile left his face. "We found another body. Ripped to shreds. Same as Syd Jaeger."

"Oh, hell," Michael said softly. Behind him Elizabeth gasped sharply.

"What I need to know," Bob Brisk said to Michael, now smiling in apparent good humor, "is your alibi."

CHAPTER FIVE

Michael stopped in midbreath, attention frozen on Bob Brisk's tight smile. For a moment he wondered if he was hallucinating, but the cop's cold, unwavering gaze was as real as a bullet. Behind him, Michael heard Elizabeth shuffle, then felt the gentle touch of her hand on his right arm.

"Bob, you can't seriously be asking that," Elizabeth said softly.

Brisk frowned, which had the effect of narrowing his eyes to glinting slits. "No joke. I need to know where you were this afternoon, Michael."

"I was here," Michael said, his voice much steadier than he had expected. A cold wave had passed through him, and he was not yet sure if it represented fear or anger.

"All afternoon?" Brisk asked.

"All day," Michael said.

"That's true," Elizabeth said. "I phoned Michael here at around ten thirty this morning. Then at noon. And Tommy and I got over here before one o'clock."

"Didn't go outside or anything?"

"Not until now," Michael said. "And we weren't gone more than half an hour."

Brisk nodded, then pulled out a black spiral-bound pocket notebook and scribbled a couple of notes.

"What's this all about, Bob?" Elizabeth said. "What's Michael got to do with it?"

Brisk shrugged, and some of the menacing confidence was pulled back into its lair. For when it's needed next, Michael thought to himself. The cop was like a bristling dog who suddenly found himself face to face with a friend rather than the expected intruder. It he'd had a tail it would be wagging, Michael thought. Michael found his own hackles settling down.

"Like I said," Brisk said, now visibly more relaxed. "We found another body. Herb Kramer, in the south allotments. Same as Syd Jaeger. Pretty badly chewed up, but also signs of dirty work just the same."

"Oh, God," Elizabeth said. "Herb was only . . . what, sixteen years old?"

Brisk nodded, focusing again on Michael. "I wasn't harassing your friend here," he said. "Been out ascertaining everybody's whereabouts. Got Sally making the rounds in the south allotments. Getting everybody riled up, I expect, but there's nothing else for it," he said in exasperation.

Michael nodded in sympathy, now sorry about his snide comments to Brisk about Elizabeth. "Anything else you need?"

Brisk shook his head, straightening out his black cap. "You're clear on this one," he said. "Gary and Ellen Kramer were inside their cabin when it happened. Herb was out back chopping wood. Doc Unger estimates time of death between three and four o'clock." Brisk grinned. "Don't suppose you folks went strolling through the south allotments at that time?"

Michael shook his head. *Clear on this one.* But what about the last one, he thought. Or the next one.

"Bob, we were here . . ." Elizabeth began.

"Yeah, I know. All afternoon." He nodded and stepped past them toward the police car, but stopped and faced them before opening the driver's door. "If I were you, I wouldn't go leaving Tommy alone like you just did. Especially not at night. Not while this sort of thing is going on."

"He was safe in the cabin," Michael said quietly, squeezing Elizabeth's hand.

"Maybe. Maybe not," Brisk said. "Found Herb Kramer's body less than a yard from his folks' cabin. Like I said, his mom and dad were inside. Didn't hear a thing. Whatever's doing this, it's quiet and it's stealthy. Damnedest animal I ever heard of." He smiled at them then slid into the car.

Once the police car had turned onto the blacktop and driven out of sight, Michael and Elizabeth entered the cabin. Tommy was sitting on the sofa, still reading his book, and he looked up as they came in. His face was troubled.

"Tommy, are you okay?" Elizabeth asked.

"Sure. You saw Bait Bucket, I guess."

"Bait . . ." Michael began.

"Tommy, that's not nice."

Tommy shrugged. "He wanted to see Michael. He wanted to look around the place. I told him to wait outside. What's the problem?"

"Another boy was killed today," Elizabeth said.

Tommy looked at Michael. "Why did he want to talk to you?"

"He's talking to everybody," Michael said,

Tommy stared at him for a moment, then nodded, apparently satisfied.

"I guess we should get going," Elizabeth said to Michael, and her voice trembled slightly.

Michael put his hands on her shoulders. "You and Tommy are staying here tonight. You can have the master bedroom and Tommy can have the guest room."

"Michael . . ."

"No arguments, please. I'd feel better about it if you'd stay."

For a moment he thought she was going to refuse, but suddenly her features were suffused with what could only be relief. She's frightened, Michael thought. And the realization came, like a flash bulb going off in the dark: *I'm frightened too.*

Tommy stood in front of the bathroom mirror and brushed his teeth with the index finger of his right hand, spat out a huge wad of foamy Crest toothpaste, and finally rinsed his mouth with cold water. In the hallway he could see that Mike had closed his bedroom door, providing them with some privacy. But Mom's door was open and she was lying on the bed reading and smoking. Tommy stepped into the master bedroom.

"Finished?" Mom regarded him with suspicion.

Tommy rolled his eyes. "I even used my finger to

brush my teeth, okay?"

"How about behind the ears?"

"Jesus . . ."

"Tommy!"

"I'm clean, I'm clean!"

Mom shook her head, then smiled. She took a puff on her cigarette, blew a cloud of smoke into the air, and then crushed it out in an ashtray on the bedside table. It took Tommy a moment to pinpoint what was wrong. After Syd Jaeger had been killed at the beginning of the week Mom had gone on and on about how even New York, Minnesota, wasn't safe anymore. But tonight, after an initial bout of anxiety, she seemed to have forgotten that Herb Kramer was also dead. Why wasn't she fluttering over him like he was a baby? Why wasn't she complaining about crime? Why wasn't she bemoaning the fact that little New York was becoming nearly as bad as its larger namesake?

Instead, she lay in bed, lips curled in a small smile that had been there most of the night.

"What are you so happy about?" Tommy asked at last, moving further into the room. He sat himself on a chair beside the closet.

Mom blinked and looked at him in shock.

"Is it that noticeable?"

Tommy shrugged. "I guess so."

Mom's smile widened slightly. "Michael kissed me tonight."

Tommy rolled his eyes backwards and retched. Is that what it was all about? "About time," he muttered.

"What?"

"I knew that was going to happen the day you

80

brought him home for dinner."

She pursed her lips and regarded him coolly. "You did, huh?"

"Yup."

"Do you like Michael?"

"Sure. He's okay."

"I like him too."

"No kidding."

Mom lifted one of the pillows as if to throw it at him, and Tommy darted from the room. He halted in the doorway and glared back at her. "Mike and Mom, up a tree, k-i-s-s-i-n-g," he began. "First comes love, then comes . . ."

"Tommy!"

He laughed and trotted through to the guest room before she really tossed something at him. In bed, he lay looking out the window. This room did not give as good a view of the sky as his own, since two large oak trees towered above the cabin on this side, but he could see the occasional star between their gnarled, naked winter branches. Soon he rolled over and faced the wall, almost relieved that there was no Iron Maiden demon to assail his senses.

Against his wishes he found his mind dwelling on the murders of the week past. He had not known either victim, but he had seen them around town. Both were older boys, effectively removed from his stratum by their age. But in New York it was hard not to know somebody by sight. Syd Jaeger had worked summers in the movie theater, and Herb Kramer sometimes worked with his father to repaint the town's peeling road signs. Both boys were dead now.

Dead. Like Dad. Just dead.

Except that Bob Brisk had wanted to talk to Michael about it. Bob Brisk who thought he was some kind of back woods Sherlock Holmes.

Tommy rolled over again, aware that sleep was slowly impinging on his consciousness and that he was not thinking entirely clearly.

What possible connection could Michael Smith have with the two dead boys?

An image of Michael formed in his mind: pale face, short brown hair, friendly grey-blue eyes. A brief image of Syd Jaeger followed, smiling stupidly behind the popcorn counter at the movie house, and then a sudden shift: the flashing red lights of Bob Brisk's police car, the crumpled body in the snow, and the pool of black blood.

Tommy groaned, shifting restlessly.

Michael's face was back, lips curled up, eyes smiling. He imagined Michael kissing Mom and remembered Mom's smile.

And then, on the screen of his mind, Michael opened his mouth to smile, and gleaming behind the pale lips were two rows of serrated shark's teeth.

Dripping black blood.

On Sunday, Michael allowed himself to be dragged on a cross-country ski trip around the entire perimeter of Great Lake, a trail of more than fifteen miles, and by the time they returned to the cabin he was a mass of aches, pains, and throbs. To Elizabeth and Tommy it had been just another Sunday jaunt. They regarded him afterward with sympathetic amusement. He would get better at it, they promised him. Michael did not believe them.

Although he tried most of the day to maneuver himself into a moment of privacy with Elizabeth, Tommy always seemed to be near. The boy's keen eyes followed them everywhere, as if he were fully aware of what was on Michael's mind. But when Michael dropped them off at their own cabin after dinner, he was shocked when Elizabeth reached up and kissed him warmly on the lips while Tommy stood silently observing.

"Drop by the bookstore tomorrow," she whispered to him.

Michael nodded. "G'night, Tommy," he said.

Tommy smiled mischievously. "Bye."

After Tommy disappeared inside, Michael whispered to Elizabeth: "Does he know about us?"

"Before we knew ourselves, I think," she replied, smiling.

Michael frowned. "He approves?"

"He doesn't disapprove. Let's take it from there."

Monday morning heralded the beginning of a bright new week. All indications that a storm had threatened during the weekend were gone, and the sky stretched open blue from horizon to horizon. Michael drove into Fergus Falls after a quick breakfast of instant coffee and toast, intending to pick up another couple of canvases and a large sketch pad. But when he arrived in Fergus Falls an hour later, he passed Frazer's Art Supplies without stopping.

He drove up and down side streets, trying to remember the layout of the town. Finally, two large corner buildings clicked in his mind, and he seemed to snap back to his childhood, when he had known this city as if it were a familiar playground. He parked the Corsica near City Hall and walked the half block to the Fergus Falls Public Library.

The librarian was a slim, attractive woman in her mid thirties, who responded to Michael's requests for help with warm enthusiasm.

"No, I don't think there's a separate publication for statistics from each individual township," she said regarding Michael thoughtfully. "But I believe each is listed individually in the statistical almanac for the entire Otter Tail County area. Would that be suitable?"

"Should be," Michael said.

She disappeared into an aisle of enclosed shelves and returned a few moments later with a stack of slim, softbound volumes. "This will take you back ten years. If you need more, just let me know."

He returned her smile and took the stack of publications from her arm. In a wooden booth next to a window overlooking a snow-covered rockery on the south side of the Library he studied what she had given him. There were ten volumes in all, each bearing the title: *Otter Tail County Sheriff's Department: Crime And Accident Statistics*. Michael began at the most recent volume and slowly worked his way backward. The design of the almanac was simple. After an overview of the entire county, each township was presented individually, with the statistics organized by types of crime. The township of New York had the smallest section in each of the books.

Apart from a few cases of minor assault, one or two scattered incidents of aggravated assault, and two nonfatal hunting accidents in the same month three years ago, New York was a relatively crime-free town. Most of the incidents of assault occurred during the summer months, when the area was flooded with tourists from the big cities, or immediately after graduation, when the local kids were a bit wild. The last murder in New York had occurred nine years ago, and although the almanac gave only the bare statistics, Michael remembered it.

Old Martin Sharpe had killed his wife during a terrific bender. She had taken the bottle of bourbon from his hands and begun to pour it down the drain. Martin had flown into a rage and had knocked her to the ground. Her head had hit the edge of the sink counter, and she had died three days later of a slow cerebral hemorrhage. The incident had been the talk of the town. Michael had been twenty-one at the time, and back in New York after a semester at the University of Michigan.

The almanac also listed incidents of animal attack. There were nineteen such incidents over the past ten years, fifteen involving wild dogs, one listed as a bear attack on a camper, and three cases of rabid skunk bite. None fatal.

He handed the pile of almanacs back to the librarian and thanked her for her help. At Frazer's he picked up two more canvases, a large Grubacher sketch pad, and a box of soft charcoal. By the time he started the drive back to New York it was close to 3:00 P.M., and a thin smatter of high cumulus clouds had appeared in the sky.

Michael drove carefully, eyes following the meandering path of blacktop as it wound through the rippling countryside of hills and lakes. But his mind was elsewhere. He was thinking of the statistics.

In the past ten years there had been only two unexplained deaths in New York.

And they had both occurred since Michael had arrived in town.

CHAPTER SIX

It was close to 4:00 P.M. when Michael drove into New York. The thin smatter of clouds had turned into a towering bank encroaching from the northwest, and the gentle morning wind had taken on a nasty, gusting edge. Particles of ice and snow stung his neck and face the moment he stepped from the car. When he entered Horn's Books, Elizabeth immediately appeared from the back room, the curious look on her face turning to pleasure.

"Thought you might have gone back to Chicago, Mister," she said, smiling.

Michael chuckled. "You don't know me well enough yet if you thought that," he said.

Elizabeth came up to the front of the store, pulling down the sleeves of the sky blue angora sweater that snugly hugged her upper body. The faded Levis had given way to a darker pair of designer jeans, the taut fabric exquisitely tracing the smooth lines of her buttocks and long legs. Michael felt his eyes widening in appreciation and seemed powerless to stop himself from gaping. But Elizabeth was not offended. Instead, the pleasant smile on her face turned decidedly lascivious. She stepped closer to him and looked up at his face.

"We never got a chance yesterday to continue . . . ," she began, and then she reached up and kissed him firmly on the lips.

Michael was too surprised to do anything but return the kiss. Soon he felt Elizabeth's soft body pressed close to his own. He ran his hands slowly up and down her back, finally lowering them until they cupped her buttocks. Elizabeth broke the kiss and slapped his hands playfully.

"I wasn't sure if the other night had actually happened or if I had dreamed it," she said softly.

"I had the same feeling," Michael said, "until now." He walked further into the store, scanning the rows of books without really seeing any of them. He could sense Elizabeth's eyes on his back as she leaned on the front counter and lit a cigarette. When he turned around she was studying him with ill-disguised interest. Her eyes followed a slow path from the black leather boots on his feet, up along the dark brown cotton pants, where her eyes widened perceptibly as they crossed the obvious bulge that had grown there, across his dark blue ski jacket, finally coming to rest on his eyes. Michael smiled and held out his arms. "Do I meet with your approval?"

She smiled, drew on her cigarette, and her eyes twinkled. "You'll do."

Michael walked slowly over to the counter. He studied Elizabeth's face carefully, and before long she began to mirror his own earnestness. "When I told you the other day that I never really got involved with anybody . . ."

"It was the truth," she finished for him.

Michael blinked. Could she read him that easily? He nodded. "I said it was because I didn't really have the time, but the truth is, I've avoided emotional entanglement for a number of reasons."

"We all have our secrets," she said quickly, silencing him.

"But you hardly know me," he protested.

"Nor you me," she said.

When he did not respond, Elizabeth sighed. "Michael, it's obvious that both of us have kept to ourselves for a long time, and I'm sure your reasons are as good as mine. I don't know what's happening between you and me, all I know is that it's something that hasn't happened to me in . . . years."

Michael nodded, hoping she read the action as an echo of her sentiments.

"Now we're getting all serious and thoughtful about something that should just . . . happen. I mean, hell, why don't we let it? Just to see what happens?" She smiled hopefully.

"There are things about me you don't know."

"If I'm meant to know them, you'll tell me eventually."

Michael reached out and touched the swath of hair lying on her left shoulder. It felt like silk beneath his fingers. She lifted a hand and pressed his hand to her cheek. "Maybe we both need what's happening," she said, and stepped into the circle of his arms. He crushed her to his chest and kissed her.

It was only the sudden warning tinkle of the bell above the door that broke them apart. Elizabeth brushed her hands over her sweater, putting on a smiling face. But as the door clicked shut her eyes narrowed and her lips tightened into a thin line.

"Damn it, Bob Brisk, if I didn't know better I'd say you were harassing us!"

Michael turned more quickly than he intended, and the look of shock was still etched in his face when Bob Brisk focused on him. Silhouetted against the bright glass of the door, Brisk looked like a teenager dressed as a cowboy. It was only when he stepped deeper into the dimness of the store that the lines on his face became clear, and the teenager's face instantly metamorphosed into that of a worried, intense adult. Brisk's wide face softened into a smile that was not completely pleasant.

"Thought I might find you here," he said to Michael.

"I think Elizabeth may be right," Michael said quietly.

"About harassing you?" Now the smile was definitely humorous. "What reason could I possibly have for harassing an ex-hometown boy on vacation?"

"Maybe you'll tell me, so we can stop playing this ridiculous game. You're like a jack-in-the-box, Bob. Popping up all over the place."

Brisk chuckled. He reached into the breast pocket of his khaki parka and withdrew a crumpled package of Marlboros. *How did I know he smoked those?* He slowly placed the cigarette between his lips, lit it, and exhaled an expansive cloud of smoke into the already musty room. He studied Michael with open curiosity. Although Bob Brisk was a good six inches shorter than himself, Michael distinctly began to feel that it

90

was he who was lacking in stature. Height has nothing to do with it, he thought. That man has *presence*.

"How are the roads into Fergus Falls," Brisk asked casually, taking another deep drag on his cigarette.

Michael paused before answering. "Clean," he said at last.

Brisk nodded. "Get everything you needed?"

"Yes," Michael said simply, becoming angry with the elusive interrogation.

"How did you like the library?"

Michael opened his mouth to respond, but shut it again angrily. For a few seconds he locked eyes with Brisk and then looked away before his emotions jumped another notch. "You followed me," he said, his voice low and even.

Brisk shook his head. "Not me. Had Sally take a run after you."

Michael shrugged, then shook his head in confusion. "But why? What have I done?"

"I was hoping you'd tell me," Brisk said.

Elizabeth slapped her hand on the counter. "Bob, if you've got something to get off your chest, then get it the hell off! Because we're both getting pretty damned tired of this."

Brisk held out his hands in a calming gesture. "Liz, keep out of this. I want to talk to Michael."

"So let's talk," Michael said.

"Maybe we should take a walk," Bob said. "It's kinda stuffy in here, ain't it?" He took another drag on his cigarette and added to the haze in the room.

"You can talk here," Elizabeth said.

Brisk turned to Michael and raised his eyebrows. "You want to talk here, Michael?"

Michael glanced from Brisk to Elizabeth, then back to Brisk. Something in the police chief's tone said that to go against him in this would bring more trouble than Michael was prepared for. Much more. "Let's walk," he said at last.

Brisk nodded, smiling. "I'll wait outside for you." He tipped his cap to Elizabeth, then opened the door and stepped out into the cold. The bell above the door tinkled, then became silent.

"That man . . ." Elizabeth said in exasperation.

"He justs wants to talk," Michael said. He laid a hand on her shoulder to calm her. "It can't hurt."

"But I can't help thinking he's just jealous, or maybe . . ."

Michael grinned. "I wish that was all it was," he said. "But two boys have been killed in this area in less than a week. I just got back in town. He's acting like any normal cop."

Elizabeth's eyes widened, and Michael realized the connection had not occurred to her before now. He could see her quickly analyze the idea from a number of angles, eyes focused on his, until finally she blinked. "That's ridiculous," she said.

"I'll talk to him," Michael said. He leaned forward and kissed her on the lips. As he was about to break away she held him, pulled him closer, and pushed her tongue past his lips. When they finally broke, Michael shook his head as if to clear it. "Whew."

"Come by the cabin later," she said.

Michael nodded, then turned and went out into the cold.

* * *

Bob Brisk was leaning against Michael's Corsica, a half smoked Marlboro hanging from his lips. He was watching us through the window, Michael realized. The thought cheered him slightly. Brisk straightened when Michael emerged from the store, dropped the cigarette to the snow-covered sidewalk, then crushed it out with his black-booted heel.

"You and Elizabeth are hitting it off," Brisk said. His face revealed no emotion.

Michael shrugged. "Yeah, I guess so."

"She's a nice girl."

Now Michael chuckled. "Yes, she is. Is this what you wanted to talk about?"

Bob Brisk did not smile. "No. Come on." He began to walk north along the street. Michael paused, glancing back at the store. Elizabeth was still leaning on the counter, gazing out at him. He locked eyes with her for a moment then followed quickly after Brisk.

Though short, Brisk had a long stride to his legs, and walked at a good speed. Michael found himself hurrying to keep up. "Y'know," Brisk said thoughtfully, "you get some small town folks who run off to the big city, and all of a sudden they start thinking there pretty damn sophisticated. Like they've shucked off the blinders kept 'em from seeing things the way they *really* are."

Michael said nothing.

"Then once in a while they come waltzing back, flashing their sharp new cars and sharp new clothes, and all of a sudden they're better than they ever were before. A step above the backwoods bumpkins they left behind. That the way you feel, Michael?"

Again, Michael said nothing.

93

"But some things don't change from the big city to the small," Brisk said, his voice now lower and less laden with sarcasm. "A dead boy in Chicago is just as dead in New York, Minnesota."

"I've noticed," Michael said sharply, and instantly wished he had kept his mouth shut.

Brisk glanced at him sternly, then smiled. "What I'm trying to say is that I don't think you're stupid."

"Thanks a lot," Michael said.

"And I don't want you to think I'm stupid either," Brisk said.

Michael glanced at him, trying to read the cop's face. "I don't," he said.

Brisk nodded. "Good. That'll make this a bit easier, both of us being fairly intelligent." He chuckled. "Sally tells me you were looking through the county's crime statistics. Find anything interesting?"

Michael frowned, not liking the direction of the conversation.

"Come on, I thought we agreed neither of us is stupid. I'll tell you what you found," he stopped walking, and turned to face Michael. "You found that New York, the little crab apple, hasn't had a murder in ten years. You found that we're a quiet little community that hardly had any use for cops at all. Until last week."

"What are you getting at?"

"I'm saying that you got home on Monday morning," Brisk studied Michael's face carefully. "Monday night we had our first murder since I joined the force. Saturday we had the second." He dug out his package of Marlboros and lit another one. He took two deep lungfulls of smoke before continuing. "Today you run

94

into Fergus Falls and show a pretty keen interest in what's been going on."

"Damn it, Brisk, I didn't kill those kids!"

Bob Brisk laughed. "Hell, I know that." He turned and began walking again.

Michael frowned, squinting his eyes against a sudden squall of ice particles.

"You got an airtight alibi for the second, and nothing to tie you to the first," Brisk said. "But I'm betting you got some good ideas about it all." He smiled at Michael, and his eyes were like chunks of ice. "You didn't kill those boys, but I think something followed you out here from Chicago that ain't so innocent."

CHAPTER SEVEN

The sudden chill that caused a shiver to run up Michael's spine was not caused by the cold, and he found himself unable to respond to what Brisk had said. And the cop was not above noticing Michael's sudden silence.

"Something sound right about that?" Brisk asked, still smiling.

"Nothing sounds right about any of this," Michael said, forcing himself to remain calm.

But Brisk was not about to be put off. "Oh, hell, I thought we agreed neither of us was stupid." Brisk took a drag on his cigarette and let the smoke trail out of his nostrils. "Come on, I've got some stuff I want to show you."

"Where are we going?"

"Station house."

Brisk stepped away, but Michael did not follow. "Do I have a choice in this?"

Brisk turned back, and although his lips were curled up it was not a smile. "Sure you do, Mike. Just make the right one."

Michael shook his head. In a moment he followed reluctantly, a vague uneasy feeling tugging at him. Ahead, the squat concrete bunker of the police station looked like an oversized pill box from a war movie. "Am I going to be allowed to leave?"

"What do you think?" Brisk snorted. "If I was going to hold you, I wouldn't have asked you to come for a walk. Not so nicely, anyhow. I said you were *connected* to these deaths. That doesn't make you guilty of anything. Not yet."

A sudden gust of wind caused both Brisk and Michael to turn their backs, as a small cloud of razor-sharp ice particles funneled around them. "The connection is purely coincidental," Michael said through gritted teeth.

"Ain't no such thing as coincidence," Brisk said. "Not in a small town like this," he turned and began moving forward again. "You need a lot of variables for coincidence to come into play. Like the population of Chicago, say. But up here, we don't have to fall back on coincidence to explain things. Usually there's a causal relationship. Sometimes it's a bit hard to see, but it always comes to light eventually."

Michael pursed his lips and remained silent. At the station Bob Brisk pulled a key from his jacket pocket and unlocked the front glass doors, holding one of them open for Michael. Michael stepped into the pocket of calm and warmth. As Brisk pushed the door closed a gust of wind sent a blast of glittering ice particles past their feet. Outside, the wind howled.

"Sounds like a storm coming," Brisk said, stepping past Michael. He unzipped his parka, shucked it off, and draped it over a seat behind the reception counter.

97

Michael unzipped his ski jacket but did not remove it. He followed Brisk through the small open area behind the reception counter and into the office he had first seen Brisk emerging from.

Brisk dropped heavily into the padded seat behind the desk. He knitted his fingers beneath his chin and regarded Michael thoughtfully. "Sit," he said at last.

Michael glanced at the open seat in front of the desk, then back at Brisk.

"I'm not going to keep you long," Brisk said.

Michael shrugged, and lowered himself into the seat.

Brisk smiled faintly. "I can see you think I'm taking a run at you for no good reason," he said. "But you gotta look at this from my perspective. You come waltzing back into town and we have two weird deaths inside a week. There's gotta be a connection. I'm not saying you know what that connection is, but it seems apparent that there is one. I mean, take the case of that little widow over in Hinton couple years back. String of break-ins over a period of a month, and the only common thread is that the owners are all friends of this woman. A connection. Obviously she ain't the perp, but maybe she knows something. Turns out her cleaning lady got the addresses of these single retired women from our gal's address book and passed them onto her sleezeball boyfriend. A connection. Innocent, but it was there."

"I don't know *anything* about the two boys that were killed," Michael protested feebly.

Brisk shrugged. "Maybe not." He pushed a file folder across the desk toward Michael. "Here, take a look at this."

Michael leaned forward and picked up the folder, almost a quarter inch thick. He glanced up at Brisk uneasily.

"Go ahead. Look."

Michael pulled back the cover of the file folder to reveal an eight by ten black and white glossy photograph. At first glance it was an abstract form, an exercise in light and shadow. It took a moment for his perceptions to shift, and suddenly the scene sprang to life. The twisted blob in the center assumed the dimensions of a human, curled into a semifetal ball. Even from this odd angle the ragged edges of a throat wound were visible, as were the dark spatters of blood around the head. The clothes had been ripped from the body, and the torso looked like it had been mangled pretty badly.

"Christ . . ." Michael let the cover fall closed.

"No, look at the rest."

"I can't, it's . . ." Michael's voice was hoarse.

"Goddamn it, look! We've got two dead kids and I don't want any more. I want you to look through those, and then I'm going to ask you some questions." Brisk sighed, stabbing his cigarette out in three violent motions. His face softened slightly, and he took a deep breath. "Please, just look."

Michael flipped open the file folder again and began to leaf through the pile of photographs. There were a number of long shots from various angles, showing the bodies in full. When he got to the close ups of their faces, and then the extreme close ups of the ragged throat wounds, Michael felt his bile rising. He groaned, and dropped the folder back on the desk.

"Okay," Bob Brisk said softly. "I'll tell you what the pictures don't show. At first we assumed animal attack. Hell, look at their throats, and look at the way Syd Jaeger's chest was scratched up. But Doc Unger's preliminary inspection revealed a deep laceration in the flesh of the throat that could not have been caused by animal jaws." He studied Michael's face carefully. "Their throats had been cut before being ripped out," Brisk said.

"Oh, God . . ." Michael felt a wave of nausea pass over him, and he held his breath until it passed.

"No signs of a struggle at either site. Bunch of muddled footprints, but nothing clear. No animal tracks at all. Damned snow covers everything."

"I've never seen anything like it," Michael said softly.

"You're sure?"

"Believe me, I would have remembered."

Brisk shook his head. "Michael, you're from Chicago. It's a big city. Lots of weird stuff going on. Cults and stuff," now he focused directly on Michael's eyes and there was no compassion there at all. "Were you involved in any sort of activity, I mean even peripherally, that might . . ."

"For God's sake, no!"

Brisk was silent for a few moments, but would not take his eyes from Michael. "Something else. Doc Unger says there was a fair amount of blood loss from each body. Much more than we can account for in the splatter patterns at the sites. Just gone."

Michael's eyes widened before he could control his reaction, and he stared down at this lap.

"Now, I could take your word for it that you've had

100

no dealings with any group in Chicago that works in this way," he smiled grimly. "But I won't. I'm a cop, right? Got to check these things out. So I've cabled the Chicago area PD. They're checking their records for a similar MO. I've also given them your name."

Michael looked up sharply, fighting back a surge of anger. Bob Brisk was still smiling. "We'll see what comes up. I hope you haven't been lying to me, Michael."

"I haven't."

Brisk nodded. "Then I better let you get back to Elizabeth."

Michael stood slowly, and walked to the door of the office. He turned and glared at Brisk. "I had nothing to do with any of this."

Brisk picked up the folder and dropped it into his desk drawer, then slowly pushed the drawer back into place. "Maybe not. But I've been a cop for twelve years, and even out here in the boonies that stands for something. I've got a cop's instincts, a cop's hunches. Yeah, I know, sound's silly, doesn't it?"

But Michael wasn't smiling.

"And right now," Bob Brisk said. "I get the feeling you aren't saying everything you know. What are you hiding, Michael?"

Michael shook his head, then turned and walked quickly from the police station. He could feel the cold, hard glare of Bob Brisk's eyes on his back. Outside, the cold had a welcome bracing effect. It was like stepping out of a dream. But he could not get the memories of the stark black and white glossies to leave his mind. The close-ups of the throat wounds were etched indelibly in his memory.

And another set of memories thrummed to life in sympathy.

But, of course, Sondra had nothing to do with the present. Absolutely nothing. In fact, she was probably dead by now. Long dead. It was foolish and paranoid to even bring her to mind.

But no matter how hard he tried, she would not leave.

CHAPTER EIGHT

After Michael Smith had gone, Bob Brisk lifted his feet and rested them on the edge of his desk. Although he knew he shouldn't, he lit another cigarette and breathed the smoke deeply. The smoked burned his mouth and the back of his throat, and at the bottom of his lungs he felt the flesh rebelling at the intake of noxious fumes. But he did not cough. The smoke calmed him. It took away some of the edge that talking to Michael Smith had left behind.

What was it about Michael Smith that bothered him? Brisk took another deep drag on the cigarette, hissing the smoke out through his nose and mouth. Hell, there was a lot about Smith that bothered him. Like the way he moved so quickly in on Elizabeth Turner when not so long ago his own advances had been . . . *spurned*. It was the only word he could think of. So there was that. Smith was a big city slicker with all the right moves.

Brisk shook his head.

Jealousy was not an emotion he countenanced easily, in himself or in others, and he felt that he was belittling himself by allowing it to prejudice him. So Elizabeth had taken a liking to Michael Smith. Big deal. Let them have their fun. It wasn't any of Bob Brisk's business, and in his heart he knew that. The boy in him felt those jealous pangs, and the man had to quell them. It was that simple.

But the cop in him had other things to worry about.

Like the fact that two very weird deaths had occurred in an otherwise quiet town, immediately after Michael Smith's arrival. The connection was so obvious, so glaring, that it could not be denied. Even Michael Smith had admitted it. Coincidence, he said.

Brisk didn't believe in coincidence. Not up here in New York. But neither did he believe that Smith was directly involved in the deaths. Not that he didn't want to believe it; he did, but he knew it wasn't true. He hadn't been joking when he'd said that neither he nor Smith were stupid. And he couldn't imagine a man stupid enough to connect himself so obviously to murder. Whatever connection existed between Smith and the two dead boys was oblique.

Michael Smith, however, knew things he wasn't saying. That was the thing that bothered Bob Brisk the most. Smith was hiding something. He could read it in the man's eyes, in his face. Smith was a man laboring under a burden, but what that burden was Bob Brisk could not immediately ascertain. He would hit on it eventually, he knew that beyond doubt. Whatever secret Michael Smith was holding inside, it would come into the light. It was just a matter of time. He took another drag on the cigarette, then crushed it out methodically in the overflowing ashtray at the corner of the desk.

The front door swung open and a sheet of snow drifted into the reception area. Sally Warner leaned into the door to close it, then turned around shaking her head. Her cheeks were bright red and her eyelashes had frosted. "I hate winter," she said evenly, unzipping her parka.

Brisk eased himself to his feet and sauntered into the reception area. He leaned against the door frame of his office. "How're the roads?"

"Not too bad. They'll get worse if it keeps up," Sally said. She pulled off her parka, tossed it over her seat, and plunked down on top of it. She turned and stared at Brisk. "Did you talk to him?"

Brisk nodded. "Yeah."

"Nothing?"

"He knows something, but I'm not sure he knows what it is."

Sally shook her head slowly. "He's a strange man."

"What do you mean?"

Sally shrugged. "I don't know, really. It's just . . . I watched him when he came out of the library. He looked . . ." she raised her hands in exasperation, unable to find the word. Finally she sighed. "Haunted. He looked haunted."

"You think he's scared?"

"No. Worried maybe." She shrugged again. "Maybe scared. I don't know."

Brisk chuckled. "Did you drop the tissue samples off with Cocoran?"

"Yup. He'll try and get back to you in a couple of days. He said don't be impatient."

Brisk laughed. "First time in ten years I give him

something to do and he tells me not to be impatient. Asshole." He went back into his office, grabbed his parka, and pulled it on. When he came back to the reception area Sally was leaning back in her seat, eyes closed. "Sally, why don't you head home," he said.

She blinked her eyes open and smiled. When she did that she damn near looked attractive, Brisk thought. He zipped up his parka.

"What are you doing tonight?" Sally asked.

"Might take a run over to Old Jack's."

"Want some company?"

Brisk thought about it, then shook his head. "Not tonight."

Sally nodded in understanding. "Think it'll stay quiet tonight?"

Brisk shrugged. "I hope so. The last two were five days apart. That should give us three more days until the next."

Sally's eyes widened and she stared at him. "You think there will be another?"

Brisk waited a moment before he answered. "Yup," he said at last, "but I'm not going to sit around waiting for it to happen. Put the phone on night service and go home and watch some TV. See you tomorrow." He smiled, then stepped out into the howling cold.

Old Jack's Tavern was the closest bar to New York that Bob Brisk could even begin to feel comfortable in. It had taken less than a month after he'd joined the force to understand that frequenting either of New York's two bars was an activity frowned upon by all six town councillors. A town with a total police force of two did not like to see half of its force sitting in a bar depleting the county's bourbon supply, no matter how regular a customer he'd once been. Fergus Falls was too far a drive for a simple drink, but Hinton was only twenty minutes away and still within range of his pager if anything should happen. Drinking outside of the township was a vice to which the councillors willingly turned a blind eye. After all, a cop who didn't drink at all was not entirely to be trusted.

Brisk had liked Old Jack's from the moment he'd first stepped through the door almost ten years ago. The dim lighting, the raw wooden siding, the juke box that played only manly hurtin' songs and ballads by female vocalists were all conducive to getting away from it all. For a while. And tonight there seemed a hell of a lot more worth getting away from than usual.

Brisk was staring at the dregs of his second double bourbon when he realized that his mind had been playing footsie with Elizabeth Turner.

"Jesus Christ . . ." he muttered, and waved for the bartender to refill his glass. Brisk watched as the amber liquid splashed over the two ice cubes and smiled when Hud added a generous splash more than a double.

"You gnawing a troublesome bone tonight, Bob?" Hud asked, taking the bottle away.

Brisk shrugged. "Just fighting the winter blahs, I guess," he lied.

Hud shrugged his massive shoulders and moved to the other end of the bar to polish glasses. Brisk was glad. He didn't really feel like talking. He focused again on the image that had tailed him all the way from New York. Elizabeth, standing behind the counter at Horn's Books, pony tail swished over her shoulder, face smiling.

Damn, she was about the prettiest woman he'd ever laid eyes on.

He sucked back half the bourbon.

But now he couldn't think about her without Michael Smith's pale, narrow face somehow intruding in the background. Michael Smith, who had been back in New York less than a day before getting the invite over to Elizabeth's for dinner. And who knows what else. A sudden flash of tangled limbs and panting mouths rippled across Bob Brisk's mind and he groaned inwardly.

Get off that track!

He wished now that he had accepted Sally's offer of company. There was no possibility that he and Sally would ever become permanently attached, but they had occasionally spent a night together in Hilltop Inn east of Hinton. Tonight her jaundiced humor and sharp laughter would be a welcome diversion from his own dangerously introverted mood.

He had decided to leave Old Jack's after finishing his drink, to seek out Sally at home, when the shape leaning back in the shadow at the other side of the room caught his attention. The booth was lit by a hooded bulb that cast a dim orange glow across the wooden surface of the table but left the upper reaches in darkness. The result was the disquieting effect of a pair of legs without a body. And the legs, he noticed, were worth looking at all by themselves.

On the floor beneath the table he could make out the glistening shape of black pumps. Above them was a long stretch of naked white leg leading to the smooth fold of a black leather skirt. Above that . . .

The woman leaned forward, coming into the light, and Bob Brisk found himself holding his breath. He caught a hint of platinum blonde hair, cut short and sleek, a long thin neck tapering into shoulders that curved exquisitely into the deeper shadow below. And the face . . . narrow, edgy, but rounded by makeup. A model's face, a focal point for the eyes. And Bob could not take his eyes away. His breath hissed slowly out, then in again.

The creature leaned further out of the shadow, and the long pale legs uncrossed themselves. She's getting up, Bob thought. She's getting up. Walk this way. Please, God, let her walk this way. Let her walk past me. . . .

His prayers were answered. She seemed to slide out of the darkness of the booth like a well-oiled machine, like a cool gun sliding out of a greased leather holster, and he saw for the first time the full length of her body in the bar's dim light. Above the short black leather skirt, which hung to a point just above her knees, she wore a smooth black leather jacket, hanging open, and beneath that a glittering silver blouse, cut low. His heart was pounding and he still had not let out his breath. I'm staring, he thought, and she's looking at me, she can see I'm staring . . . but he could not drag his eyes away. In the background he was aware of Dolly Parton's voice wailing from the jukebox, something about "I will always love you," and he echoed the thought in his mind.

The woman walked straight over and took the stool next to him at the bar. At last, Bob Brisk let his breath hiss out. She was beautiful. Her face was a perfect structure of bone, skin, and makeup. And her eyes, flat grey yet somehow gleaming beneath the shadow of her eyelids, were locked onto his. Her lips, glossy red, curled up in a smile. "Hi," she said.

Bob Brisk opened his mouth to speak and promptly forgot what he had intended to say. After a moment it came to him. "Hi," he grunted.

Her smile widened. He focused on her lips, seeing himself sinking into her mouth, pushing past those lips, those teeth. He felt himself blushing and suddenly had the distinct impression that she knew what he had been thinking. This only made him blush more.

"Uh, can, uh, can I get you a drink?" His voice was much smaller than he had intended.

"Vodka on ice," she said.

Brisk waved for Hud, glad to be able to take his eyes off her for a moment. Hud had been watching them from the other end of the bar, he realized, with a look of concern on his face. Now the massive bartender walked over.

"Vodka on ice for the lady," Brisk said, now slightly more in control.

Hud nodded and poured the drink. He appeared about ready to say something to Brisk, but thinking better of it he walked silently back to his glass-polishing post.

"My name's Bob Brisk," he said, as she reached out and took the glass. Her fingers were long, pale, and slim, and the nails were red daggers.

She smiled, raising the glass to her lips. She took a small swallow of the raw liquor, and her face did not even flinch. "What do you do?"

"I'm a cop," he said. Her perfume, whatever it was, was making him even drunker.

"Here in Hinton?"

He shook his head. "New York."

I can't believe this is happening. The thought bounced around his mind like a superball off concrete.

"I like cops," she said.

Bob did not know what to say. So he lifted his glass and sucked on the ice that was in there. Oh, shit, he thought. Don't do that! She'll think you're a kid! He lowered the glass carefully.

"I've never seen you around here before," he said.

"I'm visiting," she said carefully. "I have people here."

Brisk nodded. Had to be something like that. A creature like this would never go unnoticed. She'd be the talk of the fucking county. And I'm talking to her. The thought made him reel.

"Would you like to walk me home," she asked, her grey eyes locking onto his.

Brisk's heart hammered like it was about to explode. "Sure," he managed to say, and was surprised that the word even came out sounding like English.

She sucked back the remnants of the vodka, then placed the glass gently on the counter. When she stood she was a good two inches taller than him, an effect of the high heels. In bare feet I'd be taller, he thought. But that would not be an advantage, he realized.

As they walked to the door of the bar every eye in the place followed them. A table of young rednecks near the door gaped open-mouthed as they passed, and Brisk felt himself infused with a feeling of tremendous power. She wouldn't even talk to them, he thought. Not a word. And I'm walking her home.

Outside, the wind had died down since he had arrived, but eddies of snow and ice particles still rolled along the highway. Even in his parka Brisk felt the bite of the cold.

She's got bare legs and an open jacket.

"Aren't you cold?"

"I love the cold," she said, and began to walk east along the highway, leaving the dim lights of Hinton behind.

"Where we going?" Brisk asked, keeping up easily.

"I'm at the Hilltop Inn," she said, and glanced at him. "I don't like to stay with my . . . folks. I get privacy this way."

A lump rose in Brisk's throat and he nodded. They walked in silence after that until the Hilltop Inn appeared around a bend in the road, hidden by a wall of snow-covered pines. He walked her up to the foyer, then along the covered porch to number 16. At the door she stopped and turned to face him. They were standing very close, and he could feel the heat radiating from her. His nostrils were filled with her perfume and a heavier, more powerful odor beneath it.

"Thanks for walking me home, Bob," she said, and leaned forward.

His first instinct was to step back in disbelief, but of course he did not. Her red lips touched his own, and he felt her tongue reach through to part his lips. His own tongue responded, pushing at the warm wetness of her mouth. Her hand worked between them, and Brisk gasped as he felt the sharpness of her nails through his pants, stroking the rock-hard lump between his legs. A moan slipped from his lips.

At last they parted, and she smiled like an animal. "I don't do this all the time," she said. "But I don't know many people here. I don't have any friends."

Brisk nodded as if he understood. He did not. He studied her in a state of shock. The taste of her lipstick was strong and thick in his mouth. The kiss had hinted at an abyss of sexual depravity that he had never even imagined, just a step away. I want to wallow in it, he thought.

Please, drag me down into it.

Again she smiled, as if she could read his mind.

"I won't ask you in tonight," she said.

"Why not?" He could not stop the words coming out.

She smiled.

"I want to see you again," Brisk said.

"I'll be at Old Jack's tomorrow night."

Brisk nodded. She turned and unlocked the door to her room, taking a step backward into the darkness. Again she was partly hidden. A vague shape in shadow.

"I don't even know your name," Brisk said.

"Sondra," she said, and shut the door.

He stood there a good thirty seconds, staring at the door. She knows I'm here, he thought. She's leaning against the door, smiling. He shook his head, turned, and began to walk back to his car.

113

It was only when he sat down on the cool vinyl seat that he felt the erection straining against his pants. Almost painful. He'd had it since he'd first seen her.

"Holy shit," he whispered, and started the car.

He was halfway back to New York when he realized that he had not thought of Elizabeth Turner, Michael Smith, or the torn throats of Syd Jaeger and Herb Kramer since meeting Sondra. She had taken all of his attention.

He smiled. Just that single kiss had made him feel like he had one foot already in hell. She probably has orifices I've never even seen before, he thought to himself, and found the thought very funny.

His smile widened.

One foot in hell and halfway damned, for a kiss!

He laughed out loud. For Sondra it would be worth it.

CHAPTER NINE

When Michael arrived at Elizabeth's cabin that evening he found himself incapable of relaxing. His run-in with Bob Brisk had left him tense and far too introspective. Brisk's contention that he was in some way connected to the recent killings was more disturbing than Michael cared to admit, and the paranoia he had fought so hard to quash over the past three years began to raise its head again. To his relief, Elizabeth did not inquire about the nature of Brisk's interest, and he could not bring himself to recount the interview. The whole thing, he hoped, would blow over quickly.

Even Elizabeth's attempts to further their initial tentative physical relationship could not cut through his unease, and he found himself responding half-heartedly to her soft kisses and gentle touches. Tonight, he knew, if he wanted, he could take this relationship another step along the road to fruition, and it appeared that Elizabeth was willing. Perhaps eager. She radiated an aura of want and need that Michael had not sensed in a woman in years. His own desire was a warm glow he could not help notice, but he could not clear his mind of the stark black and white images of the mutilated bodies. Finally, knowing he was going to hurt Elizabeth, he made his excuses and left. Her disappointment was obvious, and though he could have lessened her hurt by explaining his mood he did not.

Over the next few days Michael's tension slowly dissipated, and although Elizabeth seemed reticent to continue where they had left off on Monday night, Michael knew that when the opportunity again presented itself he would not disappoint her again. He had forgotten, however, the vagaries of the virus.

Friday was Tommy's eleventh birthday, and Michael had spent Thursday morning gallivanting around Fergus Falls looking for a suitable gift. His last stop had been Stuart's Optical Supply, where the manager had offered him a complete telescope mirror-grinding kit, including designs for a moderate-sized instrument. It was a gift he would have loved to have received himself at eleven, and Tommy's interest in astronomy was far more advanced than his own had been. His choice turned out to be perfect. An astounded Tommy, after securing Michael's promise that he would help during grinding and construction, retired to his room to study the manual and supplies.

Michael sat at the kitchen table and sipped a glass of white wine as Elizabeth cleared the table.

"The jeans and sweater I bought him have been pushed aside by your gift," she said with a mock pout.

Michael chuckled. "He'll get more use out of yours than mine, believe me."

"Don't kid yourself. If he does anything but work away at that kit over the next couple of months I'll be surprised."

Michael finished his wine then rose to help with the dishes. Elizabeth moved aside to give him room at the sink, but he leaned forward, moved the pony tail from her shoulder, and softly kissed the back of her neck. Elizabeth gasped, then turned to face him. Michael put his hands around her small waist and pulled her closer. This time he kissed her on the mouth, firmly and with promise.

"Mister, we have dishes to wash," Elizabeth said breathlessly, a smile curling her lips.

"So, who says we can't have fun doing dishes?" But he grinned and began to wash.

When they had finished they retired to the living room. A made-for-TV movie about the trials and tribulations of misunderstood rich kids was nearing its end, but they did not watch the screen. Their attention was wholly upon each other. Elizabeth pressed close to him, snuggling into the crook of his arm, and her softness produced a strange feeling in Michael's stomach, a warmth and a tightness he had not felt in a long time. He was acutely aware of her smell, the enticing aura of her perfume, and below it the dusky, sensual odor of her body. When she leaned closer to him and touched her warm lips to his neck, a small groan escaped from his mouth and a shiver ran the length of his body. He placed his glass of brandy on the coffee table and faced her.

117

"You're pushing me," he said huskily.

Elizabeth's brown eyes glinted in the soft light, and her lips turned slightly in a smile. She reached up and kissed his lips, then leaned away. "Well, you'll have to control yourself. At least until Tommy goes to sleep."

Michael groaned again, but Elizabeth silenced him with another kiss. "That doesn't mean we can't begin," she said softly, and trailed her tongue down the side of his neck, probing wetly at the hollow of his throat. Michael slowly raised his hand between them and brushed the soft mound of her breasts. Elizabeth moaned into his neck.

It was almost two unbearable hours later that Elizabeth unfastened herself from Michael and tip-toed to Tommy's bedroom. When she returned she was smiling. She lowered herself carefully into the sofa.

"Sleeping," she whispered, then pressed into him. As her lips clasped his and her tongue probed gently between his lips, he felt her hand as it moved between his legs. He groaned and again touched her breast beneath the soft fabric of her sweater.

When she moaned softly into his mouth Michael pushed her away. "Tommy . . ."

Elizabeth nodded. She pulled herself to her feet. Holding his hands, she led him to her bedroom. Michael followed, eyes unable to leave the sight of her body. Once she had closed the door of the bedroom he pulled her to him and kissed her roughly, sucking on the tongue she offered him. Michael moved his mouth across hers, then down her chin and neck. He fell to his knees before her. He raised her sweater, releasing the soft white orbs of her breasts. Exposed, she exuded an aura of erotic vulnerability that had the effect of spurs on him.

He pushed her back on the bed and with her help undid her jeans and removed them. Kneeling between her legs, leaning over her, he kissed her neck, then slowly lowered his mouth across her torso, smiling at the tremor that rippled through her. He lingered for a moment at her breasts, encircling each tumescent nipple in turn, caressing each with his tongue. Then he moved lower, guided by her hands, until his mouth found the source of heat radiating from her pelvis. Elizabeth arched to meet his mouth, a deep groan slipping from her lips. The taste of her almost drove him out of his mind.

When at last, she pulled him up, he did not fight. Guided by her slim fingers he pushed against her moist heat, easing himself into her in a single motion. As the hot wetness engulfed him Michael gasped, an echo of Elizabeth's own response. And then they moved together, rhythmically, mindlessly.

It was, Michael admitted to himself afterward, purely and simply, a "fuck." There was no other way to describe it. They had become lost in pure carnality. Faceless, each with no identity for the other. Tools existing only for the pleasure of the other. Like animals rutting. This was as far from "making love" as it was possible to be, and both of them knew it. Afterward, completely spent and sated, they lay in each other's arms breathing softly.

"What are you thinking?" Elizabeth's voice was soft, hushed.

Michael shrugged. "I'm thinking we may have

lost more than we gained."

Elizabeth shook her head. "Michael, don't talk like that. We both needed what happened tonight."

"Maybe. But I think it got the better of us."

"Well, it happened and we saw it coming. Let's just go on from here. Maybe now we can focus on . . . the less physical aspects of . . ."

He kissed her. "Okay." He smiled.

He was about to kiss her again when the pain stabbed into his hip and reverberated through his entire body. Elizabeth's eyes widened.

"What's wrong?"

Michael grunted, sitting bolt upright. "I . . ." Another stab of pain from his hip cut off his words. For a moment he was aware of nothing but the sharp throb in his hip, the tendrils of exquisite tension reaching out from the locus of the hip into the surrounding muscle and bone. . . .

"Shit . . ."

He swung his feet out of bed, face pinched.

"Michael, are you alright?"

"Muscle pull," he grunted, hoping the lie would suffice.

"Oh, no . . . I'm sorry. . . ."

Now he chuckled through the slowly subsiding pain, realizing what she had been thinking. "Not from that," he said. "From the skiing earlier. I thought I'd got rid of it. Don't worry. It will be okay."

He rose to his feet and limped across the cold hardwood floor. At the bedroom door he turned and offered Elizabeth a reassuring smile, then went out into the hallway and into the bathroom. When he flicked on the bathroom light his eyes felt as if they had been poked with needles. He groaned, protecting himself with his hand until the pain subsided. Dammit, it couldn't be time yet. This was simply the midmonth flare-up. It had to be. The viral symptoms had always had a tendency to rise unpredictably in the middle of the cycle, but they usually subsided within a few hours. When had he had the incident with the mugger? Two weeks ago? He searched back in his memory. No, damn, it had been almost three weeks. Twenty one days. Only one week until the *real* symptoms began. So what was this? Just another sign of the virus's new randomness?

John Muir's words topped into his mind: *Perhaps all you've been experiencing up to now is the incubation period.*

No!

His reflection in the mirror looked back at him with a depressing mask of resignation. At thirty he looked close to forty. At sixty he'd look eighty. At eighty, if he lived that long, he'd look ten years dead. The morbid projection made him grin, even through the pain.

He thought of his own medicine cabinet and formed an image of the three unmarked bottles pressed close together in the top shelf. Could it be time for that yet? The metallic copper taste popped into his mind and he cringed reflexively. No, not yet. There was plenty of time. If this was the usual cycle, he'd be fine in a couple of hours. He turned on the faucet and poured himself a glass of water. As he raised the glass to his lips his hand trembled slightly. Not enough to spill any water, but notice-able. As the cold liquid dribbled into his mouth his neck muscles spasmed painfully, but he managed to subdue the gag reflex and to swallow. After the first sip the rest of the glass went down more easily.

Back in the bedroom, Elizabeth regarded him with obvious concern. She was sitting up in bed, covered to her waist in a sheet, smoking a cigarette. A thin veil of smoke drifted across the room. The smell was strong and harsh to Michael. He dressed slowly, limbs trembling uncontrollably at times.

"Are you sure you're alright?" Elizabeth asked softly.

Michael nodded, buttoning his shirt. His fore-head shone with sweat, and already the underarms of the shirt were stained. "Just feeling a little sick," he said.

Elizabeth did not press. She followed him to the door of the cabin and gave him a warm kiss on the lips. His attempted response came across as another uncontrolled tremor. "I'll call you tomorrow," he said, horrified at how weak his voice sounded.

The quick drive back along the road to his cabin did nothing to calm him, and even the cold air rushing in the windows only seemed to make his shivering more violent. He parked the Corsica be-side the cabin, but did not bother to plug it in. Luckily, he had not locked the front door, because his hands were trembling so badly he might not have been able to use the keys. Inside, he went di-rectly to the bathroom without turning on any lights. He did not need lights. The cabin seemed to glow with an eerie phosphorescence, the outline of furniture and doorways glowing with their own light. What he could not see, he could sense.

In the bathroom he took one of John Muir's bottles from the top shelf of the medicine cabinet and spun the cap off. The sharp odor rose up to him instantly, filling the small room. His nose wrinkled and he closed his eyes in disgust. But something inside him quaked with need.

He closed the cabinet, and gasped at the reflection of himself that swung into view. His face was that of a stranger. Gaunt, hollow-eyed, haunted. His lips were pulled back from teeth that glistened with saliva. His entire body was soaked with sweat, trembling.

It was as John Muir had told him so long ago. Anxiety and stress could prematurely bring about the onset of the virus's prodromal symptoms. Could sex with Elizabeth be considered stressful? Or had it simply been building up since his interview with Bob Brisk, since seeing those photographs? The sudden memory of the photographs sent a wave of fear crashing through him.

For an instant he thought of the thing he had withheld from Brisk.

"Sondra . . ." The name came from his lips like a hiss of air, and he shook his head in denial. No, it was impossible. His reflection in the mirror cringed in horror.

Michael raised the small jar to his lips, then tipped the thick fluid into his mouth. The taste sent a spasm of revulsion through his body, and he gripped the edge of the sink for support. When the fluid hit his stomach he bent over double, retching.

Tendrils of the thick liquid bolted back up his throat, tickling the back of his tongue, but he forced them down. In a moment the tremors subsided.

In a few moments he felt himself calm down. As if somebody had cut a surge of electric current to his brain.

Thinking of Sondra was the worst thing he could do. If one thought was stressful enough to bring about the premature onslaught of the viral symptoms, it was her. Had he been unconsciously dwelling on her this past week? The answer, he knew, was affirmative.

In another minute he went back outside, allowing the cold arctic air to surround him. He walked down to the edge of the lake, feet crunching in the shallow snow. There was no moon, but Venus was so bright over the western horizon that it cast a dim light across the jagged ice. Tiny particles of wind-driven snow bit into his face, but the sensation was pleasant, calming.

But there was something different about the lake now. When he had painted it earlier his unconscious feelings had produced images of strange life within the trees. Now those feelings had jumped to a conscious level. The darkness seemed to be hiding something. Something evil.

He tried not to think of her name.

CHAPTER TEN

The next morning, Elizabeth drove into Horn's Books, despite it being Saturday, to do a little work. The previous evening had left her full of energy. Making love to Michael had resulted in a relief of tension that she could hardly comprehend. It was as if she had been building up to an elusive, powerful sneeze that had finally erupted. There had hardly been time to appreciate that it was *Michael* making love to her; the act had swept all thoughts from her mind. In the future, she hoped, *she knew,* it would be different. Last night had fulfilled a need in each of them. Now they could move on. Even his strange behaviour afterward, the sudden *sickness* that had come upon him, did not tarnish the evening. She went about her work as if it were a pleasure.

She had decided it was time to reorganize some of the shelves and was in the process of moving the racks of Harlequins, contemporary romances, and regencies to a more prominent position near the front of the store when Bob Brisk's police car rolled to a stop outside. Elizabeth lit a cigarette, inhaled the smoke deeply, and watched uneasily as Bob climbed out of the car and walked toward the store. A gust of cold wind followed him inside.

He leaned on the counter and regarded her curiously. She had been angry at him for his harassment of Michael earlier in the week, and now those emotions rose again.

"You won't find your murderer around here, Bob," she said harshly.

His wide face flushed in embarrassment. "Elizabeth, you know I was just doing my job."

"Michael Smith would never hurt a fly. You know it." She drew on her cigarette and guided the plume of smoke towards him.

He harumphed, pulled his own smokes from his jacket, lit one, and blew a retaliatory volley of smoke at her. "I don't know any such thing. All I know is that we had no trouble around here until he arrived."

"Are you still harping on that?"

"I'm not saying he's responsible. I told him that too. That doesn't mean he's not connected somehow."

Elizabeth drew on her cigarette. Bob's logic was undeniable, of course, and the same thoughts had occurred to her. But she had come to know Michael over the past three weeks, and she was sure that he knew nothing of the murders. "I think you're just jealous," she said, and instantly regretted her words. Bob Brisk was not a bad sort, and although she had turned his attentions away he had never acted badly with her or tried to force himself upon her. Her words were a low blow against a man who did not deserve it.

But he did not seem to take offense. His smile was wide and boyish. "Hell, I admit it. I was jealous. To begin with."

Elizabeth jumped at the chance to change the subject. She grinned suggestively. "Bob Brisk, you're seeing someone, aren't you?"

Bob shrugged, but could not keep the affirmation from his face. Elizabeth felt a rush of relief. She wanted Bob to be happy, and had worried since the time she had turned him away that he would hover over her forever. "Well, who is it?"

"Nobody you know," he said softly, now obviously embarrassed. He quickly regained his composure, once again all business. "That's not why I came anyway," he said.

Elizabeth felt a stab of unease. "What is it, then?"

"I just wanted to warn you. As a friend."

"About what?" She heard the tension in her voice, but could not keep it away.

"I just got word from the pathologist in Fergus Falls, about the tissue samples I sent him from the two dead boys. He ran some tests and came up with some weird results. I didn't ask him to, but he ran the samples down to Minneapolis for further tests. Those boys there were interested too, and they did some more checking. The end result is that we now have some serious FBI interest in our two backwoods killings. I expect they'll be up here either Sunday or Monday at the latest."

"But why? What did they find?"

Bob shrugged, frowning. "Not sure I understand it myself," he took a deep drag on his cigarette and hissed the smoke out from his nose and mouth. "Something to do with saliva traces on the tissue samples from the boys' throats. Cocoran says they picked up traces of a real potent anticoagulant."

"Anti what?"

"Anticoagulant. Stops the blood from clotting, lets it flow more freely."

"I don't understand," Elizabeth said, eyes locked on Bob Brisk's shadowed face.

"Hell, neither do I. But it sounds like there's been similar killings in other parts of the country. Even in Chicago. So the feds are coming up for a look around."

"But what has that got to do with me?"

Bob looked at her steadily, as if surprised she did not understand. "Michael's from Chicago," he said softly. "The feds are gonna pick up the connection as quick as I did."

Elizabeth's mouth hung open in surprise. "That's ridiculous."

Bob shrugged. "Maybe. But I can tell you one

thing, Liz, those big boys won't be as easy on your friend as I was. There could be trouble. I just wanted to let you know."

After he had gone, Elizabeth felt a heavy depression descend upon her. Wouldn't they ever leave Michael alone? She returned to her work with a vigor she did not feel, trying to keep her mind away from the subject of the murders. But it was no use. She kept coming back to them, and back to Michael. The two notions bumped together in her head, trying to join, until she was so annoyed at herself that she wanted to scream.

When she saw him later she would tell him about Bob's visit. He would likely laugh at her for worrying so much. But even that prospect did not please her.

Michael did not wake until close to 10:00 A.M. on Saturday. He had slept fitfully and had woken twice during the night to find himself trembling and soaked with sweat. He put on a pot of coffee, waited impatiently for it to brew, then sat at the kitchen table in his pajamas. After the second cup he began to feel more awake. Outside, fat flakes of snow were drifting down slowly like leaves, no wind to drive them to fury. Michael sipped his coffee and tried to follow the descent of individual flakes. It was no good. They kept getting lost in the background. But the exercise helped take his mind off the constant throb in his hip. It hadn't been a dream.

The previous evening's events were hazy in his mind. He remembered giving Tommy the mirror-grinding kit, and he remembered, as through gauze, making love to Elizabeth, but after that it was all a blur. The early symptoms, what he'd taken for a midmonthly flare-up, had raised their heads at an inopportune moment. The result was that he remembered the evening as if he'd been drunk.

The coffee, however, was helping. Each sip pushed him closer to the edge of the precipice of wakefulness. He was halfway through his third cup when a knock sounded at the front door. Michael walked gingerly across the cold wooden planking of the porch, holding his nightgown tightly closed, and opened it on the form of a middle-aged man. He was wearing a dark green parka, hood drawn up, and grey corduroy pants tucked into a pair of scuffed hiking boots. The grizzled eyebrows, just visible below the furred edge of the hood, were thick with frost.

"Hello. You must be Michael Smith. I'm Dan Stone. From fifty-eight." He cocked his head toward the cabins closer to town. "Thought I'd drop in and say hello."

Michael frowned, then felt his eyes widen in recognition. "Mr. Stone!" He held open the front door, allowing his visitor to step past him into the

130

porch. "I didn't recognize you." He closed the door.

"Don't blame you," Stone said, unzipping the parka and pulling down the hood. "You were a kid when you last saw me."

But once the parka was off and the rugged face laid bare of its protective scarf, Michael had no difficulty in recognizing his neighbor. The Stones and his parents had been close friends, and their daughter, Monica, had had a crush on Michael for years. Michael took the parka from the older man and led him into the cabin. "I've got a pot of coffee on if you're interested," Michael said.

Dan Stone nodded gratefully. He was a big man, though lean and well-muscled. Michael guessed his age at close to sixty. The Stones had been slightly older than his own parents, he remembered. Stone had lived his entire life in New York, most of that time running a small service station just east of town. He had the look of a man who still might feel comfortable doing physical labor. Michael poured an extra cup of coffee and topped up his own. Stone accepted the cup, cradling it between two large, brown hands, and sipped eagerly. After the first sip he leaned back in one of the kitchen chairs and regarded Michael with good humor.

"You don't look at all like your dad," Stone said, smiling. "Not that you'd want to."

Michael chuckled. "I have the looks, he had the brains."

131

"He had those," Stone agreed.

Over the next hour the two men talked over old times as if they had been only a few weeks ago. It became obvious that Dan Stone missed Michael's parents almost as much as he missed his own wife, who had been dead for nearly ten years. And though the conversation seemed always on the verge of falling into a pit of maudlin reminiscences, Michael began to enjoy himself. The pain in his hip dwindled to a mere annoyance and the hangover feeling was soon replaced by an edge of sharp wakefulness. He began to wish he could sit himself in front of the easel and begin painting. Though he had not intended his impatience to show, Dan Stone soon became aware of it.

He placed the coffee mug carefully on the table, then rubbed his hands briskly together. "Hell, I guess you know I didn't come by just to say hello," he said, watching Michael carefully.

Michael blinked. In fact, he had suspected no such thing. He stared at Stone blankly, waiting for him to continue.

Stone began to look a little embarrassed. "That Bob Brisk has been asking some mighty strange questions," he said.

So that's what it was all about. Michael began to feel the preliminary warmings of anger. "What has he been asking?"

"Oh, this and that," Stone said nervously. "Seeding the idea that you might be connected to these recent killings we've had."

Michael shook his head.

"No, no, you don't have to go denying it to me," Stone said. "I know you got nothing to do with it. I've known you since you was a boy, and I knew your parents before that. You're not capable of doing what was done to those boys. I know that for a fact. That's what I told Bob Brisk."

"Thanks," Michael said quietly. He had the sudden feeling that if he ran in to Bob Brisk soon he might flatten the cop's nose.

"I come over just to let you know about it," Stone said. "Bob Brisk has a way of letting everybody but the one most concerned know about what's going on. I felt it was my duty, as a friend of the family, to make sure you were informed."

"Thanks, again."

Dan Stone now regarded Michael with what might have passed for fatherly protectiveness. "You can count on me, son, for support."

"That's good to know."

"Bob Brisk is just an uppity local boy. Kinda jealous of you, I guess, having a good education and a job in the city. Guess it's kinda natural he'd be suspicious, though." He smiled at Michael, revealing large square teeth.

Michael tried to smile back, but the mood of neighborly comaraderie had dissipated somewhat. "Bob's just doing his job, I guess," he said.

Stone nodded, smiling, and pulled himself to his

feet. "Just so you know we're behind you."

Michael wondered who "we" were, but Stone said no more. He pulled on his parka, wrapped his scarf around his head, and waved once as he stepped out into the cold. The snow was still falling slowly, taking a sharp edge off the previous icy crusting. Michael watched, feeling a vague anger as his neighbor worked his way slowly but methodically along the snow covered trail, down along the edge of the lake and back toward New York. When Stone was out of sight behind a high ridge of snow Michael went back into the porch. He poured himself the remainder of the coffee, now disgustingly strong, and sat down in front of the easel with a blank canvas. Soon he began to paint.

Dan Stone was three cabins away from his own, just behind the boarded-up windows of the Jackson's place, when he heard the crunch of snow behind him. He stopped and turned, but could see nothing but the bare trunks of trees and the unmarked carpet of fresh fallen snow. He pulled back his hood and listened more clearly. All he could hear was the sound of his own breathing. The quiet, more intense because of the lack of wind, was almost disturbing.

Ears already stinging from the cold, he pulled his hood back up and continued, lifting his feet high above the snow. Walking this trail in winter was damned good exercise. There was no getting away from that. It was just that this old body wasn't as willing to suffer through exercise the way it used to. He grunted in disgust and continued onward, his own cabin now visible around the next drift of snow. To his left, Great Lake stretched like the flat of a large dinner plate, glittering in the midday sun.

Again Dan heard the crunch of snow behind him, as if he were being followed. He stopped, twirled, pulling his hood down as he did so. This time he caught a quick glimpse of a dark shape flitting between the trunks of trees further down the trail. He squinted. The shape had been moving very quickly, away from the trail, where the snow was deep. He frowned.

"What the hell," the words slipped out by themselves, startling him.

His visit to Michael Smith was making him nervous. Smith sure as hell wasn't the killer Bob Brisk was after; that was obvious. Although, and Dan admitted this to himself reluctantly, he had rather hoped Smith might prove to be a bit more dangerous looking. He had liked the kid's parents but he had never much cared for the boy. Too quiet, too self-sufficient. He held his breath a moment, listening intently, but whatever he had seen disappearing into the trees was gone.

Leaving his hood down, despite the biting cold, he continued walking along the trail. By the time he reached the front door of his cabin his ears were numb and his heart was pounding loudly in his chest.

"Too old for this . . . ," he muttered, fumbling his keys at the lock.

He twirled again at the sudden rush of air behind him, and this time he froze in surprise. Less than two yards away, rushing toward him as if she were flying, was a woman. A woman barely covered from the cold by patches of black leather, pale legs churning the snow into dust. Her short blonde hair was soaked with sweat, sticking straight up off her scalp. Her gleaming grey eyes pierced him, as her mouth strained open in a silent scream. Stone had to time to think: *her legs are bare, she's not wearing any shoes, she must be freezing.* Then she hit him.

Although large, he was thrown backward through the door of his cabin as if he were made of straw. Where her fists had struck his chest he felt sudden stabs of pain, as if bones had been snapped.

That's impossible!

He crashed to the floor, bending his left leg painfully beneath him. By the time his eyes blinked, becoming accustomed to the darkness inside, she was bending over him. Her face hung less than six inches from his own, and Stone felt his bowels quiver. Her lips were pulled back from a set of teeth that chattered incessantly, as if her facial muscles were spasming out of control. But it was her eyes that destroyed him. Depthless, lifeless, glittering pieces of ice in dark sockets. He could not escape them.

From the corner of his eye he saw her pale hand retrieve what looked like a dangerous piece of metal from a pocket of her leather skirt.

Knife!

From some far corner of his mind he watched the glittering blade as it arched towards him. On his lips there hung the beginning of a plea for mercy, but he could not bring himself to speak it. What was the point? In those eyes he saw the answer. He was doomed.

And then she whispered something in his ear, and he knew he must have imagined it. "You're going to love this," he thought she said.

He hardly felt the sudden line of pain beneath his ear, and only realized his throat had been neatly cut open when the sheet of blood splashed down into his parka, a warm sensation crawling along his chest. And then those chattering teeth were tearing at the wound, ripping it farther, shredding the flesh of his throat as if it were no barrier at all. He tried to move, to fend her off, but his arms were bound tightly in her grasp. Her fingers were like cold metal.

She was crouched over him in a horrible parody of copulation, and his body responded in kind. He felt a stirring in his loins, but his erection was

137

feeble. Her hair tickled his ear, but the sensation was distant, unimportant. He was aware mostly of the pressure of her weight, a giant scrabbling insect sitting on his chest. His last sensation was her deep growl vibrating against his torn flesh, and the sharp, almost sexually obscene probing of her tongue into the depths of his wound.

CHAPTER ELEVEN

The painting was one of the quickest Michael had ever executed. Three hours after he had roughed in the background he laid down his brush, blade, and palette and went back into the kitchen. The new pot of coffee had mostly evaporated, leaving a residue of viscous black fluid. He sniffed it distastefully and turned off the power. It was close to 4:00 P.M. More coffee would just make him edgy. He opened the fridge and pulled out a Coors Light, popped the cap, and sucked back a large mouthful. After the bitter coffee, the beer tasted sweet, but its coldness refreshed him. He leaned against the fridge and finished the remainder of the bottle in three gulps.

Though his stomach growled for food, he decided a shower would be the wiser choice. He had spent the day in pajamas and robe and was feeling decidedly decadent. He turned the water as hot as he could stand it for five minutes, breathing in the steam, shampooing his hair, scrubbing himself with soap. Afterward he cut off the hot water and remained as long as possible under the needles of cold. His breath became short and ragged, and after a few seconds he turned off the cold and stepped out of the shower. He dried himself briskly, using two towels, then went to the bedroom to dress.

He had barely finished zipping up his Levis when the knock sounded at the front porch door. He tucked in his shirt, ran a hand through his hair, and went to answer it. If it was another neighbor, come to offer support against the suspicions of Bob Brisk, they were in for a nasty surprise. Michael did not feel very friendly.

Elizabeth smiled brightly when he opened the door, and reached up to kiss his lips. "Scrubbed and cleaned, just the way I like 'em," she said, and stepped past him.

Michael followed her back into the cabin, and took her coat after she unbuttoned it. When he turned to face her again she stepped into him, encircled him with her arms, and pulled his face down for another kiss. Her lips were cool from being outside, but after a moment they warmed beneath his own, and soon her tongue was exploring his mouth. When they parted Elizabeth was smiling, and Michael felt the tension leaving his own face.

"Feeling better today?" she asked.

Michael blinked. "Oh, yeah. I don't know what it was, but it's gone now." He turned and glanced out the window at the Volkswagen. "Where's Tommy?"

"Home, working on your gift. I did a little work at the store. What have you been doing?"

"Painting," Michael said.

"Can I see?"

He shrugged, then led her to the porch. Elizabeth stood before the canvas and studied it carefully. Michael, too, studied his handiwork closely, and what he saw shocked him. Is that what he had intended to paint? Elizabeth was frowning. "Strange," she said at last.

"I . . ." But he did not venture anything else.

"It's some sort of monster. A beast. Spooky," Elizabeth said.

She was right, Michael thought. He dragged his eyes from the painting and turned to Elizabeth.

"What is it?"

He debated lying, but decided against it. "Self-portrait," he said.

Elizabeth's eyes widened, and she glanced back at the painting. After a moment she turned to Michael again and said very carefully, "Well, it's original."

Michael grunted and went back into the kitchen. He had seen himself and had painted a beast. He shivered in revulsion. From the fridge he pulled two beers, opened them both, and handed one to

Elizabeth. She accepted the bottle and took a tentative sip. Michael took a long swallow of beer, then another. Elizabeth, he noticed, was preoccupied with something. Her smile seemed slightly forced. When she saw that he was staring at her she smiled nervously and turned to look out the window.

"Still snowing," she said.

Michael came up beside her and rested a hand on her neck. He traced a delicate pattern in the silky hair above her shoulders. Elizabeth shivered, and pressed closer to him.

"What's wrong?" Michael said at last.

"Wrong?"

"There's something on your mind."

She turned to him, smiling wryly. "It's that obvious?"

Michael grinned and nodded. He kissed her forehead. "Like an open book," he said. "Now what is it?"

Elizabeth frowned, stepped away from him, and sat at the kitchen table. She began to peel the label from her beer bottle, tearing it off in strips. "Bob Brisk came to see me this morning."

Michael's stomach muscles knotted tightly. "Oh?"

"He was . . ." she would not look into his eyes. ". . . he was concerned. He wanted to warn me."

"About what?" Michael tried to keep his voice even and calm, tried to strangle the flaring anger at Bob Brisk.

"He sent tissue samples from the throats of the two dead boys to a pathologist in Fergus Falls, and the pathologist sent them to Minneapolis. They found traces of a . . ." she frowned, trying to remember the word. ". . . an anticoagulant. It's something that stops blood from clotting. They found it in the wounds on the boys' throats."

Michael stared at her, unable to speak. The coldness that had begun in the pit of his stomach lurched outward in a wave that encompassed his entire body. Beads of sweat broke out on his forehead.

"Apparently the FBI is interested now," Elizabeth said softly. "Bob thinks they might want to talk to you."

"Jesus . . ." Michael slumped into the seat across from Elizabeth. His thoughts were in turmoil.

Elizabeth reached out and touched his hand. "I told Bob you weren't involved. But he says the FBI people will want to talk to you anyway. Just because the killings started after you got here."

"Coincidence," Michael said feebly.

Anticoagulant. The word activated long quiet memory traces. Michael frowned, trying to silence them.

"Listen," Elizabeth said, squeezing his hand again. "Tommy wants to go to Fergus Falls to see a movie. You want to come with us?"

Michael nodded absently, hardly hearing her voice. Some animals had anticoagulant in their saliva, he thought. Some snakes, some bats, even some insects. The presence of anticoagulant didn't mean . . .

"Michael, are you okay?"

He blinked, startled, and looked up at Elizabeth. The look of concern on her face cut through the confusion of his thoughts.

"Are you okay?" she asked again.

Michael nodded, and smiled. "Yes. I'm sorry. It's just . . . this thing with Bob Brisk is getting to me." His smile widened, turned almost into a grin. "One of my neighbors visited me today, offering support. I mean, this story I'm somehow connected is spreading quickly."

Elizabeth nodded in sympathy. "It's a small town, Mike. Secrets don't last."

Michael nodded, still smiling. "I'll talk to Bob Brisk or whoever else. I have nothing to hide."

Now Elizabeth's features softened. "I know that. I think Bob knows it too. He's just doing his job."

Michael tried another smile. "Let's go pick up Tommy. We can go for pizza before the movie."

Elizabeth leaned across the table and kissed him on the lips. "The movie won't last all night," she said softly.

They left Elizabeth's Volkswagen at Michael's cabin, plugged in, and drove the Corsica over to Michael's. It was not yet 5:00 P.M., but already dusk had rooted itself firmly, and a few twinkling stars were poking through the intermittent cloud cover. Lights shone out of almost every window of the cabin, casting the surrounding snow in weird patterns of shadow and light. Michael cut out the Corsica's lights and shut off the ignition.

"One of these days you're going to have to come and help Tommy with your gift," Elizabeth said as they climbed out of the car.

"Hell, he knows more about it than I do."

"He'd still like you to help."

Inside the front porch they stamped the fresh snow from their feet, and as they did so the inner door opened and Tommy greeted them.

"We going to a movie?"

"Yup," Elizabeth said, kicking off her boots. "And dinner too. So hurry up and put on some nicer clothes."

"Alright!" Tommy grinned, spun on his heels, then turned back to them. "Hi Mike!"

"Hi!" Michael said, chuckling.

"Did you see the lady?" Tommy asked.

"Lady?" Michael bent to unfasten his boots, prying them off with his toes.

"She came here to see you," Tommy said. "I said you were probably at home."

Michael straightened up quickly, a horrible hollowness blossoming inside his chest. "Tommy, when was this?"

Tommy shrugged. "Couple of hours ago, I

145

guess." His eyes widened. "She left something for you." He spun around and darted through to the kitchen.

Elizabeth was frowning. "What lady?"

Michael shrugged, mirroring her frown. His stomach was knotted tightly and he forced himself to breathe slowly and calmly. Tommy came trotting back with a small jar and handed it to Michael. Inside the jar a thick liquid, almost black, sloshed back and forth. Only the light refracting through the edge of glass revealed the liquid to be dark red. Michael moaned softly, taking the jar from Tommy. He lifted a hand to cover his eyes, and leaned against the porch wall for support.

"Michael, what is it?" Elizabeth's voice was soft, full of concern.

Michael shook his head. He turned his attention to Tommy and knelt so that he was on the boy's level. Voice calm, totally controlled, he said, "Tommy, what else did she say?"

Tommy, sensing he had stumbled into something very important, furrowed his forehead in concentration. "She said, uh, say hi to Michael. She said, uh, give him this."

"That's all?" A frantic edge had entered Michael's voice.

"Uh . . . she said tell him it will make him feel better." Tommy shrugged. "That's all."

Michael reached out and held Tommy's shoulders. "Tommy, what did she look like. Try and remember everything."

Tommy's face pinched in pain, and Michael softened his grip on the boy's shoulders.

"She was pretty," Tommy said. "Like a model from one of Mom's magazines. She was dressed kind of funny. She didn't have a coat. She had really white hair, kinda short."

Michael stood up, shaking his head. "Oh, God."

"Michael, who was she?" A sharp edge had now entered Elizabeth's voice.

Michael continued to shake his head. "I have to talk to Bob Brisk." He stepped into the cabin, went to the phone by the kitchen door. Elizabeth followed closely behind. She held out a hand and stopped him from picking up the receiver.

"What's going on, Michael. I have a right to know."

Michael nodded. "It's about the murders. I have to talk to Brisk."

Elizabeth's face turned white, and she lifted her hand. Her lips tightened and a coldness entered her eyes. Michael turned away and dialed the police number. After two rings it was answered by Sally.

"Sally, this is Michael Smith. Is Bob Brisk there?"

"Sorry, Mr. Smith, he's off tonight."

Michael muttered something foul. "Do you know where he is?"

"Probably at home," Sally said.

"I need his home number."

147

There was a long pause, then Sally's voice became very careful. "I'm sorry, Mr. Smith, but I can't give out that number."

"Damn it, this is important!"

"I'm sorry . . ."

Michael slammed the receiver back in his cradle. He turned to Elizabeth, who was watching him carefully, face emotionless. "You know his home number, don't you?"

Elizabeth nodded slowly.

"I need it. It's important." He tried to keep his voice calm.

After a moment Elizabeth nodded again, and reached for the small phone pad. After a quick scan she read him the number. Michael dialed, and waited impatiently as it rang. *Come on, damn it Brisk, come on!*

"Hello?"

"Bob, this is Michael Smith. I have to talk to you."

After a short pause, Brisk coughed softly. "I was about to head out," he said.

"This is important. It's about the killings."

Another pause. "What about them?"

"Damn it, I need to talk to you in person!"

"Okay, okay, calm down. Where are you?"

"I'm at Elizabeth Turner's cabin, but . . ." he turned to see Elizabeth's white face and shook his head. "Meet me at my place."

"Now?"

"Right now."

"This better be important, Michael."

Michael hung up the phone and saw his hand trembling as it came away from the cradle. His forehead shone with sweat and his underarms were soaking.

"Michael, what's going on?" Elizabeth's voice was soft.

He reached out and touched her arm, but she backed quickly away. Michael regarded her a moment, then shook his head. "Let me talk to Brisk first. I'll come by later. I'll explain everything."

She held his eyes for a few seconds, then nodded almost reluctantly. Before he left, she kissed him lightly on the lips. But there was no passion there.

Feeling hollow, Michael drove back to his own cabin. His hip throbbed painfully, incessantly, and even the headlights reflecting off the snow made him squint his eyes in pain. The stress, he realized, was causing a resurgence of the symptoms. He would have time to consume some of Muir's concoction before Bob Brisk arrived, but even as the thought occurred to him he discounted it.

Brisk would be skeptical. He would demand proof.

He parked the Corsica behind Elizabeth's Volkswagen, but did not plug it in. One thought echoed through his mind, blocking out all others.

She found me. She found me.

The past he had run from had caught him up. Sondra had kept her promise. She had sought him out.

And now there was no more running.

CHAPTER TWELVE

Michael sat at the kitchen table and waited for Bob Brisk. He left the cabin dark except for a single lamp in the living room, the dim light reaching feeble fingers into every corner. When he heard the crunch of tires on snow outside he rose and walked to the front porch. A light snow was falling. Bob Brisk was dressed casually in dark slacks, a plaid shirt, and a light blue ski jacket that heightened the lines of his trim torso. He offered an impatient nod as he walked past Michael and into the cabin.

The cop slowed as he entered the dimly lit interior. He peered into the living room, into the open bathroom, into Michael's bedroom. The living room light cast his face in stark relief, accenting the rugged, chiseled look of his features. His eyes glittered watchfully. He seemed tense, as if he was expecting something to happen. Michael closed the front door, turned to face Brisk.

"Can we have some lights in here?" Brisk said, slowing down as he entered the darkness.

"Sorry," Michael said. He flicked on the kitchen

lights and squinted in pain at the sudden brightness.

Brisk gave the kitchen a thorough inspection without seeming to do much more than glance quickly around. But his eyes missed nothing. Michael felt a brief flare of admiration for the cop. At last Brisk's eyes came back to Michael and focused squarely on his face. "It's Saturday night, Michael. This better be important."

Michael nodded. "Sit down, this will take a little while."

Brisk seemed to debate this suggestion, but finally lowered himself into the hard wooden seat. "Mind if I smoke?" He had his pack out and his lips around a Marlboro before Michael could answer.

"Will you have a cup of coffee?"

Brisk shook his head. "Don't suppose you have beer." He expertly lit the cigarette and exhaled a plume of smoke into the air.

"I do," Michael said. He went to the fridge and came back with two bottles of Coors Light. Brisk accepted the bottle with a brief smile, twisted the cap off easily, and sucked back a deep swallow.

Michael sipped his beer slowly. He was finding it difficult to look directly at Brisk. Brisk, accustomed to nervous suspects, noticed immediately.

"Listen, you dragged me over here in the middle of the night. Don't hedge now. What is it?"

Michael nodded and sipped his beer. His throat tightened as the bottle touched his lips, but he did not gag. "You said earlier that I might be connected to the killings and not know anything about them. I didn't want to admit it at the time, but you were right. I know something."

Brisk took a long slow drag on his cigarette, then hissed the smoke out of his nostrils. Eyes still focused on Michael, he lifted his bottle and took a draw on the beer. His eyes were cold and hard. "What do you know?"

"It's a long story, actually. I should start at the beginning."

Again, Brisk took a drag on the cigarette. It was obvious he had somewhere to go, that he did not want to be trapped here too long. But finally he nodded.

Michael took a deep breath. "It starts three and a half years ago. I had just finished university, was kind of edgy, not ready to settle down. I traveled down to Mexico with a friend for a couple of months. Sort of a last fling before finding a job and getting on with life." He smiled, but Brisk did not smile back. "That was in October. We didn't have much money. We were basically staying away from the resort areas, taking the trains, second class all the way. We worked our way down to Mexico City, stayed there a few days, and then rode further south, into the jungles. We wanted to see the ruins at Palenque."

Brisk took a drag on his cigarette, eyes impatient.

"We stayed in a place called the Maya-Bella campground. Right in the middle of the jungle. They provide a thatched roof on poles and you sling a hammock up to sleep. Really popular with American kids, hippies, sixties rejects. But cheap. Most of them were there for the ungos, psilocybin mushrooms."

Brisk sighed impatiently. "Does this have a point?"

Michael nodded. "I just want to give you the background. Otherwise you won't believe me."

Brisk's eyes widened slightly, and an amused smile curled his lips slightly. "Okay."

"We stayed there a couple of weeks," Michael said. "One morning, toward the end, we woke up and found we'd both been bitten pretty badly by insects during the night. I had a lump the size of a plumb on my neck, didn't go down for a couple of hours. Itchy as hell. But this was just routine. We didn't think much about it. By the next day we were both feeling pretty bad, feverish, body tremors, diarrhea. We'd already had our bout with the water, so we figured this was something to do with the insect bites. The next day it was worse. Neither of us could bring water even close to our mouths without gagging."

"Hydrophobia," Brisk said quietly, sipping his beer.

"Anyway, we were getting pretty worried. We packed up our things and hitchhiked back into the town of Palenque. There was a doctor there and he had a look at us. His diagnosis was that we were both exhibiting the early stages of some sort of insect-borne encephalitis. It might get better, it might not. We didn't want to take the chance. Maybe in Mexico City there would be adequate medical treatment, but not out here in the middle of the jungle. We had enough cash left to stay in Mexico another few months, or enough to get us back to the states by plane in a hurry. We opted for the latter. Two days later we were in McAllen, Texas, booked into a dinky little motel at the edge of town, spread out on the bed, feverish and almost hallucinating."

Brisk said nothing. He lit another cigarette, sipped his beer, and kept his eyes on Michael.

"By this time it was pretty bad," Michael said. In his mind he felt himself transported back to that room, and felt again the terror of the initial symptoms. "Our eyes were sensitive to light. All our senses seemed heightened. The sheets on the bed felt like sandpaper. Every sound was like a cymbal going off in our ears. And there was . . . a hunger. Not for food or water, but for . . . well, we didn't know what at the time."

"This is sounding less and less like encephalitis," Bob Brisk said in good humor.

Michael nodded. "I just lay on the bed and fought it. I mean, I wanted to run out into the street and break things. I had these incredibly violent images in my head. But I knew it was the fever and I tried to fight it. But my friend . . ." The memory made him shiver. "I sort of snapped out of it once in a while, had brief moments of clear thinking. One of those times I found myself alone. I was terrified, knew I should call the police or something, but I was back under in a second. I remember the sounds of sirens, and these incredibly bright flashing red lights. It was like a war outside, it seemed to me. And then the door opened and my friend came it. And she looked like she was over it."

"She?" Brisk's eyes widened.

Michael nodded again. "She'd snapped out of it. The fever had broken. But I was still fighting it. She knelt beside the bed and smiled at me, and somehow I knew all those sirens and flashing red lights had been for her. She had done something, and it scared the shit out of me. I didn't want to think about it. 'I know what you need,' she said to me. She had a jar with her, filled with some dark liquid. I could smell it, and it made me shake. I just lay there, teeth snapping, eyes open, with her beside me, smiling. I didn't want what was in that jar. But she poured it into my mouth. Maybe I didn't fight her off. Maybe I . . ." Michael shrugged, looked away from Brisk, and sipped his beer.

"Definitely not encephalitis," Brisk said.

"Nope," Michael said. "It took about fifteen minutes for my fever to break. Half an hour later I felt better than I'd ever felt in my life. But I was also terrified. 'What did you give me?' I asked her. 'Don't you know?' she snapped back. And I did know. The taste was still strong in my mouth. It was blood."

Bob Brisk sighed. "I hope this comes to a point soon."

"It does," Michael said. "We got into a big argument. She said that whatever virus we had contracted, it had changed us. She said we were better now, that we were stronger. The trick was, not to fight it. Let it take control. Let it push. Let the hunger take the driver's seat. Like she had done. When I asked her where she had got the blood she

156

laughed. We'd both heard the sirens. Later, in the news, they showed a body lying behind a building. The police thought a wild animal was running loose and had ripped out this kid's throat. They hunted down a couple of big cats in the area, and that was that. But it wasn't any cat. When I confronted her with it she just laughed. But I thought there was still hope for us. I told her we were going to Chicago. I had a friend there who could help us, or get us help. But again she laughed. 'We're better now,' she said. 'Why go back?' "

"And I did feel better. A lot better. Stronger, quicker. But I could also tell that the virus was still inside. Who knew when it might erupt again? Anyway, I split off with her. I told her I was going to find help. She said I was crazy. She said whatever we had, it was something new. There would be no cure. We would need each other and eventually we'd have to get back together. I didn't believe her."

"That's it?" Brisk said angrily.

"No. Almost. I went to Chicago, like I told you. I have a friend, a doctor. It *was* something new. Not encephalitis. His tests revealed a mutated form of the rabies virus. It took us almost a year to get a handle on it. The virus followed a rigid monthly cycle. Every twenty-eight days the symptoms reasserted themselves. But worse, it had induced biological changes, especially in the digestive system. Blood had assumed the role of a digestive enzyme. Without a regular intake, it was impossible to digest any other food. He wanted to go public and do some serious research, but I refused. For the past three years he's been providing me with supplies of modified human blood compounds, which I consume whenever the symptoms appear. It was only last month that I finally consented to some serious research. I can't live like this any longer."

"What about your friend?" Bob Brisk said.

"I thought she might be dead. I hadn't heard from her in three years. I didn't want to believe that the killings here had anything to do with her. I mean, why should they?"

"So why did you call me?"

"Because Tommy was visited today by a woman. The way he describes her, she could be my friend. She gave him this. She told him to give it to me and tell me that it would make me feel better. Who else would know?" He reached behind him to the sink counter and handed Brisk the small jar.

Brisk held the jar up to the light, squinting at the liquid within. He placed it gently on the table. "You think your friend killed those boys?"

Michael paused, then nodded. "I think so. I don't know why, but I think so."

Brisk polished off his beer and began to peel the label. "The FBI is sending a couple of men up here on Monday. They'll want to talk to you."

"Elizabeth told me."

Brisk smiled grimly. "Thought she might." The smile faded as quickly as it had appeared. "In the meantime, I want you to give me your friend's name, and a description. I'm not saying I believe any of this, but . . ."

"I can prove it," Michael said quickly.

Brisk's eyes widened slightly. "Oh?"

Michael leaned forward in his chair. Since driving over from Elizabeth's his body had been racked with exquisite pain from his hips to his neck to his eyes. Never before had he attempted to intentionally bring on the symptoms, but Bob Brisk's belief was necessary if this was ever going to end. He closed his eyes, shivered, and allowed the symptoms to carry him. Soon his teeth began to chatter, and even behind closed eyelids he seemed to sense shapes and patterns of light and dark around him.

"That's good," Bob Brisk said hoarsely. "I can clack my teeth too."

Michael opened his eyes. Brisk's quickly hidden reaction of shock was gratifying. Michael smiled, and the tendons of his neck and face became taut. "I'm under control," he hissed. "But I must show you. The virus does some weird things. Heightened awareness. Speeded muscle response and reflex."

"Uh huh," Brisk said uneasily.

In a sudden explosion of muscles and limbs Michael jumped from his seat, circled the astonished Brisk twice, pinned the cop's arm behind him, and brought his mouth close to his neck and left ear. He felt his own hot breath reflecting off Brisk's skin. Beneath his hands Brisk's arms strained to be free, but Michael's grip was tight and easy.

"You see," he said, his voice cracking, barely recognizable. "I'm very fast. My strength is abnormal."

"Goddamn it, let me go!" Brisk strained vainly.

Michael loosened his grip and the cop broke free and jumped to his feet. He spun on Michael, his

159

face a mask of rage. But the rage was overcome by a look of shock and revulsion. Michael tried to smile, imagining what his constricted face must look like. He could not close his lips over his teeth, which clattered and clacked spasmodically.

"Jesus . . ." Brisk whispered.

Michael turned away. He went to the bathroom, opened the medicine cabinet, and brought down one of John Muir's bottles. He brought it back to the kitchen and held it up for Brisk to see. Then he spun open the top, groaning at the sudden odor, and lifted the bottle to his mouth. With difficulty, hardly able to control his gag reflex, he spilled some of the liquid down his throat. The effects were immediate. His face muscles slackened, relaxed, assumed their normal contours. Soon he was able to close his mouth.

Brisk sat down again, eyes trained incredulously on Michael. "This is crazy."

Michael shrugged, and took his seat again. The symptoms had subsided to a level he was comfortable with. It was not often they disappeared entirely. "I've never done that before. Given in willingly."

Bob Brisk shook his head. "Okay. So I believe you. It's still crazy." He lit a cigarette with a shaky hand, suppressing a shiver. "Now who's this friend of yours and what does she look like?"

"Her name is Sondra," Michael said. "Sondra Palmer. She's about my height, very attractive. Short blonde hair. Looks like a model, Tommy said. I always thought she could be."

Michael frowned. Bob Brisk's face had suddenly

160

gone completely white and his eyes were staring at Michael blankly. "What is it?" Michael said.

Brisk blinked, eyes coming to a focus. "Nothing. Still finding it a bit hard to believe," he said.

"Believe it," Michael said. "And what I showed you is nothing. You've got to realize that this was a first for me. Sondra has been doing this for years. She'll be in complete control. Very, very dangerous. Definitely not human."

Brisk nodded, still far away. It was as if he had blocked his mind to any outside stimulus. "And this jar she gave Tommy," Michael said. "I doubt it was from one of the two boys. My bet is there's another dead body somewhere."

Brisk nodded. "Expected there'd be another one," he said softly, not looking at Michael. "We won't find it tonight. Have a good look tomorrow."

"We have to find Sondra," Michael said.

Brisk nodded absently. "Sure. We'll start looking tomorrow. FBI will be up Monday. Don't worry."

The cop stood, took a deep breath, and turned his attention to Michael again. "Thanks for telling me all this."

Michael nodded. "I didn't want to believe it myself, otherwise I'd have told you sooner."

Brisk smiled grimly. "What about Elizabeth? Does she know yet?"

Michael shook his head. "I guess I'll have to tell her."

"Guess you will," Brisk said, breathing out a cloud of smoke. He walked to the front porch, opened the door, and stepped out into the snow.

"Don't worry, we'll clear all of this up," he said, then walked over to his car.

Michael watched the Chevy roar to life, back up, and disappear down the blacktop, lights flickering between the trees. He went back inside and opened himself another beer.

He sat at the kitchen table and sipped the beer slowly, washing the other taste from his mouth. Something about Bob Brisk's reaction was not right. The cop had seemed very tense. Almost frightened.

The tables were turned. Now it was Bob Brisk who knew something he wasn't saying. The thought made Michael very uncomfortable.

He sipped his beer, and looked over at the phone on its small table. It was time to call Elizabeth. Time to tell her everything.

He took another sip of his beer, but did not move.

CHAPTER THIRTEEN

Bob Brisk twisted the car radio's dial to off, interrupting Willie Nelson in midsentiment, and filling the Chevy with silence. The strange reversal of being cheered by depressing ballads was not working properly tonight. Silence was preferable. The blacktop of 210 just east of New York was patchy with drifts of snow, but out here in the clear the wind had done a fair job of keeping the road clean. He drove at moderate speed, faster than the road conditions dictated, but not nearly as fast as he wanted. The studded rear tires whined on the asphalt.

Since leaving Michael Smith's place he had been unable to think clearly. He kept getting flashes of Michael jumping up from his seat, a blur of motion, circling him like a tornado. His arms still ached from where Michael had gripped him and held him fast with fingers that felt like iron. No man could move that fast, no man could be that strong, least of all Michael Smith. But the action had added a strong sense of verisimilitude to the preposterous story Michael had told. And Michael had said his friend's name, the one who had contracted the virus with him, was Sondra. Sondra Palmer.

Bob gritted his teeth, grinding them together noisily.

It had been a week since he had met the woman in the bar, the woman who said her name was Sondra. He had seen her every night since then, meeting her first at Old Jack's, then accompanying her to her room at the Hilltop Inn. In the dim lighting of room 16 she had done things to him that he still could not believe, things he had never imagined doing. She had raised him to almost painful heights of ecstasy and expectation, using her sharp fingernails, her full red lips, and her moist, pointed tongue as surgically precise tools. Yet not once had she allowed him to climax. Not once had she relieved the tension she had produced.

"Not yet," she kept saying, her breath hot against his ear. "Soon," she promised, tracing small circles on his abdomen with her tongue.

Every night after he left her he stopped the car a mile out of Hinton and masturbated furiously. Remembering those nights he burned with shame. He had never been like this with a woman. He had never met a woman like Sondra. But even as he hated himself for doing so his erection grew and throbbed against his thigh as he drove, and every subtle movement of his leg against the accelerator or brake pedals brought to mind a touch or a kiss she had given him.

It had been that way since the first night.

Now, as he drove, he felt not only the edge of expectation and desire that had been his constant company this past week but also a cold hard ball of anger and fear pressing up into his sternum. He parked the Chevy at the edge of Old Jack's parking lot and left an obvious trail of footprints in the snow as he walked across the black asphalt. As he stepped inside the bar, a gust of snow particles followed him in, and outside the wind howled plaintively.

It was Saturday night, and Old Jack's was packed. A smokey haze hung in the air like dirty sheets of cellophane, and the smell of cigarette smoke and spilled beer was strong. The juke box was playing "Lucille," and a table in the corner added a drunken cacophony to the chorus: *"You picked a fine time to leave me. . . ."* Brisk quickly scanned the booths against the far wall, then turned his attention to the scattered tables. Even in the dim lighting he could see that Sondra was not here. He meandered through the room and leaned against the bar. Hud, seeing his arrival, smiled sympathetically, put down the glass he was wiping, and came over. Beneath his Minnesota Twins T-shirt, rolls of flesh moved languidly, as if his immense body were suffering tidal effects from an invisible moon.

Hud leaned his immense, hairless forearms against the countertop and regarded Bob Brisk with a patented bartender's sympathetic-yet-cynical-I-don't-give-a-shit-but-tell-me-anyway look. "Double bourbon?"

Brisk shook his head. "Has Sondra been in?"

Now the look of sympathy, so far peripheral, became the prominent aspect of Hud's face. "Yeah. She was here. Left about half an hour ago."

"Alone?"

165

Hud smiled. "Yes."

Brisk turned away so he would not have to look at the bartender's face. The sympathy, the pity, sickened him. The first night he had walked out of here with Sondra the faces around him had been wide-eyed and astonished. *Envious.* But now, a week later, they were laughing at him. They could see what Sondra was doing to him, see how she was wrapping him up, controlling him. He fought back the blush that had started at the roots of his hair, then turned back to Hud. "I'll be in later," he said.

Hud nodded, neither belief nor disbelief evident on his chubby face. Brisk walked back across the smokey room to the exit, ignoring the looks he was getting. Let them talk. Let the fuckers talk. It's *still* envy.

He drove the three hundred yards to the Hilltop Inn and parked the Chevy outside the front office. The old woman sitting at the desk smiled at him through the frosted front windows as he drove by. Likely she considered him a regular by now. Brisk smiled grimly, not at all pleased at the thought.

He paused outside of room 16, shuffling his feet. There were tracks in the snow in front of the door, but he could not tell if they were made by one or more persons. He studied the crushed snow with an expert's eyes, but the anger inside him destroyed his impartial vision. He saw only a tangled trail that told him nothing. Groaning in dismay, he raised his hand and knocked three times on the hard wood. He waited. Cold wind tugged at his ears, caressed his neck, stung his cheeks. Wind-driven flakes made him squint his eyes. It seemed he stood there forever.

Finally the latch clicked and the door swung open.

Sondra stood framed in the doorway, and Bob Brisk caught his breath. She was wearing a sheer black negligee that hung to a point just below her hips. Beneath the diaphanous material her flesh looked radiant and pink. Her breasts were firm, high, and the nipples poked obviously against the thin material. Her legs were naked, pale. Unable to help himself, Brisk let his eyes travel the length of her body, returning at last to her face.

"I knew you'd come eventually," she said. Her voice was smokey.

"You weren't at Old Jack's," Brisk said, his voice weaker than he had intended. The hard ball of anger was melting in the quickly growing flames of his desire.

Sondra stepped aside to let him enter. Brisk walked past her into the room. A single lamp in the bathroom cast dim but warm lighting across the remaining walls. She closed and latched the door behind him. He stood still as his eyes grew accustomed to the dimness. Sondra came up behind him and began to unbutton his jacket. He remained still as she pulled it off.

"I waited for you. You were late. I hoped you'd come here."

Free of his jacket, Brisk turned to face her. Before he could open his mouth to speak she kissed him, pressing her lips hard against his own, pushing her tongue into his mouth. She tasted sweet, yet dusky. Brisk brought his hands between them, pressed his palms against the flat of her stomach. Beneath his hands she felt warm. He slowly raised his hands until

167

he cupped the mounds of her breasts, stroked the nipples beneath the silky material with his thumbs until the tiny protruding points became even harder. Sondra moaned into his mouth. She nipped his tongue with her teeth.

"Why were you late?" she asked softly.

Her question suddenly dragged Brisk back to reality. He reluctantly stepped out of her grasp and turned his face away from her. From his shirt pocket he pulled a crumpled pack of Marlboros, placed one in his mouth, and lit it. The burning smoke did not have its usual calming effect on him. He took three deep drags, hissing the smoke out slowly before turning to face her again.

"Do you know a man named Michael Smith?" he asked.

Sondra blinked. Her gleaming grey eyes were locked on his own. "I did once," she said carefully. "Why?"

Brisk drew on his cigarette and held the smoke in his lungs before letting it out. "He's living in New York."

"Little New York?" She seemed startled.

Brisk nodded. "I met with him tonight. That's why I'm late. He told me . . . a strange story."

Sondra kept her eyes locked on his, then turned away to the night table where a bottle of vodka and a glass rested. She lifted the bottle and poured a healthy amount of the clear liquid into the glass. "What kind of story?" she asked, not turning around.

Brisk took a deep breath. "He said you and he traveled to Mexico three years ago. He said you contracted a virus. Something weird."

She spun around now and took a step toward him. Brisk took an involuntary step backward before stopping himself. Sondra came closer. The smell of her perfume, mingled with the blank alcoholic smell of the vodka, tingled in Brisk's nose. "So?" she said softly, stepping closer.

Brisk found himself focusing on her icy grey eyes. "He said you might be responsible for a couple of killings we've had recently. He said . . ."

"Do you believe him?" Her voice was flat, emotionless. Her red lips hardly moved as she spoke.

Brisk shrugged. "He showed me some strange stuff. I believe him about the virus."

"About me?"

"I don't know," Brisk said quickly.

Sondra stared at him steadily a few seconds, then stepped closer to him. Her breasts pressed into his chest, and even through his shirt he could feel the firm points of her nipples. His erection throbbed against his slacks. "I did travel with him to Mexico," she said, and kissed his lips softly. "Both of us contracted the virus," she said, and kissed him again, sucking gently on his lips. "We split up after that," she said, and trailed her tongue down the side of his neck, leaving a glistening trail of saliva.

"Was he telling the truth?" Brisk said hoarsely, knees feeling weak.

Sondra smiled. She unbuttoned his shirt, pressed her lips to his chest, and began to move her mouth lower, her tongue tracing wet patterns on his skin. "We split up," she repeated, "and he's been following me ever since."

She lowered herself to her knees before him and began to unbuckle his belt. Soon she unbuttoned his slacks and slowly pulled down the zipper.

"Did you kill those boys?"

Her sharp red fingernails hooked over the top edge of his briefs and pulled them down, freeing him. His erection jutted out, almost touching her lips. "Michael Smith is mad," she said softly. "He hates me." She encircled him with the fingers of her right hand, running her nails across the smooth, hot skin. She opened her mouth wide and held him steady before her.

Brisk groaned at the sensation of her hot breath. Looking down, he could hardly believe what he was seeing. She had never taken him this far before. Never come close to this. All thoughts of Michael Smith vanished from his mind as he concentrated on the moment. Sondra's grey eyes looked up at him, and her pink tongue darted out to lick her lips. "Guide me," she said.

"What?"

She reached for his hands and placed them on the sides of her head. "Guide me," she repeated softly, and opened her mouth again, holding him on target with her right hand.

Brisk groaned. Beneath his hands her blonde hair was silky and smooth. Her eyes looked up at him, waiting. Brisk slowly pulled her head toward him, and as he did so she guided him into the glistening opening of her mouth. Her lips encircled him, a hot ring, and her tongue probed and licked. Brisk shuddered and pushed her away. Looking down he could see that Sondra was smiling up at him.

"As much as you want," she whispered. "All that you want."

Brisk breathed deeply, slowly. "Did you kill those boys."

She stared up at him a moment. "Do you think so?"

"I don't know."

She smiled again. "Guide me."

He pulled her head forward again, and she swallowed him completely. Using only his hands to guide her mouth, he pushed his whole length into her, over and over again, as deep as he could, and she took it all. Her tongue was in constant motion and her cheeks hollowed as her mouth worked. Brisk felt the explosion of orgasm building within him, and Sondra seemed to sense it too. She pulled her mouth away, encircled the base of his erection with her fingers, and squeezed tightly.

"Not yet," she whispered.

Soon the threat of orgasm receded, and Brisk's breathing quieted. Sondra stood before him, eyes level with his own. Her tongue reached out and traced a delicate line across his lips.

"Now it's my turn," she said. "Can you support my weight?"

Brisk nodded. Sondra smiled. She put her arms around his neck and pressed close. "Lift me," she whispered into his ear.

Brisk placed his hands around her smooth buttocks and lifted her. She helped him by jumping slightly, supporting her weight with her arms around his neck, until her pelvis was pressed against his belly.

"Are you ready?" she said.

Brisk nodded, unable to speak. It was happening tonight. *It was happening!*

"Feel me," she whispered.

Brisk moved one hand across her buttocks, to the joining of her legs. He could feel her heat radiating against his fingers. "Oh, God," Brisk said.

"Will you help me?" she said.

"With what?"

"With Michael Smith. He wants to destroy me."

Brisk groaned, his erection throbbing painfully.

"I need you to protect me," she whispered into his ear. She pushed her tongue into the hollow of his neck.

"I'll protect you," he whispered, caressing her smooth buttocks with his open hands.

She moaned into his ear. "I knew you would," she said. "Let me go."

Brisk obeyed. He lowered his hands away from her so that she was suspending herself on his body, supported by her arms around his neck, and by her legs scissored around his waist. Her heals prodded the backs of his thighs.

"I've wanted this for so long," she said.

Her body began to move. With exquisite control she lowered her pelvis, until she was touching him. He groaned involuntarily, clenching his fists. Her mouth clasped his own and her tongue darted out to probe between his lips. He opened his mouth to her.

And then she engulfed him, inch by inch, squeezing almost painfully, taking him deeper than he had thought possible. He wanted to scream, wanted to jump and thrust and rut. But she held him in complete control. She moved against him, taking him in, sliding off, taking him in again. Moving slowly, slower. When Brisk came close to orgasm she seemed to sense it, and with unbelievable control she squeezed him until it was safe to move again. He did not know how long he stood there with the woman moving over him. But the muscles in his legs began to burn painfully. He did not care. The sensations rippling through his body were unbelievable, and undeniable. He had no choice.

"My lover, my protector," Sondra whispered in his ears, moving over him, engulfing him, squeezing him.

At last there was a flood of hot wetness at their joining, and Sondra's mouth opened in a pink "oh." "Now, lover," she said hoarsely, almost gasping. "Now!"

Brisk thrust and thrust and bucked against her. She raised her legs so her knees were pressed into his underarms, opening herself completely to him. When the climax came it was as if an earthquake passed through him. He shook and shuddered, and his legs wobbled beneath him. He would have screamed if Sondra had not clamped her mouth across his own.

Afterward, still carrying Sondra, he stumbled over to the bed and toppled them both onto it. They did not speak. The sound of their heavy breathing filled the small room; the smell of their sex began to taint the air. Her head rested on his chest and he stroked her hair.

Presently Sondra disengaged herself and moved higher, so that she was facing him. Brisk could hardly move. He felt completely drained. Every muscle on his body had been wiped out.

"Michael is the killer," Sondra whispered in his ear. "Not me."

Brisk blinked, but said nothing.

"Do you believe me? Will you help me?"

Brisk nodded slowly. "Yes," he said.

In a while he rose from the bed and dressed. Sondra remained on the bed, curled languorously around a wad of sheet and blanket. Her eyes were thin slits, but he knew she could see him. He pulled on his coat, buttoned it up, and went to the door. He turned to her once more and let his eyes travel along the smooth pale length of her body. His groin ached.

Outside, the cold air made him shiver. He walked slowly to his car, savoring the bite of the wind. He let the motor of the Chevy run for five minutes before putting it in gear. The whole time he stared out the front windshield, mind blank, unseeing.

He drove back to New York in silence. The trees passing at the side of the road were a blur. He was driving on automatic pilot.

He did not know if he believed Sondra.

But it didn't matter. The realization hit him without the slightest bit of shock or surprise. It didn't matter at all.

After tonight he would do anything for her. He was hers. Completely. Utterly. Without question.

CHAPTER FOURTEEN

Michael fought into wakefulness with some difficulty. He felt trapped on the lip of a cavern of sleep intent on dragging him deeper. His internal clock, well off kilter, informed him he'd slept less than three hours, but the bright swaths of winter sunshine slicing through the bedroom's airborne dust told him otherwise. At last, with a grunt, he heaved his legs out of bed, blinking furiously as he did so. There had been no dreams. None that he remembered, anyway, and those were the only ones that counted.

As he sat on the edge of the bed he breathed deeply, stretching his chest muscles while moving his arms in wide circles. His ribs creaked. The alarm radio said it was 9:47. So he'd slept a good ten hours. Too much sleep. No wonder he felt so tired.

After Bob Brisk had left Michael had remained seated at the kitchen table, debating the merits of calling Elizabeth. He had decided, after due consideration, that the subject of his call was not worth disturbinh her night. She would be in bed, and Tommy might be wakened. Better to wait until the morning when both of them were fresh, when she might be more receptive to what he had to say.

But now, ten hours later, the time still did not seem right. Can there ever be a right time for telling someone that you are a monster? He rubbed the sleep from his eyes and went through to the bathroom. He splashed cold water in his face, rubbed his eyes, then wet the back of his neck. Half an hour later he was feeling more human. He had finished half a pot of coffee, eaten a bowl of cereal, and was watching the steady fall of snow outside the kitchen window. There was still no wind.

It occurred to him that he was procrastinating. He could not deny it. Yet he could not fight it. He found himself dwelling on his relationship with Elizabeth and Tommy, speculating upon the damage his admission would cause. The exercise depressed him.

Finally, coffee finished, nerves frayed, he found himself in a hopeless state. In a mood of resignation he picked up the phone and called Elizabeth. When she answered he was at a momentary loss for words.

"Michael, is that you?"

"Uh, yes. Good morning."

"You sound strange."

"Tired."

Long pause. "I thought you would call last night."

"It was late . . ."

"I waited for your call."

"I'm sorry," he said, wishing now that he'd had enough guts to phone her earlier. "Bob Brisk didn't leave until late. I didn't want to disturb you and Tommy."

Another thoughtful silence. "You said last night,

when you were here, that you were going to explain everything.,"

"Yes . . ." Michael coughed, sniffed. "Can I come over?"

Elizabeth's voice softened. "Sure. Have you had breakfast?"

"No," he lied.

"I'll set a place for you. Don't be long."

He hung up, feeling more depressed than ever. In a sort of blind stupor he pulled on his coat, tied up his boots, and stepped outside. The cold was refreshing, and he enjoyed it so much he decided to walk to Elizabeth's cabin. By the time he was on the blacktop he was feeling much better. He would tell her everything. Everything he had told Bob Brisk. Either she would accept it, and accept him, or she would not. There was nothing he could do about it. But to continue this relationship without telling her . . . it would not be right. Better to end it honestly than continue in a lie. And now, at least, he was *doing* something. He had admitted Sondra's existence to a person in authority, someone in a position to act.

The running, at least, was over.

Elizabeth listened to his story with a look of earnestness that frightened Michael. She sat, leaning across the kitchen table, sipping occasionally from a mug of milky coffee, smoking continuously, eyes locked on his own. Michael was aware of Tommy's presence too, as the boy flipped through a book in the living room, obviously listening to every word. Elizabeth did not interrupt with questions, did not

177

seek clarification on any point. When at last Michael had told her everything he had told Bob Brisk, she did not respond.

"That's it," Michael said, sipping his coffee nervously.

Elizabeth blinked. "That's quite a story."

Michael shrugged.

"What did Bob Brisk think of it?"

"He believed it. He had no choice."

Elizabeth frowned. Michael began to wonder if she had taken him seriously, or if she thought he had been joking.

"I thought rabies was fatal," she said, eyes still locked on his own.

"It is, normally. But this isn't your usual run-of-the-mill rabies, it's a radically mutated version of the virus." Talking specifics made Michael feel more at ease.

"Is it contagious?" She asked this so casually that Michael almost missed it.

"No," he said. "When I first went to John Muir, we tried infecting laboratory rats with the virus, using my blood, using my saliva, even using isolated cultures of the virus. But we could not induce contagion. That's what's so strange about it. It's like it has become part of me, and only me."

"This Sondra," Elizabeth said, her voice now more wary. "What does she want?"

Michael shrugged. "I don't know."

"But it's something to do with you."

"I think so," Michael said. "I don't know. All I know is that I fought the effects of the virus and she gave into them. In a way, they augment her natural

178

personality. She was always somewhat of a predator, even back in college."

"You have a strange taste in women," Elizabeth said, looking away from him and exhaling a plume of smoke.

"That's not fair," Michael said, feeling hurt. "I was a kid then. Besides, maybe she chose *me*. I was never very good with . . . I mean, I never really had much to do with . . ."

"What about us. Me and you?"

"What about us?"

"I mean, with Sondra here. What does it do to us?"

"Nothing," Michael said gently, reaching across the table to touch her hand. "There's nothing between me and Sondra. I want nothing to do with her. If she's the killer, then Bob Brisk will hunt her down. I'll help him if I can. That will be the extent of my involvement."

Elizabeth turned to him, her eyes softer. "I'm sorry if I'm sounding bitchy, it's just that you never mentioned any of this before."

"I never really admitted it to myself. My past is something I've been hiding from for years."

When the phone suddenly rang, Elizabeth hunched her shoulders as if she were about to be slapped, a movement so sudden and small that Michael wasn't quite sure he had seen it. She's tense, he thought. She smiled nervously and rose to answer the phone. Michael sipped his coffee, trying not to listen in on the mumbled voice. When Elizabeth came back to the table she looked worried.

"That was Bob Brisk," she said.

179

Michael felt his eyebrows momentarily rise. "What did he want?"

"He wants you to meet him at the station as soon as you can."

"Did he say why?"

Elizabeth shook her head. She tapped her cigarette pack and pulled one out with her lips. She lit the cigarette, drew deeply, and exhaled the smoke with a sigh. "Michael, I'm frightened."

"There's nothing to be frightened about," he said.

"There is. Even Bob sounded worried on the phone. And this woman, this Sondra, she's already contacted Tommy."

Michael frowned. He could not argue with her. "Listen. I'll go and see Brisk. I'll call you later."

Elizabeth did not respond. She was looking worriedly at Tommy in the living room. The boy seemed absorbed in his book, but Michael knew he had been listening to everything.

"Okay?" he said.

"What?"

"I'll call you later."

Elizabeth nodded distractedly, then grunted noncommitally.

When he left Michael felt confused. Telling Elizabeth everything had not been what he had expected. He had been prepared for something more confrontational. But now he felt . . . empty. As if he had lost something. As if Elizabeth had taken a step away from him, putting some distance between herself and him. The thought deepened his depression.

At his cabin Michael brushed the snow off the Corsica, let it warm up a few minutes, then drove into New York. At the police station he found Bob Brisk alone in his office. The cop smiled grimly when Michael entered, then motioned for him to take a seat. Brisk lit a cigarette, inhaled deeply, then blew out the smoke in a lazy plume.

"You think maybe there's another body somewhere?" Brisk asked.

Michael was startled by the question. "Another..."

"You said last night there was probably another murder. The jar at your cabin?" Brisk regarded him with professional patience.

"Oh, yes. I'd say there was."

Brisk nodded. "We'll look for it today."

"What about Sondra?"

Brisk's eyes narrowed slightly. It was as if a thin veil had been drawn over his features, an extra bit of tension in the muscles. "What about her?"

"We have to find her."

Brisk nodded, drew on his cigarette. "So you said."

Michael felt a chill in his stomach, a welling of anger. "I wasn't joking last night, Brisk. Not one bit. If Sondra Palmer is involved in this, and I think she is, then we have to get her."

Brisk sighed. He had the look of a man who did not want to rise from his desk, a man who was being pestered by an annoying underling. "If this woman is like you say, if she has this virus, what can she do?"

"She'll be very, very dangerous."

"So, how do we get her?" His lips curled in a half-mocking smile.

Michael shrugged. "You can't think of her as a woman, not as a human being. She must be hunted down. Like an animal."

Brisk shook his head and smiled, but the smile was empty of humor. "Crazier every minute."

"Goddamn it, Brisk, you believed me last night. What's happened since then?" Again, Michael had the distinct impression that Brisk was hiding something, that the cop knew more than he was saying.

"I just had time to think." He drew on his cigarette. "Did you tell Elizabeth your . . . story?"

"Yes," Michael said simply.

Brisk nodded. "Well. It's not easy to believe."

"But I showed you . . ."

"I know what you showed me." Brisk swung his legs off his desk, landed his feet on the linoleum floor with a thump, and rose slowly. "We'll look for another body. One thing at a time."

Michael wanted to shout, to scream, to force this obtuse cop to act. But Brisk would be immune to those tactics. "When are the FBI men coming up."

Brisk regarded him cooly. "Tomorrow." he said.

Michael nodded. "We can get their help."

"You think they'll believe it?" Brisk walked past Michael and into the main room of the station. He picked his parka off Sally's seat and shrugged it over his broad shoulders.

"They'll have to."

Brisk paused, staring at him. Michael did not like the look in those eyes. There was something missing there, he decided.

"If we find another body, the feds will be the

182

smallest of our worries. The sheriff will send men from Fergus Falls. We'll be crawling with law."

"Good. The more the better."

Brisk chuckled. "This girl's got you running scared."

Michael returned Brisk's gaze. "Very scared."

He followed the cop through the reception area then out into the cold. The fat flakes of snow still drifted down, covering the ground in a soft layer. An older model Parisienne cruised slowly past the station, and Brisk raised his hand in greeting. Michael listened as Brisk spoke into his car's radio, giving instructions to Sally.

"Come on, get in," Brisk said to Michael.

"Where are we going?"

"Body hunting," Brisk said. "I want you to stick with me."

Michael nodded silently. As Brisk turned the car and drove to the east end of town, Michael pressed his face to the window and watched the snow falling. *We're coming, Sondra. We're going to get you. I'm not running any more.*

He wondered if he was making the biggest mistake of his life.

CHAPTER FIFTEEN

"You want me to do *what?*" Sally's voice sounded tinny over the car's radio.

"I want you to check the north allotments," Brisk said. He guided the cruiser through the arch of downtown New York, slowing perceptibly where snowdrifts encroached upon the blacktop.

"What exactly is the purpose of this exercise?" Though warped by electronics and a cracked diaphragm in the speaker, the sarcasm in her voice was sharp.

Brisk drew on his cigarette and smiled apologetically at Michael. *Good help is hard to find,* his look said. Michael did not smile back. "Hadn't you better tell her?"

Brisk shook his head, frowning now. He drew on his cigarette again and guided the exhalation of smoke out the partially opened window. He pressed the "talk" button and held the black plastic of the microphone close to his dry lips. "Just do as I ask, Sal."

There was a short silence, filled with static. "Okay,

Bob," Sally came back, resignedly Michael thought. "But what am I looking for?"

"Oh, anything suspicious," Brisk said, now slightly more at ease at Sally's apparent acquiescence. "Break-ins, prowlers, strangers lurking about." He took another drag on his cigarette, then brought the microphone back to his lips. "Anybody missing."

This time Sally's silence was longer, and even the static did not seem to fill it. "Missing?"

"Hell, I don't know. Just take a goddamned look around and let me know what you find!" He slammed the microphone back into its cradle and shook his head. "Jesus, can't get a friggin' thing done around here."

Michael maintained his gaze through the passenger window, watching the frozen slices of Great Lake sweep by between the dark trunks of trees. Since the light snowfall, the depression of the lake had begun to merge with snow on the bank, giving the appearance that the trees and cabins were sprouting out of the ice itself. Elizabeth and Tommy would want to go skiing soon. The thought popped out of nowhere, and with it an image of mother and son. A feeling of unexplained loss, a physical hollow, blossomed inside Michael's chest. To get his mind off it he turned again to Brisk.

"If you'd been honest with her, she might have been cooperative."

Brisk chuckled. "What would I have told her?" He smiled at Michael. "Good old Mike Smith thinks there may be another body lying about somewhere, Sal. I don't know why, but I believe him, so I'm diverting one hundred percent of our man power to act on his hunch. . . ." Brisk took another drag on his cigarette, and this time his face pinched in pain. He exhaled the smoke in small coughs, each one rattling wetly in his chest. After the coughing retreated he stabbed the cigarette angrily into the car's already overflowing ashtray. "Gotta quit this," he said softly. "Killing myself."

Michael kept quiet after that, kept his face pressed to the window as a solemn silence filled the car, somehow fortifying the already existing barrier between himself and the cop. When, a few minutes later, Brisk slowed the cruiser and turned onto a narrow access road, it was the cop who spoke first.

"This is Mary Ferguson's place," Brisk said. "No point taking it farther than this. Only summer places the rest of the way round the lake." He brought the car to a stop, snow crunching loudly beneath the tires, and put the transmission in park. He did not turn off the ignition. "I'll have a quick chat, be right back."

"Mind if I tag along?" The question was out before Michael could think through what he was saying. *I need to be doing something,* he realized. *I need to be taking positive action.*

Brisk, who had been in the process of opening his door, closed it again slowly. He turned to Michael, frowning. Despite the coughing fit only a few minutes earlier, he dug out his crumpled pack of Marlboros, stuck one between his lips, and lit it, exhaling a thick gout of smoke into the car. For a moment it looked as if another rack of coughing was imminent, as the cop's shoulders shook violently, but in a moment the tremors passed. An obvious flush crept into

Brisk's face.

"I don't know if that's such a good idea."

"I don't want to sit around," Michael said. "You asked me to come along."

Brisk took another drag on his cigarette, squinting his eyes in pain. "So I did," he said, "but just to keep an eye on you."

Now a flush of anger rose on Michael's cheeks. "You . . ."

"Now don't jump all over me," Brisk said. "It's just that folks around here might not take too kindly to seeing you right now. What with the killings, and you being a stranger in town."

"I wonder where they got that idea," Michael said tightly.

Brisk frowned, then shook his head. "Suit yourself, city boy." He opened his door and stepped out into the snow. Michael followed.

The cabin was a clone of every small cabin around Great Lake, most having been constructed at the same time back in the late forties and early fifties, but this one had been maintained carefully over the years. The original imitation log paneling had been covered with plywood, horizontal wood siding had been added on top of that, and Michael suspected that the white paint had been kept crisp and clean with yearly coats. The grey roof tiling looked almost new. A brick chimney rose from ground level at the east side of the cabin, spreading a stream of dark smoke across the sky. The air was redolent of burning logs.

"Don't say anything," Brisk warned as they approached the cabin.

Michael nodded.

Brisk knocked three times on the door, and in a few seconds it swung open. A small wiry woman in a long, flower patterened dress, regarded them suspiciously, clutching a pink cardigan tightly to her bosom. She looked from Brisk to Michael then back to Brisk again.

"Good morning, Mary," Brisk said, tipping his hat.

The woman's wizened face seemed to wrinkle further, but Michael could not tell if it was a smile or a scowl. "Been seein' a lot of you lately, Bob Brisk," she said. Her voice was a hacksaw drawn over the edge of a tin sheet.

"Busy days, Mary," Brisk said, adding a pathetic tone of weariness to his voice.

"Who's that with you?" Mary asked without looking at Michael.

"This is Michael Smith," Brisk said carefully. "You remember Henry and Barbara from the north allotments, don't you? This is their son."

The glittering slits of her eyes widened momentarily, and her attention shifted to Michael. "Never much liked Barbara Smith," she grated, and again the flesh of her face receded into a spasm of wrinkling skin. "And I've been hearing about *you*."

Having consciously decided not to let the old woman's antagonistic stance discourage him, Michael held out his hand and smiled warmly. "Nice to meet you, Mrs. Ferguson."

Equally deliberately she lowered her eyes from Michael's, regarded his extended hand with what appeared to be mild curiosity, then hid her own hand behind her back. She looked up at Brisk again. "I'd invite you in, if you was alone," she said, and curled her lips in a gummy grin.

Michael withdrew his hand. Brisk coughed in embarrassment.

"What we're out here for, Mary, is to check up on you," Brisk paused to let this fact sink in, but Mary did not react at all. "Everything fine with you?"

She nodded, looking past the two men at the car, as if there might be others waiting.

"Haven't seen any strangers poking around?"

"Just you," Mary Ferguson said.

Brisk tipped his hat at the scored point. "Well, if you notice anything out of the ordinary, Mary, you be sure to give me or Sally a call. Hear?"

She nodded, now distracted, hugging her cardigan closer around her withered body, interested neither in Brisk nor in Michael nor in anything they might have to say. As they walked back to the car, the door thumped closed behind them.

"Nice," Michael muttered, climbing back into the cruiser.

Brisk flicked the remnant of his cigarette into the snow, where it smoked and sizzled momentarily, then slammed his door closed. "I told you what to expect."

Michael nodded, feeling depressed. "I didn't think it would be this bad." He sighed. "I've only been back for three weeks."

Brisk chuckled, but would not look at Michael. "News travels fast around here," he said, and backed the car out onto the blacktop.

After that, while Brisk approached each cabin and questioned the occupants, Michael remained in the car. The inactivity was annoying, and with each passing minute Michael became progressively more frustrated. *Time is of the essence.* The phrase ran through his mind continually, a damning litany. And although Brisk was not above noticing Michael's discomfort, the cop did nothing to ease it. After each stop Michael turned to Brisk and asked, "Anything?"

Brisk's response was always the same. "Nope."

But Michael was impressed with Brisk's no-nonsense, professional attitude toward the job at hand. The cop knew every cabin owner by name, knew which cabins were occupied year round and which only seasonally, and knew which of the empty cabins had been tampered with since his last visit. If nothing else, Michael decided, Brisk was a good cop.

At 1:17 P.M., by the cruiser's digital dash clock, Brisk picked up the microphone and buzzed Sally. "Sally, it's Bob."

He lit a cigarette, breathing the smoke in deeply. "Come in, Sal." His voice assumed a singsong lilt, as if he were playing a game. But Sally did not answer. Michael imagined her talking to the north allotment version of Mary Ferguson. The thought was not amusing.

Still holding the microphone, Brisk smoked his cigarette halfway down before trying again. "Sally, it's . . ."

"What is it, Bob?"

"S'lunch time, Sal. Want to meet at Chuck's?" As

190

an afterthought, he added, "I'm buying."

There was a short pause as this undisguised offering of peace was digested, then Sally said, "Not yet. Ten more minutes."

"Something up?"

"No." Then: "I don't think so. I'm over at Sixty-three North."

Michael blinked. *My cabin.*

"Michael Smith isn't here," Sally said. "But Liz Turner's Beetle is parked here. I've already been at the Turner place, and Smith isn't there either."

Brisk coughed. "S'okay. He's here with me."

Long pause. "Okay, Bob." Again that note of resignation. And unspoken: *Why didn't you tell me?*

"We're heading over to Chuck's. Get there when you can."

There was no response. Brisk hung up the microphone, lips pinched thoughtfully. Michael had the impression that he'd stepped into the midst of a lover's quarrel and that each of the participants was acting out of character.

This was not the way Brisk and Sally usually worked, he decided. His first impression had been that they shared information honestly and quickly. Brisk's recent reticence was affecting their working life. Michael said none of this to Brisk, but he believed that the cop knew it anyway. *He knows something and he's not saying what it is. Not to me and not to Sally.*

They drove in silence around the curve of the horseshoe, back into the arch of New York proper, while outside the car flakes of snow began to drift down through the trees.

"This keeps up we're gonna be snowed in," Brisk said quietly, turning the car slightly to avoid a particularly large drift.

"Better this than a storm," Michael said.

Brisk shrugged.

Brisk was slowing the car to a stop outside Chuck's Grill, two doors down from the police station, when the radio buzzed.

"Bob!"

Brisk picked up the microphone. "Got you, Sal."

"I'm over at fifty-two North," Sally said. She sounded breathless. It took only a moment for Michael to identify the emotion: she was frightened.

"You okay?" Brisk asked; there was honest concern in his voice.

"Yeah, I'm okay." Sally said. "And I've got a body." Her words were accusative.

Brisk was silent a moment. He inclined his head slightly and looked at Michael. "Be right there," he said, still looking at Michael.

"It's messy," Sally said, and then the radio clicked off.

Brisk hung up the microphone and pulled the car out onto the road, tires spinning on the new-fallen snow. The transmission whined in effort.

"Fifty-two North. That's old Dan Stone's place," Brisk said. "Just three cabins away from yours."

Michael sat rigidly upright in his seat. Thankfully, Brisk did not notice. Michael hissed in a deep breath and held it in, trying to calm himself. He wondered, briefly, if the falling snow had covered the tracks Dan Stone had left after his visit to Michael's yesterday.

Dan Stone's cabin was identical to Michael's, but over a period of years the older man had constructed an addition that gave the entire structure an L-shape, a picture-window living room overlooking the lake. The site of Dan Stone's demise was, as of yet, inconspicuous, having neither the morbid beating of red police lights nor the crowd of onlookers that would have gathered in a bigger city. They found Sally leaning against the outside door, smoking a cigarette, looking very pale.

As Brisk parked the cruiser she dropped the butt of her cigarette and approached the car. She offered Michael a quick nod of recognition, then turned her attention to Brisk.

"You knew something was up, didn't you?" There was an undisguised note of anger in her voice, an almost concealed sense of hurt. She feels betrayed, Michael realized.

Brisk stepped out of the car, closing the door with quiet precision. "Had a hunch," he said evasively. He zipped up his jacket and walked toward the cabin, sidestepping Sally easily. She turned away from Brisk and studied Michael openly. There was no hostility in her gaze, he decided, only curiosity. *You knew too,* her eyes seemed to say. Thinking she wanted, or needed, an answer, he found himself shrugging. She shrugged back at him, and the two of them followed Brisk into the cabin.

Dan Stone lay wrapped around a leg of his kitchen table, surrounded in a viscous pool of blood. Against the white linoleum the blood looked almost beautiful, crisp in its definition, pure in color. *Aesthetically appealing*. The phrase popped into Michael's mind uninvited, and he felt horrified at having thought it. But already he had mapped the scene out for a transfer to canvas.

On closer inspection there were speckles and splashes of blood throughout the kitchen, across the counters, even on the roof. The smell of blood and death was like a solid presence. It reminded Michael of the jars in his medicine cabinet. Only when his mind had made this connection did the force of the scene before him hit home, and a wave of nausea passed through him. He reached out to lean on the door frame for support, but instead found Sally holding him up by the elbow.

"Don't touch anything," she said quietly, breathing as shallowly as possible. "Prints."

Michael nodded.

Brisk leaned over Dan Stone, placing his booted foot between one twisted arm and the blood-soaked torso, missing the pool of blood by less than an inch. He looked closely at the dead man's face and neck.

"Same thing," he said. "I can see a knife wound on the throat, but the flesh is torn and bitten. See how the slit is pried open beneath the left ear?"

Michael turned away. Another tremor passed through him. This time, the smell of blood was waking a sensation other than nausea. His stomach rumbled and his saliva suddenly began to flow. For a moment he felt lightheaded, almost dizzy.

"You okay?" Brisk said, standing upright, now looking at Michael.

Michael nodded again, not trusting himself to speak.

Brisk regarded him curiously for a few seconds, then turned to Sally. "Who've you contacted?"

"Just you," Sally said. She was looking down at the body.

"Okay. Call Doc Unger, and get him over here with his ambulance. But nobody else. Especially not that bastard Neff. Nothin' in the papers this time."

"What about the sheriff's office?" Sally said.

"No," Brisk said. He dug out his pack of Marlboros and stuck one between his lips. After it was lit he breathed the smoke deeply and let it out slowly, directing it toward the slack face of Dan Stone. "I'll get in touch with them later."

"But we should get help out here right away," Sally protested. "This is out of hand."

"Sally, don't argue."

"But Bob . . ."

"For Christ's sake, what do I have to say to you?" He stepped away from the body, toward Sally. She took a step back, face shocked.

"Okay, Bob," she said, voice subdued.

They stared at each other a few seconds, then Sally turned and went out of cabin. Divorce coming up, Michael thought.

When the door had swung closed, Brisk turned to Michael. He took a reflective drag on his cigarette, eyes squinted. "I'll need that jar of blood you got at your place," he said. "And I'll want to talk to Tommy Turner."

Michael nodded. "Sure. But what about Sondra? Now do you believe me? She's out there somewhere

195

and she's killing people. We have to find her."

Brisk drew on his cigarette. "So you say," he said.

The urge to lash out verbally at Brisk was almost overpowering, but Michael managed to subdue it. He shook his head, fighting the newly awakened feeling of hunger, and his anger. Not wanting to, but fearing that the later discovery of the fact might incriminate him further, Michael said: "Dan Stone came to visit me yesterday morning."

Brisk stared at him straight on.

"That's a nice piece of information to be revealing at this time," Brisk said. His gaze did not waver from Michael.

"I'm only telling you because somebody probably saw him anyway."

"Thanks for saving us some work," Brisk said.

"He stayed for coffee. We talked over old times. That's all."

"Friendly," Brisk said.

Michael held his breath, calming himself. There was no point taking this further. Brisk was simply argumentative.

At Brisk's continued silence, Michael chuckled and shook his head. "I'm going home," he said at last. Then: "To my cabin," in case Brisk had misunderstood. "You can get me there, or over at Elizabeth's."

Brisk nodded distractedly, not listening any more. Michael gave a final glance to the body of Dan Stone, locking the image away, then went outside. The fresh air was like a slap in the face, and he took a deep breath to calm himself.

Sally emerged from her cruiser and came toward

him.

"What do you know about all this," she said, regarding him openly.

Michael shrugged. "Brisk will tell you."

"Maybe." She shook her head in dismay, thinking about Brisk.

"If he doesn't, I will," Michael said. "The feds will be up here tomorrow, I hear. Everything will be out in the open then."

Sally nodded. Feeling that some sort of bond had been established, Michael lowered his voice conspiratorially. "Did you find anything else here? Tracks, or any indications of somebody other than Dan Stone?"

Sally pursed her lips, obviously debating whether to discuss police business with a civilian, and a suspect at that. Finally she shook her head. "The snow covered everything."

She knows Brisk is hiding something, Michael thought. We both know it.

"This is getting scary," Sally said.

Before he could stop, Michael said: "It's going to get worse."

CHAPTER SIXTEEN

Michael cradled the mug in both hands, letting the radiating heat warm his fingers and loosen the grip of the cold, savoring the strong aroma of the coffee within as it rose to meet his face. Elizabeth had been in the process of taking a sip from her mug, but now she lowered the cup to the kitchen table and looked at Michael with an incredulous expression.

"You can't be serious," she said.

Michael sipped his coffee carefully. It had been close to 3:00 P.M. when he arrived at Elizabeth's cabin. From Dan Stone's place he had walked back into New York and picked up his car in front of the police station. At first Elizabeth had been happy to see him, but the situation had deteriorated quickly, and Michael was not quite sure where the slide had begun.

"It's a matter of priorities," he said, trying to explain the logic of his thoughts. "How much does our relationship mean to you?"

Elizabeth sighed and reached for her pack of cigarettes on the table. Her fingers trembled as she raised one to her lips and lit it. Only after two long puffs did she seem to calm down. In the living room, Tommy was packed into a corner of the sofa watching television with the sound turned very low. The boy would know everything that transpired in the kitchen, Michael knew.

"That's not fair, Michael," Elizabeth said plaintively. With one hand pressed to her forehead, shading her eyes, she sipped her coffee. The posture was one of thoughtful defiance. "It's not so easy for Tommy and me to pack up and leave. We *live* here, remember. You're on vacation. Your home is somewhere else."

"I know that," Michael said, trying to hide the exasperation he felt. "I don't mean to imply that it would be *nothing* to leave. All I'm saying is that it would be worth the trouble."

Elizabeth shook her head. Michael sighed. It wasn't going as he had foreseen. He had thought, God only knew how, that Elizabeth might be eager to leave New York, to come to Chicago with him. In Chicago he could give her, and Tommy, the type of life they could only dream about out here. His salary from the business was substantial, certainly enough to support a small family. Whatever good was supposed to have come from staying in New York was now unattainable. The tension he had been attempting to leave behind had somehow followed him, in spades.

"We haven't known each other long enough to abandon our lives," Elizabeth said softly.

"But we have something, something between us, that's worth protecting," Michael said. "I believe that, I really do. But there's too much going on in this town that I don't understand. Or maybe I understand it too well. I thought that by confiding in Bob Brisk I could shrug this thing off my shoulders, but it hasn't worked. I've somehow been drawn deeper into a situation that's getting worse by the hour. And Brisk, that son of a bitch, knows something."

"Bob Brisk may be jealous, but he's a good cop," Elizabeth said.

"Hell, I know that. I've seen him at work. But he knows something about the case, something he's keeping secret."

"That sounds slightly paranoid, Michael."

"I know what it sounds like, believe me. That doesn't change the fact. You can ask Sally Warner, and I'll bet she'll confirm it. She knows there's something wrong with Brisk, she just can't put her finger on it."

"I thought Bob was the childish one," Elizabeth said, looking away.

Michael sighed, realizing he wasn't making his point. "Forget Brisk then . . ."

"He's a good cop," Elizabeth repeated.

Michael nodded, defeated. Perhaps he was becoming paranoid. It would be hard to tell from the *inside*. "I know that. I just feel . . . caught."

Elizabeth reached across the table and touched his hand, her expression now sympathetic. "Whatever is happening here, running away from it isn't going to solve it," she said. "You told me earlier you'd been running from something for years. Isn't now as good a time as any to stand and face whatever it is?"

"You don't understand."

Elizabeth stabbed out her cigarette and stood quickly. Her seat jumped backwards with a clatter. "No, maybe I don't," she said, folding her arms across her breasts. "Maybe I don't understand any of it at all. All I know is that in three weeks we've become close. I know we've got something that could grow and be good for both of us. For all three of us," she jerked her head toward the living room, where Tommy was still pretending to be enthralled by his TV show. "But I also know it's too soon for me to throw up everything I had here before you came along. No matter how confused *you* feel about it."

Michael tried to remain calm as he listened. After Elizabeth had finished he motioned for her to sit again. After a moment's hesitation she did so.

"Point taken," Michael said softly. "I agree, I'm not a good enough reason to throw everything away. . . ."

"Oh, Michael, you know that's not what I meant."

Michael held out a hand to quiet her. "Assume I'm right. But let me attack from another angle."

Elizabeth sighed, leaning back in her chair. In a moment she nodded with great reluctance.

"Forget about you and me for a minute," Michael said. "And think about yourself. About you and Tommy."

Elizabeth's stricken look became slightly more attentive. "I'm thinking," she said.

"You know there's been three murders here in as many weeks," Michael said. "You know Tommy was approached by a stranger the other day. Probably the damned murderer herself. It seems to me this isn't the best atmosphere to be in right now."

"Bob Brisk can handle it," Elizabeth parried. "Besides, you said yourself the FBI will be up here tomorrow, and likely a pack of uniforms from the sheriff in Fergus. Whoever's responsible will be caught."

Michael scoffed. "Maybe."

His reaction angered Elizabeth. She leaned across the table toward him, her face pinched. "And if you've got such a strong connection to this thing," she said, voice a hoarse whisper, "I'd think you'd want to stick around and get it cleared up!"

Michael closed his eyes for a moment and bent his head back as far as it would go. His neck muscles creaked at the effort. In a moment he relaxed and turned to Elizabeth again. "This is getting us nowhere."

"And fast," Elizabeth agreed. She reached for her cigarettes and lit another.

"Okay, then let me try explaining from another . . ."

"Michael."

"What?"

"Don't," she said softly. "I don't want to hear any more."

"But . . ."

"I think, perhaps, we've been moving too quickly," she said, and looked away from him and out the kitchen window.

Michael felt something hitch in his guts, and the hollowness he had experienced earlier while in Brisk's cruiser now blossomed in full. "Elizabeth . . ." The word emerged as a croak.

"I think," she said slowly, and it was obvious that

202

she was speaking with great difficulty. "I think we should stop seeing each other for a while. Until we can both better understand what's going on, here, and between us."

Michael forced himself to speak. "If that's the way you feel . . ."

"It is," Elizabeth said.

Michael nodded. He took another sip of his coffee, then pushed the cup away. He stood and zipped up his jacket. Elizabeth had turned away from him and was looking into the living room.

"Elizabeth, I . . ."

"Please, Michael."

Michael nodded silently. He walked to the door. In the living room, Tommy continued to stare at the TV and did not turn as Michael passed. Michael paused and glanced back at Elizabeth. She was still looking into the living room, but her face was streaked with tears. Emotions Michael could not identify bubbled up within him, but he clamped them at his lips. Without another word he opened the door and stepped out into the cold.

As Michael drove back to his cabin his mind was a blank. It was only after he had parked the Corsica that the full emotional blow of what had just transpired hit him. When he stepped out of the car he was reeling as if drunk. He leaned against the roof of the car, face pressed into his forearm, and breathed deeply. The sense of loss within him was so great he felt that at any moment he might collapse.

You don't feel loss unless there's something to

lose, he thought. And there had been something to lose, hadn't there? Both he and Elizabeth had been perfectly aware that there had been something between them, something precious, but they had been forced into a position where abandoning that thing had seemed the best move.

Michael stumbled away from the car, dizzy with a sense of anguish deeper than he had ever known before in his life. Elizabeth Turner and her son had begun to fill a hole in his life that he had hardly been aware of until three weeks ago. Now that hole gaped like a chasm, unfathomable and unfillable.

Despite the biting cold, made worse by a tight northwesterly wind that drove the ice particles into his face, Michael began to walk. He walked down to the shore of the lake, where the snow rose to encircle his boots. The wind tugged at his ears, stinging his cheeks and eyes. Above, the sky was dark grey, heavy with moisture. A storm was possible. To the west, above the tree line, the sun illuminated a cloudy arc of sky. Dusk was coming quickly.

Michael raised his boot and kicked a funnel of snow into the air. The wind drove it back into his face, and on his cheeks the snow melted.

Not knowing why he did so, Michael craned back his neck and screamed into the night. The sound, like a sword whistling through air, echoed around the lake.

Damn you, Bob Brisk, Michael thought.

He shivered, and in his guts something quaked. For a brief instant he focused his attention on his hip, became aware of the single tendril of pain reaching out for him. He did not care.

As he looked out over the lake the emotions within him began to alter. The anguish seemed to soften, to recede. But in its place another emotion rose, a much sharper emotion. Because of it, Michael soon stopped feeling the cold.

In the past three weeks he had found something worthwhile, had begun to get his life back into a semblance of order. But that facade had been shattered. Stolen away from him. By a foe he had long been trying to forget, a foe that had long inspired fear within him.

It was not fear he felt now.

"Bitch," he murmured, and the word seemed to fall dead to the snow.

He inhaled deeply. This time he shouted his anger and his hatred: "Sondra! You fucking bitch! I'm going to kill you!"

"BITCH!"

The sound of his hatred echoed around the lake, shattering the northern silence. Soon it echoed back to him, changed by the snow and the trees and the cold, until it sounded like the high tinkling sound of a woman laughing.

CHAPTER SEVENTEEN

Despite Tommy's protestations, Elizabeth opened up the bookstore early on Monday morning; early opening meant that Tommy had a half-hour wait at the store until his school bus came by. He said that the smell of the books made him feel sick, but this morning his complaints were not as strident as they might have been. His awareness of what had transpired between Michael and his mother yesterday was keeping him in check. For this, Elizabeth was grateful. She had no wish to deal with a temperamental Tommy on top of the acute depression she was feeling.

Tommy parked a chair beside the door and flipped through one of the counter rack's magazines while waiting for his bus. Elizabeth moved to the back of the store and began to sort through the boxes and bags of trades she'd been neglecting. Her mind was not on the job, but a few solid hours of work would keep her attention away from other matters. Like the hollowness inside of her, the sense of loss. . . .

When Tommy called "Bye, Mom!" she stuck her

head through the storeroom door and waved at him.

"Stick in!" she called.

He raised his arm in a perfunctory salute and pushed out into the cold. She could see the yellow body of the school bus in the street beyond, bright and cheerful against the pervasive grey drabness of the early morning, the pink faces behind the glass smiling and laughing, a sharp counterpoint to her own emotional barometer. She watched as Tommy climbed into the bus, waited for him to find a seat and wave to her. But he must have found a place on the opposite aisle, for the bus shuddered, roared, spewed a cloud of diesel exhaust into the street, and moved beyond the narrow view provided by the store's front.

Elizabeth sighed, suppressing a pang of self-pity.

The men in my life, she thought wistfully. *Both gone.*

She pulled herself back into the storage room and resumed the chore of sorting.

Though she tried not to, she found herself dwelling on Michael Smith, running through her mind the course their relationship had taken, trying to pinpoint what had gone wrong. Everything had seemed so perfect. Storybook perfect. Until Michael had come up with that bizarre story about the mutant rabies virus and the woman who was following him. It was that, she decided, that had initiated the collapse of the relationship.

She had known from the beginning that Michael was vulnerable in some way. She had sensed it that first night. It had been his vulnerability that had attracted her so strongly. But she had never imagined that the problems of his past would turn out to have something to do with . . . his mind. The apparent relationship between his arrival in New York and the recent killings had destroyed whatever fragile balance he had been living with.

"This is a therapeutic holiday for me," he had said. But she had not probed beyond this initial offering of trust. If she had, she might have foreseen the impending trauma, she thought, might somehow have averted it.

The thought depressed her. *It's not my fault.*

With her feet she shoved a pile of books slightly to her right, making room for the next group. The top book in the pile was a contemporary romance. The cover showed a young woman lying on a beach towel, sunglasses pushed down to the tip of her nose, looking with wistful longing at the tall figure of a man who seemed, by the painting, not to have noticed her at all. The cut of the man's hair reminded her of Michael Smith.

"Damn!" She kicked out and knocked the book off the pile.

But it was too late. An image of Michael formed in her mind, gripping tenaciously to the remnants of emotions she had been trying to wipe out. He smiled, and his eyes revealed the vulnerability that had attracted her to begin with.

A small voice whispered callously in her ear: *You should have given him the benefit of the doubt.*

But it wasn't that she had doubted him. Not really. It was just that his suggestion of packing everything up and leaving was . . . paranoid. How could he have expected her to drop her whole life to follow him to Chicago? There was a child involved. It didn't make sense. It wasn't right.

He was worried about you.

He had no reason to worry. . . .

The moment she articulated the thought, the doubts assailed her.

Had there been justification for concern?

Her hands automatically continued the sorting procedure, dropping romances, science fiction, mysteries, and horror into their respective piles. Her thoughts raced.

Three killings. She remembered the flashing red lights in the trees that first night. The crumpled body in the snow. Tommy's morbid interest. Then Bob Brisk's suspicion of Michael. "The killings began after he arrived."

Poor Michael.

Then the stranger who had approached Tommy with the jar for Michael. *Blood,* Michael had said, but that was impossible.

It had all been too much, too quickly. It was no wonder that Michael had snapped under the strain.

Or else it's all true.

She stopped what she was doing and cursed herself for allowing her mind to unravel. If she kept this up it would be her, not Michael, scurrying to leave. Panic breeds panic.

She angrily slapped the dust from her hands and went into the store. She'd been sorting for almost two hours. Enough of that. She lit a cigarette and poured a cup of the coffee she'd put on to brew earlier. In a few minutes she was feeling better, much more clearheaded.

No more of that nonsense!

While the day grew slowly brighter she sat at the front counter, smoking, and delved into a Robert Parker mystery. As Spenser's troubles grew, her own seemed to dwindle. The store slowly filled with a delicate tracery of smoke, like the rippling mist of dream.

It was close to 3:00 P.M. when the bell above the door tinkled. The thirteenth customer of the day, Elizabeth thought, mentally chalking up another. The other twelve had been housewives mostly, and a couple of teenaged boys from Hinton who dropped by periodically to check out the science fiction Tommy left untouched. She stopped her sorting at the back and walked up to the front counter. The customer was standing in the aisle with the bestsellers, slowly running a long pale finger along the spines of the books.

Elizabeth leaned her forearms on the counter.

"Anything I can help you with?"

When the woman turned around Elizabeth forced herself not to gasp. She was looking at the "model" Tommy had described. The woman smiled, waxy red lips curling up to reveal a row of gleaming white teeth. The grey eyes, almost silver, seemed to glitter beneath her eyebrows. The smile looked incongruous in the angular face, as if it had been cut there, unnatural. The fur coat she wore, something glossy black, hung down to mid-shin, but did little to hide the definitely feminine form beneath. Blonde hair, almost white, protruded from a black fur cap. "Just looking," she said. A picture of contrasts. Woman, animal. Flesh, ice.

Elizabeth nodded. It was all she could do. The woman turned away and walked further down the aisle, high heels clicking on the floor, precise and sharp. It was a moment before Elizabeth realized she was holding her breath; she let it out with a soft hiss. When she inhaled again the smell of perfume was strong. Sexy. Musky. But there was something else, an underodor she could not quite identify. Her nose wrinkled involuntarily.

She should phone Bob Brisk, she realized. Right now. All day she had watched the cars pass by the front of the store. There had been two cars from the Fergus Falls Sheriff's Department and a squarish looking unmarked grey sedan she had never seen before. She imagined it might be an FBI car; the two men in it had looked efficiently anonymous, like Jehova's Witnesses. *Call them now!* At the very least, they should want to talk to this woman. She matched Tommy's description. This was the one Michael had been talking about. . . .

This vindication of Michael's suspicions did not immediately hit home. The strange woman's presence in the store demanded all of Elizabeth's attention, all she was willing to give and more. She dared not reach for the phone. Not yet. Instead she tried to stay calm, remaining at the front counter. After what seemed an interminable time, the black coat appeared from behind the other end of the aisle, caressing the smooth pale legs that protruded beneath it, and came toward her.

Elizabeth found herself smiling against her will, a brittle thing that twisted her lips upward at the corners. The woman stopped before her and mirrored her smile. This is ghastly, Elizabeth thought. Her urge was to step back, to put some distance between herself and the apparition before her. But she fought it off. Overtly, nothing was wrong. A sudden retreat would reveal otherwise. Instead she watched, enthralled, as an exquisitely manicured hand snaked across the counter toward her own, a porcelain appendage protruding from a black sheath of fur. The sudden touch was cold, almost icy, and it broke the spell that had been binding Elizabeth.

She jerked her hand away, but found that she was caught. Her shoulder wrenched with the effort and she groaned. The grip on her hand was as solid as if she had tightened a bench vise around her wrist, and as painful. Tendons and flesh slid away to avoid being crushed against bone.

"Aaaaah!" Elizabeth said, more an exhalation of air than anything else.

The red lips smiled. The face leaned closer. Elizabeth stared into the grey eyes and realized with sinking horror that there was no life there. Windows on the soul. Death. Suddenly the strength of perfume took on a new meaning: like antiseptic in a funeral parlor. Camouflage.

"Hello, Elizabeth," the woman said. The smile on

her face did not vary.

"Aaaah!" Elizabeth said again, bending over as if to do so would relieve the pressure and the pain. The thought suddenly came to her: *I should have gone with Michael.*

As if the woman had read her mind, she said, "Michael Smith is mine." The smoothness, the calmness of that voice, terrified Elizabeth.

"I . . ."

"You have a nice boy," the woman said.

Suddenly the pain lost all meaning. Her body tensed as if a thousand volts had passed through her, and she locked eyes with the pale face before her. The other woman, sensing she had finally gotten a reaction, smiled more widely. As if this had been the cue she had been waiting for she leaned closer to Elizabeth, her lips twisting out of the smile formation into something else. A grimace or a snarl. The teeth behind the lips seemed to vibrate, top grating against bottom, a noise that sent a shiver of revulsion along Elizabeth's spine. The mouth leaned closer to her neck until she felt the prickling sensation of hot breath against her skin.

"Don't . . ." she gasped.

Outside, a rusty yellow pickup truck passed along the street, leaving behind it a billow of exhaust. Elizabeth watched, as if hypnotized, as the cloud of exhaust rose and began to dissipate. *This is the last thing I'll see.*

Then the phone rang.

The teeth at her neck stopped chattering, and the face, chiseled out of makeup, backed away. The talons released her wrist. The sudden flow of blood made her hand throb painfully, and Elizabeth cradled her wrist and groaned. She stumbled backward, leaning against the cash register for support.

The phone rang again.

The woman in the black coat smiled. The flesh of her face, which had molded itself into something inhuman, again found the lines of a beautiful woman. "He's mine," she repeated.

Then the bell above the door tinkled, and she was gone.

Elizabeth blinked. A sudden sob escaped her lips and she bent over, massaging her wrist. "Jesus . . ."

The phone rang again, insistent and angry. She reached for it and picked it up. At the sound of the voice on the other end she almost broke into tears.

"Bob!" She leaned against the counter, shuddering. "Oh, God, Bob."

"What is it?" His voice was wary.

"It's . . ." She did not know what to tell him. "Michael was right. About the woman."

"Not you too, Elizabeth?"

"She was here!" Elizabeth protested. "I saw her."

The silence from the phone was unnerving. At last Brisk sighed. "When?"

"Just now. She just left. Ten seconds ago."

Again that unnerving silence. "I phoned to say," Brisk said at last, his voice now calm and business-like, "that we'll be over later to talk to Tommy."

"We?" The sudden change of track caught her by surprise.

"Me. The FBI. The sheriff's department."

214

"What about the woman?"

"We'll talk about it later," Brisk said.

After she hung up, Elizabeth shook her head in confusion. She had sensed in Bob Brisk exactly what Michael had been talking about. A reticence to discuss the matter. As if he knew something he wasn't saying.

With a shaking hand Elizabeth put a cigarette to her lips and lit it. She was nearly halfway through it before she began to calm down.

Michael had been right about the woman. For the first time that afternoon the name came to her. *Sondra.* Such a nice name for such a horrible creature. It had not been in Michael's imagination. She felt a stab of remorse at how she had treated him.

And the thought suddenly occurred to her: *If he was right about Sondra, then how much of the rest of his story might be true?*

She tried not to think about it.

CHAPTER EIGHTEEN

As he turned onto the access road for Elizabeth's cabin, Michael raised his eyebrows in surprise. The Corsica's headlights had revealed a line of cars surrounding Elizabeth's rusted Volkswagen, jutting into the road at odd angles like the magnum opus of a mad new-wave auto artist. He parked the Corsica behind the blue Ford with the Fergus Falls Sheriff's Department insignia on the trunk, then stepped out into the snow and walked toward the cabin.

When Elizabeth had phoned him at 5:30 he had been surprised and unsure of how to react. He had planned on leaving that morning, but somehow he had found himself lingering. All day he had sat in the cabin, brooding, painting. The resulting canvas had reflected his mood. Even looking at it made him cringe. When he had answered the phone, expecting Bob Brisk, his tone had been harsh. But Elizabeth's voice had been like a gust of fresh air in a tomb.

"I've been thinking about what you said." But her voice did not reveal what exactly she had thought.

"Can you come over tonight?"

"Okay," he had replied immediately.

"Michael . . ."

"Yes?"

"There will be others here." She paused a moment. "The FBI. Bob Brisk."

Michael had let those words sink in. This was not to be a social visit. Before the pause became uncomfortable, he said: "I'll be there."

Now, walking past the veritable parking lot of official looking vehicles, he was not sure it had been a good idea. *I'm a suspect in this case,* he thought uneasily. So far, his offering of information had not been taken seriously. Not by Bob Brisk, at least.

At the door he paused, breathed deeply, and gathered his wits. *Be calm.* He knocked twice, and the door was quickly answered by Elizabeth. She wore her faded Levis and a handsome Icelandic woolen sweater that hugged her closely. Michael tried to keep the appreciation off his face as he stepped past her.

"Hi, Michael," she said.

"Hi." He sounded more surly than he had intended.

He shucked off his coat and draped it over the back of a chair next to the door. The air was thick with cigarette smoke and the smell of brewing coffee. From the living room he could hear the bark of voices, argumentative in tone.

"Come on," Elizabeth said.

As they passed the kitchen Tommy looked up from his place at the table. His lips turned into a smile when he saw Michael. Michael mouthed a silent "Hi" and smiled back. *I'll miss the kid if I run away,* he thought. He followed Elizabeth into the living room.

Conversation ceased, cut off instantly, the moment Elizabeth led Michael into the room. He scanned the room quickly, counting six bodies. The only two he recognized were Sally Warner, sitting on a kitchen chair in one corner looking uncomfortable, and Bob Brisk, sitting in the easy chair across from the TV, coffee mug balanced on his knee, almost diminutive in appearance. It was the others in the room that made Brisk look small.

"I'm still not clear on your names," Elizabeth said. "So I'll introduce Michael and you can do the rest."

Michael stepped past her. The two men on the sofa, both dressed in grey slacks and darker sports jackets, stood as he approached. The older of the two, at least three inches taller than Michael, smiled gruffly. The wrinkles around his eyes became more pronounced and his lips split to reveal a set of perfect teeth. He was the only person in the room not smoking, but he looked like he wanted to. Badly. He held out a large, hairy hand.

"Mr. Smith," he said. "I'm Browning, and this is my partner, Franklin. FBI."

Last names only, Michael thought.

Michael shook the offered hand, nodding.

The two other men, rose from seats brought through from the kitchen. These two were more rugged looking, faces windburned, and both middle-aged. "Smith. I'm Sheriff Willson. This is Deputy Harper. And you know Brisk and Warner."

Michael shook the offered hands, then nodded at Brisk and Sally. Behind Michael, Elizabeth pushed through another chair. He sat down, and the others followed.

Browning, the senior FBI agent, put a pen to his lips. *Pretending it's a cigarette,* Michael thought. His face was stony, but there was something in the eyes that Michael liked.

"Let's not beat around the bush," Browning said. "You arrived in New York the same day these killings started. You're our number one suspect."

Michael nodded reluctantly. "But I have an alibi for at least one of the killings."

Browning turned to Brisk. "That so?"

Brisk shrugged, uncomfortable with the sudden attention. "It's possible, but not definite."

Behind Michael, Elizabeth gasped. "Not definite? Bob Brisk, you know damn well that Michael was with me when Herb Kramer was killed."

Brisk blushed. "Apparently. But time of death wasn't determined accurately enough to pinpoint Smith's . . ."

"He was with me all day!"

"Now, now, Mrs. Turner, there's no need to get angry. Brisk here is following standard police procedures. If there's even the slightest possibility that Smith could have made the scene, then it's got to be considered."

Partially vindicated, but still uncomfortable, Brisk kept his mouth closed.

"But there's a hell of a lot more than a reasonable doubt," Elizabeth said curtly, still pinning Brisk with her angry eyes.

Browning lips twitched in a faint smile which he wiped off immediately. His blue eyes focused on Michael's. "Smith, I'll tell you why the Bureau is interested." He pretended to draw on his pen/cigarette. As he talked, he flicked the pen as if it were gathering ash. "The pathologist in Fergus Falls found traces of a rather unique natural anticoagulant in the victim's wounds. Know what that is?"

Michael nodded. Browning's eyebrows rose momentarily, then his face resumed its stony countenance.

"We've got a string of similar killings across the country," Browning said slowly. "Dating back about three years. About one hundred fifty deaths to date, mostly male victims. Possibly many more never discovered. Probably a lot written off as animal attack. So many missing people these days. Up to now we have no connecting thread, except the anticoagulant found in the wounds. And no suspects."

At the mention of the number of deaths, Michael's eyes widened. "A hundred and fifty?" The thought of that many humans killed, slaughtered, to satisfy . . . He closed his eyes, breathing deeply.

"Now," Browning continued. "Brisk here, tells us you have a crazy story to tell. He says it makes no sense."

Michael looked up, but Bob Brisk was looking down at his hands.

"I'd like to hear that story from you. I'll decide

how crazy it is for myself." He drew a deep breath, let it out in a sigh. "And then we'll decide exactly what to do about it."

Sheriff Willson and Deputy Harper nodded in agreement. Sally Warner looked up, face expressing interest. Elizabeth's hand suddenly rested on Michael's shoulder, and he glanced around. She offered an encouraging smile. Michael turned back to Browning, then began to speak.

As he spoke, Michael felt Elizabeth's grip on his shoulder tighten, until at one point it was almost painful. His grunt caused her to loosen her grip, and she patted his shoulder apologetically. Nobody interrupted as he spoke, and the look of earnest interest on the faces of his listeners, except for Brisk, was heartening. When he had finished, Michael looked from one face to another. He shrugged. "That's it."

Sheriff Willson shook his head. "Hell, I hate to say it, but I agree with Brisk. That's a crazy story."

Michael sighed. He could retell his story until he was blue in the face. It would never be believed.

But Browning, pen held close to his lips, was studying him carefully. "Crazy?" he said, exhaling a deep breath. He shrugged. "Maybe. But there's a lot of crazy things going on around here. Anybody available to confirm your story, Mr. Smith?"

The question caught Michael off guard. "Well . . . I . . . There's my doctor in Chicago."

Browning nodded. "Good. Give me his name and

number. We'll call him."

"Now?"

Browning sighed. "Mr. Smith, I like you. I want to trust you. I need confirmation."

Michael blinked. "Okay. But let me call him first. Otherwise he won't tell you anything."

Browning paused, frowned, then nodded. He turned to Elizabeth. "Is there an extension?"

"Bedroom," she said.

"May I?"

Elizabeth nodded. Browning stood slowly, easing his large frame to its full height, and followed Elizabeth to the bedroom. Using the phone in the living room, Michael dialed direct to John Muir's home. The phone rang three times before being answered by a woman.

"Betty? This is Michael Smith. Can I speak to John please?"

"Oh, Michael. I'm sorry. He's napping at the moment. Rough day. But I'll have him call you. . . ."

"Betty, this is an emergency. Please."

After a brief pause Betty sighed. "Okay. Just a moment."

It seemed hours later that John Muir finally picked up the line. "Michael, what's wrong?"

"Nothing. Not really. It's just . . . There's someone on the line with me, John. An FBI agent. I'd like you to tell him anything he wants to know."

"Michael, what's going on? Are you alright?"

"I'm fine. Really. Just do as I ask."

"Hello, Doctor." On the phone, Browning's voice sounded more gruff than it did in person. "I'm

Agent Browning, FBI. I'd appreciate it if you could answer my questions."

After a brief pause, John grunted. "Go ahead."

"Can you confirm Mr. Smith's story about contracting some sort of virus approximately three years ago?"

Again, the pause. "I can confrim it."

"He stated that the virus causes a condition where human blood is required. . . ."

"Agent Browning, Michael Smith was telling you the truth."

Browning sighed. "Alright." He paused thoughtfully. "How do I know you're a doctor?"

"I'll give you the number of my answering service. You can call them, they'll put you through to me, and we can have this conversation over again."

Browning chuckled. "No. That won't be necessary. Thank you for your help, Doctor."

The line clicked as Browning hung up.

"Thanks, John," Michael said.

"What the devil is going on up there, Michael."

"It's Sondra."

For a moment all he could hear was John Muir's breathing. "Oh my God. Has she . . ."

"There have been some deaths," Michael said. "But I can't talk right now. I'll get back to you later."

"Would you like me to come up there? I could . . ."

"No, don't do that. I'll get back to you."

He hung up and went back through to the living room. Browning had already seated himself in the sofa. Browning looked over at Sheriff Willson. "His story is confirmed. I believe him. I suggest we all do."

Sheriff Willson nodded reluctantly.

"We talked with the boy, Tommy," Browning said. "I believe him. I trust his description of the woman. Since your pathologist in Fergus Falls has confirmed that the blood in the jar came from Dan Stone, I suggest we begin operating under the assumption that this woman is the one we're after." He looked at Michael. "I just don't understand why she's come chasing you after three years. Do you?"

Michael frowned in confusion. "No, I don't."

Browning shrugged. "Well, we've got a good idea of what this woman looks like from the boy. And with Mrs. Turner's description we're sitting pretty."

Michael turned, frowning up at Elizabeth. "What description?"

Elizabeth looked worriedly toward Browning.

"I thought you knew," Browning said.

"Knew what?" Michael said, confused.

"A woman matching the description Tommy gave us visited Mrs. Turner in her bookstore today. Nothing threatening, as I understand it, but she inflicted a nasty bruise."

Michael spun around and stared up at Elizabeth. "Why didn't you tell me?"

"I didn't want to worry you," she said softly.

"Where did she hurt you?"

Elizabeth held out her right hand, rolled up the sleeve of the sweater. Purple against the pale flesh of her wrist, fading into yellow at the edges, was a

224

large bruise. "It's okay now," Elizabeth said.

Michael turned away. His breath hitched in his chest.

"I understand you were thinking of leaving," Browning said.

Michael snapped his head toward the FBI man, face livid. "I was. But not anymore."

Again, that faint hint of a smile, amused, appreciative. "That's good. We could use your help."

Michael turned his attention to Bob Brisk, but the cop was still looking down at this hands. In this room, surrounded by these large men, he looked small, withdrawn, almost childlike. To everybody in the room, Michael said what he had originally said to Bob Brisk: "We have to get her. We have to hunt her down."

Browning pretended to draw heavily on his pen, and exhaled a noisy breath. "Son, that's why we're here."

CHAPTER NINETEEN

When the others had left, Michael stood at the kitchen window watching the car lights blinking through the trees, flickering and fading as they moved toward New York proper, until the darkness outside was inky, impenetrable. Elizabeth leaned against the closed porch door and sighed. Throughout the night they had not found themselves alone together, and now that they were, a palpable tension existed between them.

"I didn't think there would be so many of them," Elizabeth said, but did not look at Michael.

Michael nodded, still looking out the window although there was nothing to see. "All for the better, I guess. It will make it easier."

"Michael, about last night."

He turned toward her and held up his hand. "Listen. There's no need to go into that. You were right."

"No. I don't think I was. But I don't think you were right either. I think both of us . . ."

Michael smiled. "Yeah. Okay. How about we

226

both apologize for our despicable behavior and start over?"

The smile that blossomed on Elizabeth's face made Michael feel weak-kneed. The empty space that had grown within him over the past few days suddenly filled, as if a dam had burst. He covered the space between them in three steps and put his arms around her, holding her tightly against his chest. With his cheek against the soft hair at the side of her head, Michael stroked her back. Soon Elizabeth pushed slightly away so that she could look up at him. He leaned forward and kissed her. Afterward, he held her close again, her taste still on his lips.

"Making up isn't so hard to do," Elizabeth said.

Michael smiled. "Not with you it isn't," he said.

In the kitchen a chair clattered. Michael and Elizabeth parted, heads turning toward the noise. Tommy stood in the kitchen doorway, regarding them with quizzical good humor. "I'm going to bed," he said.

"Good night, darling," Elizabeth said.

" 'Night, Tom," Michael said.

For a moment Tommy's eyes locked onto Michael's, and something passed between man and boy. Michael was not sure what it was. A bond of some sort had been established, he felt. Something to do with Elizabeth. Intuiting that a response of some kind was needed, he nodded slightly. In return, Tommy's head inclined, only a fraction of an inch, and then the boy turned and disappeared into his bedroom.

"What was that all about?" Elizabeth said, looking confusedly toward Tommy's closed door.

Michael turned to her and pulled her close again. "I'm not sure," he said honestly. "I think I just made some sort of promise."

In his arms he felt Elizabeth shrug, and then her face was pressed into his neck. "Can you stay?" she said.

Everything in him, every muscle of his body, every desire in his mind, wanted to say yes, but a voice of rationality spoke loudly in his ear. This was too soon after what had transpired last night. Neither he nor Elizabeth had fully sorted out their feelings. Tonight's impromptu meeting with the FBI and the Fergus Falls Sheriff's Department had added an air of danger to the proceedings, had somehow given Michael's story a feeling of verisimilitude. It was the situation itself that was drawing them together, not their own feelings, and that was not good. Such a bedrock would crumble in the long run, especially if he took advantage of it now. Better, he decided, to wait until this thing was cleared up completely.

Reluctantly he shook his head. "Not tonight. I don't think it would be a good idea." For some reason, he remembered Tommy's cryptic nod. *The kid would approve of this,* he thought, and the realization strengthened his resolve.

"But . . . I don't want to be alone," Elizabeth said softly.

Michael hugged her fiercely. "I'm only a phone call away. And Tommy's here."

For a moment he thought she was going to protest, but the same thoughts had obviously occurred to her. She nodded. "Okay."

Michael picked his coat off the chair by the door and pulled it on. Elizabeth would not meet his eyes. At the edge of her sweater's sleeve he could just discern the beginning of the discoloration where Sondra had gripped her. A surge of anger rose in him.

"Do you have a gun in the cabin?" he said.

Elizabeth's eyes darted toward him warily. "Why?"

"Do you?"

Almost reluctantly, she nodded. "Bobby was a hunter."

"Where is it?"

Her eyes were now locked onto his, and they were narrowed in concern. "It's in the bedroom. But . . ."

He reached out and touched her shoulder, calming her. "Get it. Please."

For a moment she did not move, and her eyes searched his for some clue to what he intended. At last she turned away and went to her bedroom. Michael zipped up his jacket, leaned against the door, and waited. In a moment Elizabeth returned. The gun was a Winchester repeater rifle. It hung across the crook of her arm, barrel directed at the floor. The magazine chamber was open and empty.

She knows how to carry it at least, Michael thought.

She approached him but did not hand him the gun.

"Can you use it?" Michael asked.

Elizabeth nodded. "Bobby showed me. A few times." She ran her hand along the polished wooden stock, gently, almost lovingly, as if the touch of the weapon brought back fond memories. "It's a Winchester M94 30/30."

"What about ammunition?"

Elizabeth frowned, then turned to the antique bureau beside the door leading to the living room. She pulled open the top area and rummaged about until she retrieved a yellow and green box. She flipped the cap with her thumb and glanced inside.

"Three rounds," she said.

"I'll get you some more tomorrow," Michael said.

Now the look of concern that had wavered on the edge of Elizabeth's face became full blown. She stepped closer to him. "But why?"

"I want you to be able to protect yourself," Michael said. "Sondra visited you once. She might come again."

"But I can't take this thing to the store!"

"I meant here."

Elizabeth's eyes widened. She placed the rifle on the floor, stock down, barrel resting against the wall, and dropped the near empty box of ammunition on the phone table. She stepped close to him, encircling him with her arms.

"I don't like this," she said.

Michael hugged her. "I don't either," he said.

"Yesterday, I hardly took your story seriously at all," she said. "But now . . ."

"Yes?"

"Now I believe it. And . . . and now I'm scared."

Michael said nothing. He pulled back and kissed her, a brief touching of lips, then opened the door. The outside air was crisp, cold, and clear. The snow had stopped falling. The dark clouds above were beginning to break up, and in the open spaces a few stars peeked through. Michael's breath billowed about his face. "I'll come by tomorrow."

Elizabeth nodded. She stood shivering in the doorway. Michael smiled reassuringly, then turned and began walking toward his car.

"Michael."

He turned. The look on Elizabeth's face almost drew him back. "Be careful," she said, then closed the door. The darkness swallowed him utterly.

It took a moment for his eyes to grow accustomed to the dark, then he moved again toward his car. He was glad Elizabeth had a gun. Tomorrow, after he picked up a box of rounds, he'd be even happier. Guns were reassuring things to have around, especially if you knew how to use one.

He tried to smother his doubts about how effective bullets would be against a Sondra at the peak of fever, but the answer came to him anyway:

No fucking good at all.

After leaving Elizabeth's, following the taillights of the bastard FBI agents, Bob Brisk turned his car into the access road for Michael Smith's cabin. He sat in the warmth of the car, lights out but still running, and smoked, while the radio filled the darkness with the soft strains of Loretta Lynn. He let the music calm him, without lulling him.

He had watched Michael and Elizabeth carefully during the evening, and it was obvious that something had happened between them. All was not sweetness and light; something was amiss in the land of love. He was not positive that Michael would spend the night at his own cabin, but the odds, he figured, were in his favor.

He did not have to wait long. He was halfway down his third cigarette when the lights sliced through the trees, a scythe in the darkness, and Smith's Corsica turned onto the access road. Brisk reached for the headlight toggle and flicked it on briefly as the Corsica rolled slowly toward the cabin, letting Smith know he was there. He drew on his cigarette, holding the smoke in his lungs despite the pain, as Smith stepped out of his car and walked toward him. Even in the darkness he could see that Smith was scowling as he approached. He released the smoke with a hiss and opened the car door to step out, but Smith blocked him.

"What are you doing here?"

Brisk flicked the cigarette past Smith's leg; it disappeared into the soft snow with a sizzle. "Wanted to see you." He stepped out, forcing the other man to take a step backward.

"About what?"

"Just to talk."

The slight tightening of Smith's mouth was not exactly a smile. "What's there to say that couldn't have been said at Elizabeth's?"

Brisk studied the taller man carefully. He remembered clearly the earlier display of viral augmented reflexes, but the speed and strength demonstrated that night were not apparent in Smith's stance. Tall but skinny. A rope. If it wasn't for that damned virus, a weakling, Brisk expected. "That you're a bloody fool," Brisk said.

Whatever reaction he had been expecting from Smith, it did not come. The pale, narrow face remained impassive. Smith seemed to contemplate what he had said, and in a moment the iffy curve of his lips turned into a definite smile. "You're angry because they believed my story," he said.

The accuracy of the statement caught Brisk off guard. He opened his mouth to respond, but found his mind empty of ammo.

"I'm going inside," Smith said, turning away. "If you want to talk, come on."

Wishing now that he had not engineered this confrontation, disturbed by Michael's apparent equanimity, he followed almost reluctantly. Inside the cabin, Smith pulled off his coat and went into the kitchen. From the fridge he pulled a beer and twisted off the cap. He held the bottle toward Brisk, but Brisk shook his head. If there was one time in his life he wanted to be clearheaded it was tonight. It seemed as if it were a long time ago that his mind had not been clouded with . . . hell, he didn't know what it was. An image of Sondra's slightly parted lips filled his head, and he imagined her tongue tracing a line down his abdomen.

"You said earlier you had thought about leaving. You should have."

"I thought you guys always said things like 'Don't you go leaving town till this thing's cleared up,'" Smith said sarcastically.

Brisk shrugged. "Mostly. But this is different." He eyed Smith carefully, weighing whether or not he should continue. "I believe your story. Now. Some of it, anyway."

"Thank you very much." Smith sucked a huge mouthful of beer from the bottle, swallowed it noisily.

There was something in those eyes that Brisk did not like. Something he recognized. "So maybe you didn't do the actual killing," Brisk said, and realized that he wasn't at all sure he believed that. "But, like you say, you're connected. You stick around, more people are going to get hurt."

Smith stared at him, lips tight.

"Maybe Elizabeth. Or Tommy," Brisk said.

Smith carefully placed the beer bottle on the kitchen table and stepped toward him. Brisk resisted the urge to back away. His hand itched to caress the butt of the revolver inside his jacket, but he did not move a muscle.

"I think," Smith said quietly, "I think that you're scared, Bob." He smiled, and it was not a pleasant thing. "I think that once this crew gets hunting for Sondra, they're going to find out that you knew something and didn't say it. Yes, sir, I think you're real worried." At each word he poked Brisk lightly on the chest. "I just wish I knew exactly what you know."

Brisk forced himself to smile back. "All I'm worried about is that you've brought death to this town."

This time, as a ripple of fierce anger passed across Smith's face, Brisk did take a step backward. For a moment, it seemed that the soul of Michael Smith departed from his eyes, and Brisk found himself looking into two empty, black holes. He tried to sidestep Michael's swing, but the fist caught him at the right shoulder, close to the neck, and he fell backward into the wall. Smith took another step toward him, and suddenly his face slackened. Arm cocked, he lowered it slowly.

Brisk straightened up, rubbing his shoulder.

"I'm sorry . . ." Smith began. He seemed confused.

"Yeah," Brisk said. "You don't have much control over that virus, do you?"

"That wasn't the virus. That was me."

Brisk guffawed. He could sense that Smith was now in complete control. To goad him now was much safer than it had been a few moments ago, and he took immediate advantage. "Bullshit. I saw you disappear, Michael. Something else came in to take your place."

Smith stepped over to the kitchen table and sipped his beer, looking thoughtful.

"You should be the one who's scared, Michael," Brisk said. "You're the one who's seeing Elizabeth."

Smith swung around and pinned him with eyes squinted in anger. Brisk smiled. "How long are you going to be able to maintain this charade? How long is it going to be before Elizabeth says something that pushes you over the edge?"

Smith looked down at this hands.

"Or maybe it will be Tommy," Brisk said.

"You son of a bitch."

Brisk smiled callously. "Just think about it, Michael. Your first idea was your best. Get the hell of here and save us all a lot of trouble."

For three very long seconds Smith locked eyes with him, and then the taller man turned away. Brisk smiled. He turned, leaving Smith standing at the kitchen table, beer clasped tightly in his hand. The cold air sharpened his senses, and he breathed it deeply. That had been close. Too close.

In the car he lit a cigarette, then turned the ignition, flicked on the headlights, and moved out onto the blacktop. As he drove, he thought about Sondra. Dealing with Michael Smith had brought to the surface a lot of nagging questions. Questions he would put to Sondra as soon as he saw her.

Between the two of them, Michael or Sondra, one of them was a murderer.

Michael Smith is not a killer. The thought came unbidden, a sudden flash across the back of his mind, and he knew it as truth.

Which left Sondra.

What scared him more than anything else was the knowledge that he no longer cared.

CHAPTER TWENTY

The night opened up before his headlights. Bob
Brisk kept both hands on the steering wheel as he
guided the Chevy through New York, slowing as he
passed the police station to glance through the
glass doors. The light he had left burning in his
office tripped long shadows across the reception
area, but the place was empty. Sally had gone over
to Vinning after the meeting at Elizabeth's and
would not likely return until tomorrow morning.

Downtown was quiet. The Starlight Theater was
in the middle of its last show and, against the curb
under the marquee, covered in a light dusting of
snow, four or five cars were parked closely. A single poster beside the box office advertised:

MONSTER DOUBLE FEATURE!
ALIEN & THE THING

Brisk had seen neither, never would.

He breathed deeply the smoke of his cigarette, letting it drift out his nostrils. A couple of half-tons were running outside Chuck's Grill, billowing exhaust into the street, while inside the restaurant their drivers warmed themselves over cups of coffee and maybe something else. Chuck Patterson had been known to spike his coffee with home brew in the winter months. Brisk suppressed a smile as one of the faces turned to watch his car drive by. A quiet night in a quiet town.

The night closed in again once he moved into the south allotments, tightened by the walls of trees crowding the blacktop, and the car's headlights were swallowed by the cavernous darkness on either side. Driving this slowly it took him a good five minutes to travel from Michael Smith's cabin to his own. He parked the Chevy at the east side of the cabin, but did not plug it in. He noticed with satisfaction that the afternoon's snow had covered the tire tracks leading to the storage shed. Behind the leaning wooden door, Sondra's rented Sunbird sat quietly, its rear end covered by a ratty green tarpaulin against any eyes that happened to peer through the crack in the door.

Brisk took a final drag on his cigarette and crushed it beneath his boot heel. At the front door he paused, gathering himself as he fumbled for his key, then entered the cabin. As he had asked, Sondra had left the place dark except for a light in the bedroom. He stripped off his parka, flinging it onto the arm of the sofa, and carefully unstrapped his holster and belt. He removed the revolver, hung the empty holster in the cupboard, and carried the gun through to the bedroom.

Sondra was lying on the bed, naked, arms at her sides. *Like a corpse.* The image of her lying in a coffin flashed across his mind uninvited, and he blinked trying to clear it away. Her pale breasts poked up like perfect cones. Her nipples were hard in the cold air. Against her white flesh, the tight pubic mound between her legs looked almost dark, a shadow, and her nails looked dipped in blood. Although her eyes were closed, her mouth curved up in a smile when he entered the room. Her eyes slowly opened, and the glittering grey behind the lids focused on him.

"I thought you might have run away," Sondra said.

Brisk smiled, and chuckled nervously. "Meeting went on for a while."

"What happened?" She pushed herself up on her elbows so she could look directly at him. Her knees parted slightly, and within the tight nest of hair between her legs he caught a glimpse of pink. His groin ached, and he swallowed.

"Not much. Michael Smith told his story." He looked directly at her. "They believed him."

Her right eyebrow arched slightly, but the smile on her lips did not waver.

"They're going to start looking for you tomorrow." He paused a moment, then said: "Hunt you down like an animal."

This time her smile widened. "Those are Michael's words."

240

Brisk nodded, stepped toward the bed table. He placed the revolver beside the lamp. Sondra's eyes followed the movement of his hand and remained on the gun after he stepped away.

"What else?"

Brisk shrugged. He began to unbutton his shirt. "They talked about the killings. Other killings." He moved his hand lower and unbuttoned his pants. "There were a couple of guys there from the FBI. They said there had been at least one hundred and fifty identical killings across the country in the last three years."

"Ah!" She sounded delighted.

Brisk kicked off his pants, picked them up, then folded them across the seat next to the bed table. He shrugged out of his shirt and hung it from the cupboard door handle. With a sigh of relief he sat down on the edge of the bed and lay back beside Sondra.

"Michael Smith thinks I know something," he said. The ceiling was a halo of orange light, and he focused on the center of it.

Sondra lifted her weight and moved closer to him. The touch of her hip against his thigh was cool, smooth. She placed one arm across his abdomen and rolled slightly so that she was facing him, face resting against the crux of his armpit. He inclined his head slightly to look into her face. Though her grey eyes were locked squarely on his, he imagined she was not seeing him.

"You *do* know something," she whispered. "You know me."

Brisk swallowed. Sondra's arm moved lower across his abdomen until her fingers brushed through his pubic hair. A shiver ran through him, and he groaned softly. Her hand moved lower, cupping his testicles, until the pressure of her sharp nails against his scrotum was almost painful. His face made expressions he was hardly aware of. All he could see was Sondra's smile. Soon she began to stroke him, pulling, pumping, until he was hard.

"Poor Bob," she whispered. She changed her position so that her face was close to his, and her tongue slid out and touched his lips. Again. Again. Then she pressed her mouth against his, open, probing. Below, her hand moved slowly, purposefully. "Poor Bob," she said again, leaning back to look at him.

Brisk shuddered. Whatever semblance of order his thoughts had maintained up to this point vanished in a sudden rush of desire. "You killed those people," he said hoarsely, cupping one of her breasts in his hand. Her nipples poked into his palm, a hard button in the smooth mound of flesh.

"Poor Bob," she whispered again, and brought her mouth to his neck.

Brisk stiffened, waiting for the pain. When he felt her tongue sliding across his skin he sighed in relief. Her mouth moved lower, brushing across his chest. He looked down at the top of her head. Smears of lipstick and saliva had bruised his skin.

"Don't worry, darling," she said between kisses. Her free hand was splayed across his chest, long fingers kneading his flesh. "When this is all over, when it's all done, we'll be together. Away from here."

"But . . . ah . . ." he closed his eyes at the pleasure. "But I'm not like you," he forced out.

She raised her head slightly and her eyes were smiling, the tiny wrinkles radiating from their corners somehow deeper, sharper. "But you can be, darling. You can be *exactly* like me." His stomach muscles contracted as the cool sharpness of her teeth scraped across the skin.

"How?" The question emerged as a moan.

"I've been waiting for the right one. The one to accompany me. I want you."

Her lips danced across his abdomen, and for a second her tongue probed into his navel. Brisk shuddered at the strangeness of the sensation.

"It's a virus, darling, and I can pass it on to whomever I choose."

For a very short time he was not aware of the stimuli that bombarded his body. His mind had jumped to the future. He imagined himself moving with the speed of Michael Smith, a blur of motion, of concentrated strength, of lightning reflexes. *Better than all the rest*. He held his breath in a pang of exultant expectation.

Then she took him into her mouth, and he was back.

And he smiled.

On Tuesday morning Michael Smith woke with a

feeling of eagerness to get on with the day. A cursory glance at the clock radio told him it was 7:00 A.M. He rose, showered quickly, and dressed. By 7:30 he was sitting at the kitchen table with a mug of steaming coffee and two slices of toast. He smothered the toast in peanut butter and ate each slice with deliberate slowness, looking out the kitchen window. Between the black patches of the trees the sky was that clear, crisp blue that can only be found in winter. He chewed his toast and smiled grimly.

By 8:00 he was standing at the door of the cabin, zipping up his ski jacket. Outside, the cold was sharp but not bitter. The slightly damp hair above his ears and at the back of his neck stiffened in seconds. He started the Corsica then stood beside it a few minutes as it warmed up. The freshness of the day seemed to invade him as he stood there. Nature seemed a thing alive, pressing down, encompassing. But not crowding. For an instant an image of the towering Chicago skyline superimposed itself upon his vision and a shiver of revulsion passed through him. Dark skies, grey concrete, herds of people.

When the Corsica's automatic choke kicked in and the engine slowed he climbed in and backed out onto the blacktop. The quick drive into New York seemed more scenic than ever. The rising sun brought the glittering expanse of Great Lake to life, brilliant white, glittering like diamonds with a billion ice particles. Ice mist floating above the frozen surface diffracted the sun's light into myriad rainbows, and behind them the dark line of trees on the opposite shore had the look of a painted backdrop, intentionally placed there to highlight the beauty in the foreground. Even the arch of New York exuded the rustic, northland quality he remembered from boyhood. Swaths of sunlight speared from the openings between buildings, giving the main street a checkerboard appearance of light and shadow.

He had intended to stop at the police station, but a quick pass revealed it was empty. Horn's Books, too, was still dark. Elizabeth would arrive any minute, he expected. Four cars, however, were parked outside of Chuck's Grill, and he recognized Bob Brisk's cruiser and the unmarked grey FBI sedan from Elizabeth's the night before. He parked behind the line of cars and walked slowly to the entrance. The doorbell tinkled as he pushed open the door, and the six faces at the table near the kitchen turned to face him.

Bob Brisk did nothing to hide the anger pinching his features. Sally looked worriedly from Brisk to Michael. *She knows something happened between us,* Michael realized. Apart from Agent Browning, the rest of the table seemed disinterested. Only Browning's wide face split into a smile when he saw Michael. He motioned with his arm for Michael to approach.

"Come on in, Smith," Browning said. "Grab a bite. Maybe you can give us some ideas."

Despite Browning's invitation, Michael felt as if he were crashing a private party. Browning jiggled his chair a few feet to the left and dragged over a chair from the neighboring table. Michael unzipped his coat, draped it over the back of the chair, and sat down. From the kitchen a large, florid man in white slacks and a dark green T-shirt appeared. His arms were hocks of flabby meat, capped with club hands. His face was a wax dripping, folds of flesh melting down into a quadruple chin that somehow did not quite reach his chest. Tight blonde curls gave the immense man a babyish look. Chuck Patterson had put on a lot of weight in the last ten years, Michael thought.

"Another breakfast?" he asked.

Michael shook his head. "Just coffee."

The mound of flesh returned in a moment with a brimming mug of coffee for Michael, and proceeded to top up the other mugs at the table. Michael sipped his coffee carefully, and his eyebrows rose in pleasure. Even black, the brew had a full-bodied flavor and was pleasant to taste. Rounded out with chicory, he thought.

"We were just discussing the plan for today," Browning said, sipping noisily. On a paper napkin beside his plate he had scratched some brief notes with a ballpoint pen. "We've agreed that the perpetrator, this Sondra, would likely have to be staying somewhere close." He made a small mark beside one of his notes, tearing the napkin. "So Franklin and me are going to take a run over to Hinton, and Sheriff Willson here and Deputy Harper are going to have a look around Vinning. That covers us east and west. I can't see her being beyond those towns, can you?"

Michael frowned. He shook his head. "But . . ."

"That's not all," Browning said. "Bob Brisk here, and Sally . . . ," at this he looked up and smiled warmly at Sally, ". . . are going to have a real good look around New York, in case she's somehow managed to slip your notice so far."

Micahel looked up at Brisk. The cop's eyes revealed nothing. "We'll check the empty cabins," Brisk said softly. "Ask around. Who knows? Maybe this Sondra of yours is staying with somebody around here."

"She's not from here," Michael said. "She wouldn't know anybody."

Brisk smiled. "Except you."

Michael sipped his coffee, forcing himself to remain quiet. He turned from Brisk, to Browning. "What can I do?"

Browning raised his mug to his lips and after a loud sip lowered it again to the table. He said carefully, "There's not much you *can* do, son."

"But I want to help."

"You're a civilian," Sheriff Willson said.

"You can stay out of the way," Brisk said. He had placed a cigarette between his lips, and now he lit it. A cloud of smoke spilled across the table. This acted as a catalyst for the others, and soon a thick cloud filled the air.

"It's not that we couldn't use the help," Browning said. He was not smoking, but Michael had the distinct impression that he was enjoying everybody else's second-hand smoke. "But if anything should happen . . ."

"I may be the only one . . ." Michael began.

"Forget it," Brisk said. "Stick to your painting."

Michael made a move to stand, the anger rising inside him.

Browning put out a hand to stop him. "You've got more important things to worry about," the FBI man said, brown eyes intense.

For a moment Michael strained against Browning's friendly restraint, but the arm beyond the large hand was well muscled, and it tensed as Michael pushed. In a moment Michael relaxed into his seat with a sigh. Browning nodded, pleased.

"I think you should spend the day with that young woman of yours."

"Elizabeth?"

Browning nodded. "She may not have acted like it last night, but she was frightened. The visitor she received yesterday was not very pleasant. I'd hate to see it happen again."

Michael's brow furrowed in thought. Would Sondra try to see Elizabeth again? Outside, a school bus passing the restaurant belched exhaust and roared loudly on it's way to Fergus Falls. He thought of the mottled bruises on Elizabeth's wrist, and the anger within him turned to a vague feeling of guilt. He nodded his head, turning away from Browning's scrutiny. *Those eyes see too much,* he thought.

"We'll meet again tonight," Browning said, now talking to the table as a whole, but including Michael. Again he turned to Michael. "We won't keep you in the dark, son," he said.

Michael nodded, feeling useless. The eagerness he had felt upon waking had departed quickly, and now he looked upon the remainder of the day with a vague sense of dread. The sharp lighting outside, revealing everything in stark clarity, had assumed in his mind a sinister quality. He was not sure he wanted to discover what it might reveal.

CHAPTER TWENTY-ONE

Agent Browning, who used only last names when addressing those outside his family—sometimes even within it, because he was embarrassed by his Christian name (who could trust an FBI agent named Ivan?)—leaned against the window of the Plymouth Reliant and watched the trees slide by. Franklin drove the car with the expertise of a man who has been driving for a living all his life, slowing down for the numerous snow drifts with nary an indication he had changed speed at all, never pushing past the speed limit on the straights. Since they had been partnered, five years ago, Franklin had done all the driving. The younger man enjoyed the illusion of being in control that driving allowed, and Browning was not petty enough to worry about it. But now he wished Franklin would step on it. A little. There seemed to hang in the air the atmosphere of a pressing engagement.

We'll miss something if we don't hurry.

During the twenty-minute drive, Browning forced himself to inspect the evidence again, running over the jigsaw puzzle of half-related facts juggling in his mind. The enigma in the whole affair, and possibly the key to it all, was Michael Smith.

Browning's first impression had been favorable. Michael Smith was a likeable fellow, on the surface at least. But he had sensed a veneer of some sort, a shade pulled over the inner man. *Hiding something?* No, he didn't think so. More of a protective shield. Michael Smith gave the impression of vulnerability, but also of a man who kept his inner feelings in the shadows. Nothing wrong with that. There were too many men around these days who carried their hearts on their sleeves. Smith was old-fashioned in that way, Browning thought: keep the tears on the inside.

Smith had admitted a connection to the case, but his story had been hard to swallow. Even now, Browning was not sure he believed it. If it hadn't been for the records dating back three years he'd have slapped the cuffs on Smith last night. There was enough evidence to tie the kid to the killings, in New York if nowhere else, and time to saddle him with the others before it came to trial.

But something about his story rang true. It fit the facts, in a weird sort of way. The case, a back-burner at the Bureau, had been percolating since the first reported killing in McAllen, Texas, three and half years ago. Possible animal attack, possible foul play, no suspects and no manpower to pursue further. The trail had continued after that, moving east through Louisiana, into Florida, then north through Washington, Philadelphia, and Big New

York, then back inland, across to the west coast. Always the same MO: torn throat, sometimes augmented with suspected knife wound, presence of human saliva in wound, sometimes traces of lipstick, semen, and other substances, and when toxicology tests had been conducted, the presence of a natural anticoagulant. But the Bureau was always dragged in too late to do any good.

In most instances, the information didn't get to the Bureau until months after the killings, after the locals had done their work and thrown in the towel. In such cases it was impossible for the Bureau to move in. Cold tracks are no tracks. There had not been a man assigned full time to the case since the beginning. There had been no opportunity. Until now.

When the pathologist from Fergus Falls had contacted the forensic lab in Minneapolis, the indicator light had started flashing. Browning and Franklin, fresh off a forgery bust in Chicago, had been sent up. Less than a week ago Browning had read the file for the first time. The sheer number of killings had been awesome. One hundred fifty recorded, assuming a maximum known of fifty percent (a high estimate), indicated a likely three hundred deaths within the past three years. At least. Historically, there weren't many murderers who had that many notches on their belts.

Stepping into the investigation had been no pleasure, either. It was always difficult to break into an ongoing. Lines of tension were already drawn, personality conflicts already established, working ground already agreed upon. Stepping in was usually a matter of determining whose toes it was acceptable to crush under one's heel. But this one was weird. It was a mine field of as yet undetermined conflict. Left alone, Browning decided, Bob Brisk and Michael Smith would have been happy to smash each other's faces in.

At first he had thought the reason might have been Elizabeth Turner. An attractive woman and a local. She was obviously attached to Michael Smith. An outsider. A situation like that could breed bad feelings with other locals. Especially if they'd been nursing their own private fantasies. He'd seen it before in other small towns. He'd seen violence erupt from it. Would Bob Brisk have pressed Michael on the killings because of jealousy? He didn't know enough about the cop to answer that. Probably not. But maybe. Who could tell?

By the time they reached the outskirts of Hinton, Browning was moody and irritable. The bacon, sausages, eggs, hashbrowns, juice, and three cups of coffee from Chuck's Grease Pit were a heavy ball in his gut. He wanted to fart, but was afraid it might come out hard. On top of that, he ached for a smoke. It had been three months now, and his hunger for nicotine was getting sharper.

"Where do we start?" Franklin said.

"Where do you think?" Browning snapped, and was immediately sorry he had done so.

Franklin looked at him carefully, then turned his head back to the road. "I don't know. You're the boss."

Browning sighed. "Sorry, Rich. Heartburn." The lie slipped out easily.

"S'okay."

"Let's find the local flophouse. Sheriff Willson said something about an inn. If this broad's around, she had to stay somewhere."

Franklin nodded. He kept his eyes on the road as they drove through town.

The old woman behind the desk at the Hilltop Inn was called Mabel Field. She regarded Browning with a strange mixture of suspicion and pleasure; the suspicion he was used to, an understandable result of his narrow eyes, short hair, and nondescript clothing, but the pleasure was something new. He decided to write it off as a backwoods anomaly. It wasn't pleasure at seeing *him*, exactly, more a pleasure at seeing *anybody*. Her eyes were wide, blue, and sharp; they took in everything at a single glance. The grey drabness of her hair, summarily brushed back off a high domed forehead and forgotten, reminded him curiously of his mother toward the end. The perfunctory nod of inspection she offered Franklin was almost insulting in its recognition of who was boss. Browning found himself smiling.

"Le'me see that badge again," she said, leaning over the counter. The loose-knit brown cardigan hugged to her bosom rode higher as she leaned across the desk, opening to reveal the pink polyester dress beneath. Her arms looked like empty sacks of skin.

Browning obediently produced the badge, and this time she studied it closely. Her eyes locked onto the photo on the other half of the wallet, and she looked back and forth between it and Browning before handing it back. "Must have been taken a long time ago."

"Thanks," Browning said. *She's enjoying this!*

"But like I said. We ain't had anybody here of that name," Mabel said.

"Might have been under an alias," Browning said, infinitely patient. If there was one thing he had learned in his nineteen years with the Bureau, it was *don't push.* Not on your everyday good old American citizens, anyway. They had a nasty habit of pushing back. Behind him, neither as patient nor as experienced, Franklin shuffled on his feet.

She cupped her cauliflower chin in two cadaverous fingers and looked thoughtful. "Good looking, you say? Blonde. Tall."

"Like a model," Browning said.

She nodded. "What'd this gal do?"

"Maybe nothing," Browning said casually. "But she might be able to help us."

More thoughtful nods. A playful smile. "Might have had a guest like that."

It took a moment for these words to register with Browning, and another moment before he dared speak again. "What was her name?"

"Paid up until tomorrow," Mabel said. "Been here near on a month."

"What name did she use?" Browning repeated.

She frowned. "Not her real name, I expect. Nope, I doubt it. She signed in as Mrs. Smith."

Browning refused to let the shock show on his face. "What number?"

"Oh, she ain't here now. Ain't nobody here now."

Franklin touched Browning's elbow, leaned closer, and said, "There's *somebody* in one of the rooms."

The whisper had been loud enough for the old woman. "Locals," she said, grinning. Her teeth were perfect and square, early model dentures. "Second honeymoon."

"With two cars?" Franklin said.

She shrugged. She kept her attention on Browning.

"When will she be back?"

"Don't know. Left yesterday. Didn't stay here last night."

"May we look at her room?"

The old woman's eyes narrowed. "Don't you need a search warrant for that?"

"Not if you let us in." He smiled conspiratorially.

Mabel Field studied him for a moment without moving a muscle and then nodded. She pulled on a knee-length corduroy coat hanging from a wooden rack in the corner behind her, then came round to the front of the desk. Standing, she was barely as tall as Browning's midriff, and looking down at the top of her head as she walked past he was not surprised to see an almost bald scalp, pink and gleaming beneath strands of grey, misty hair. The followed her outside and down the sidewalk that ran the length of the motel. When she passed room 12, where the two cars were parked, she slowed and peered in the window. Browning shook his head and kept his eyes on her back. At room 16 she stopped, waited for Browning and Franklin to catch up, then opened the door.

The room smelled strongly of disinfectant. The double bed was neatly made, blankets tucked in. The glass ashtray on the bed table gleamed. The brown carpet was criss crossed with the lines of recent vacuum cleaner passage. Browning walked through the room and opened the bathroom. The faucets reflected his image perfectly, and the mirror might as well have been an opening into another room.

"The place has been cleaned," he said, coming back into the bedroom. "We won't find a single print. Guarantee it."

"Clean 'em every day," the old woman said, eyeing the faint tracks on the carpet from Browning's shoes. She ushered them outside impatiently.

"Did she have a car?" Franklin asked.

She nodded and began walking back to the office.

"What model?"

"Don't know."

"What color?"

She paused and looked back at the younger agent in disgust. "Purple."

"You mean burgundy?"

"I mean purple." She shook her head and began

walking again.

At the office door she blocked their entrance. The look she now turned on Browning was of suspicion only.

"Did she register her license plate number with you?" Browning asked.

"No."

"Mrs. Field, it's the law that . . ." Franklin began.

"She didn't give it," the old woman said, shooting him a nasty glance. "But it was a rental plate."

"That's okay," Browning said, motioning with his hand for Franklin to shut up. "Is there anything else you can tell us, Mrs. Field?"

"She had a fella," Mabel said. "Saw him near on every night this past week."

Browning gave Franklin a quick glance, then turned back to the old woman. "What did he look like?"

"Don't know."

"Was he local?"

"Don't know."

"Did he drive a car?"

"Yup."

"But you can't remember what model," Franklin piped in.

"It was brown," Mabel Field said. She stepped into the office. "And that's all I know." She let the door swing shut.

Franklin made a move as if to follow, but Browning held out a hand to stop the younger man. "Forget it, Rich," he said, intentionally using the other agent's first name to calm him. "Dry well."

Reluctantly, Franklin followed him back to the car.

"What now?"

"We'll try in town," Browning said. He glanced at his watch, it was almost 11:00 A.M. "Maybe someone saw her. Maybe we'll strike it lucky." He stroked his nose thoughtfully. "Maybe somebody recognized her beau."

Browning started on the north side of the main drag, moving east, and Franklin on the south side, moving west. Hinton was about twice the size of New York, and its main street had the look of small town commercialism trying to be big. Almost every storefront sported an illuminated sign, some in multicolored neon. Browning liked the look of these towns. Even when they strived for the glitter and decay of their larger counterparts they looked somehow innocent.

The job was relatively easy, the time passed quickly, and he did not have much opportunity to dwell on the innocence of small town USA. In most of the establishments he visited there was no indication of recognition at Sondra's description. The name "Mrs. Smith" drew a blank everywhere. But a couple of times he hit a nerve. A carpenter replacing a windowsill in a small restaurant perked up when Browning had been talking to the manager. He stopped Browning on the way out.

"I seen her around," he said.

"Where?"

"Around," he said, scratching his head. "Don't really remember. Old Jack's, I think. For a week or two."

"Old Jack's?"

"The bar. Few doors down. Just before the Hilltop Inn."

Fifteen minutes later, when he hit the same nerve, Browning walked directly to Old Jack's. The bar was a pleasant surprise. He felt like he'd walked into a western movie. Rough-hewen planks lined the inside walls, and the lighting came from imitation kerosene lamps at each table. The hooded lamps gave off a dim orange illumination. The place was almost empty except for a group of old codgers at a corner table playing cards and a middle-aged woman drinking alone at the end of the bar. Browning stepped up to the bar and climbed into a stool.

The bartender was a mountain of a man who seemed to roll rather than to walk. He placed hands the size of dinners plates on the counter and stared at Browning out of eyes like finger holes in lard. "What'll you have?"

"Coffee," Browning said.

For a moment it appeared that the bartender would refuse. Finally he shrugged, slapped a mug on the counter, and hastily splashed a foul-looking liquid into it. "A buck," he said flatly.

"What?"

"A buck, I said. This ain't no charity institution."

Browning shook his head and pulled out his wallet. He slid a crumpled bill across the counter and flipped out his badge. The empty eyes scanned the badge quickly, then grabbed the bill. "So?"

"I'd like to ask a couple of questions."

A heaving sigh ensued, and the flesh beneath the T-shirt jiggled. Browning could hardly keep his eyes on the man's face.

"We're looking for a woman."

"Every dick in this town is looking for a woman."

"I'm looking for a specific woman. Very attractive. Might be a model. Blonde. Maybe wearing leather clothes. I was told she came in here sometimes."

The eyes widened slightly. Not in shock, but more in an attempt to see Browning more clearly.

"What'd she do?" The perennial question.

"We don't know yet," Browning said. He sipped his coffee, and immediately wished he hadn't.

"Well, she's been around," the bartender said.

"When?"

"Not for a couple of days." He picked up a perfectly clean glass and began to polish it distractedly with his apron. "Good thing, too. Getting sick of that bitch. Something wrong with her. Strange. Icy. Wouldn't talk to anybody." Again the eyes receded into the pale flesh.

"I heard she was seeing a local boy," Browning said, and watched carefully for a reaction.

The bartender shook his head. "No, not local."

261

"But you know where he's from?"

"Sure. You should'a gone to him in the first place."

Browning waited, not saying more. *Don't push.* The answers would come eventually.

"You feds are a slow bunch, ain't'cha?"

"What do you mean?"

"Hell, the law around here got to that woman weeks ago."

Browning blinked. He could not bring himself to speak.

"The chief of police over in New York. Bob Brisk. Poor fella. He's been seeing her every night for a while now."

Browning dropped from the stool and ran.

CHAPTER TWENTY-TWO

At 2:30 P.M., after his lunch had settled comfortably, Michael Smith accepted the offer of a cup of coffee. Not particularly because he desired a cup at that moment, but because Elizabeth looked like she needed something to do. She was becoming increasingly nervous and jumpy as the day wore on. At one point she had yelled at Tommy to turn down the volume on the TV. Michael had not heard a sound. It might have been better, he thought, if she had remained at the store. Work, at least, would keep her mind off other things.

After the brief breakfast meeting at Chuck's Grill, Michael had walked past Horn's Books to find Tommy moping at the front counter and Elizabeth involved in some sort of mindless sorting activity at the back. When he had entered, Tommy had looked up at him with a self-pitying slant to his mouth.

"I thought I just saw your school bus go by."

"It did," Tommy said petulantly. "Mom wants me to hang around here."

Elizabeth had poked her head through the storage room door, but he could not tell by her expression if she was glad to see him or not. He nodded sympathetically at Tommy and went to the back. Elizabeth sighed as he approached.

"I didn't want him alone at school," she said defensively. "She approached him once already."

Michael nodded. "No. That's a good idea." He had glanced casually around the store. "Will you be busy in here today?"

"Not likely."

"Would you get in trouble if you closed up?"

She looked up at him sharply. "Well, no, but . . ."

"I was going to suggest we could all spend the day together at your cabin. I don't know about you, but I'd feel better about it. Otherwise I'll have to spend the day pacing around my place."

She had smiled, trying not to show her relief, and nodded.

Michael had walked over to the other side of the street where Anderson Hardware was just opening. He had purchased a box of 30/30 rounds, again wondering how effective they would be against Sondra. *You have to hit the target for these things to work.*

On the way back to Elizabeth's cabin they had passed Bob Brisk's cruiser moving at a leisurely pace in the opposite direction. The cop had cocked his head at Michael and Michael had returned the greeting. We're civil, at least, Michael thought.

Civil enough, he hoped, that Brisk would inform him of any developments.

But as the day wore on he became increasingly doubtful of Brisk's amicability. When Elizabeth brought him the cup of coffee he checked his watch: 2:35. He raised the cup to his lips and sipped the dark liquid, grateful for something to do with his hands.

"Do you think they'll get her?" Elizabeth asked.

Michael shrugged. "I think they'll *find* something. A trail, maybe. She's been here long enough to leave one."

Elizabeth wrung her hands. "I wonder . . ." She looked over at Tommy, then back at Michael. "I wonder if I should try the rifle. I mean, it's been so long since . . ." Her eyes widened. "Michael, what's wrong?"

Michael had suddenly paled, and his hand trembled as he lowered the mug. Coffee splashed over his fingers and across the kitchen table. Unable to stop himself, he bent over slightly, face pinched.

"Are you . . ."

Michael shook his head. "No, no. It's that pulled muscle in my thigh. From skiing. Just bothering me a little." But the icy stab of pain in his hip had nothing to do with skiing. He suppressed a groan as a tendril radiated out from his hip, reaching for his knee, fine and sharp, like a long splinter of glass sliding down the bone.

And then, as suddenly as it had come, the pain was gone. His leg throbbed, echoing its own scream. Michael sighed and felt the color returning to his cheeks. He smiled, but felt his lips tremble. "See," he said to Elizabeth, "it's gone."

She looked at him worriedly, then after a moment nodded. "About the rifle . . ."

Michael nodded. "Oh, sure. A couple of shots. Just to see if it works."

Elizabeth put on a pink ski jacket and carried the gun outside. Michael pulled on his own jacket without zipping it up and followed. Tommy, curious, stood at the porch door and watched.

She knew more about guns than he did, and he was relieved about that. She popped the magazine and loaded ten rounds into the black metal, eyes far away and blank, then slid it back into place. She turned to Michael and smiled. He smiled back encouragingly. As if she did this every day, she raised the stock to her shoulder, turned sideways to a tree about twenty yards away, pumped the finger lever once, and squeezed off a shot. A small piece of bark dropped from the center of the trunk, then the sound of the shot echoed through the trees like the crack of a whip, fading to nothing. Across the lake the echo sounded like faint thunder. The acrid smell of cordite filled the air.

"Good," Michael said.

Elizabeth smiled. "One more."

She raised the rifle, pulled the lever, and fired again. Another chunk of bark dropped away, revealing the glistening white meat below, and again the whip crack echoed and the thunder rumbled across the lake.

Elizabeth nodded, satisfied.

"Your husband must have been a good teacher," Michael said.

Elizabeth cradled the gun across her arm and stepped closer to him. "He was," she said softly, then reached up and kissed his lips.

"Let's hope you won't need it," he said.

Elizabeth nodded. She backed away, looking up at the sky. "The station in Fergus says we're going to get a storm tonight."

Michael followed her gaze. The clouds were flat and grey, moving with ponderous grace. As he stared, his eyes involuntarily closed and a lance of pain shot to the back of his head. He groaned, raising his hand to his eyes. His hip throbbed.

"Jesus . . ."

"Michael, are you okay?"

He breathed slowly, hand still pressed to his eyes. He felt Elizabeth approach and place her arm around his shoulder. He shook his head.

"It's the symptoms," he admitted.

For a moment Elizabeth was silent, and then she began guiding him toward the cabin. "C'mon, let's get you inside."

He lowered his hands and blinked. The snow was as bright as the sun. Once inside the cabin, the pain slowly receded and he slumped into the kitchen chair.

"Do you need that stuff you have at your place?"

Michael nodded, then shook his head. "No. Not

yet."

Tommy, who had seen everything from the porch door, was watching Michael curiously. Michael could not bring himself to look at the boy. He made himself breathe slowly, deeply, pushing at the curtain of pain that was waiting to close in on him.

Again he felt the futile anger against the virus. Why was it changing? Why, after three years, was it weakening the control he had fought so hard to gain? What could it possibly have in store for him that it hadn't already revealed?

He groaned as the pain suddenly intensified in his hip. His skin felt like it was alive, crawling, covered with a million clicking insects.

Fight it! Push it back!

Muir's compound would help. He knew that. It would end the symptoms, subdue the pain, and cut the hunger that was beginning to expand in his belly.

But if they found Sondra . . .

He concentrated, directing all his will inward until he sensed the symptoms receding somewhat. The pain slowly became tolerable. But he sensed it waiting, lurking in the shadows, ready to pounce.

Muir's compound would bring quick respite, supplying what his body needed, demanded. But it would also make him normal.

And if they found Sondra, they might need him. Need what he could do when the viral cycle was peaking.

Elizabeth stroked his hair, and he smiled up at her.

"You okay?" Her voice was filled with concern, and it sent a shiver through him.

"Fine," he said, gritting his teeth. "Just fine."

Bob Brisk lit a cigarette, drew deeply, and held the smoke until his lungs hurt. He exhaled with a small cough and took another drag. The smoke was sucked out the partially open driver window of the cruiser into the trees. He pressed his neck back into the headrest, made himself comfortable, and closed his eyes. He placed the cigarette between his lips and left it there, drawing periodically on the smoke and letting it drift out his nose.

It was almost 3:00 P.M., and he'd been parked at the empty Granger cottage, lot 89 South, since before noon. Sally had called twice, checking in. She had found nothing in the north allotments, of course, and Brisk felt mildly guilty about sending her on such a wild goose chase. She was working her way slowly out along the arm of the horseshoe, and if she kept at it she'd circumnavigate the lake in a day or two. He did not find the thought very funny.

Even less funny was the thought of the two FBI men over in Hinton. It wouldn't take them long to hook up with someone who had seen Sondra, and after that it was only a short hop to connecting Sondra with himself. And that would be the end of it. He had taken the precaution of disconnecting the base transmitter at the station. That would make it difficult for the FBI men to make contact with Sally or himself. It gave him a little more time to think.

He'd seen Michael Smith following Elizabeth and her boy back to the cabin this morning. They were all together now. It occurred to him that the smartest thing he and Sondra could do would be to pack up and disappear right now. Leave Smith where he was. Forget him. Forget everything, just get away. But somehow he could not imagine Sondra agreeing to that.

He picked the cigarette from his lips, inspected it briefly, and flicked it out the window. Thinking time was over. He started the car, revved the engine a moment, then backed out onto the blacktop and headed for his cabin.

When he entered the cabin his nose wrinkled involuntarily. He had expected the sharp odor of Sondra's perfume, but there was something else, an underodor he'd only detected hints of previously. The smell went right for the back of his nose, made him feel almost dizzy. It reminded him, somehow, of . . . sex. The moment he made the connection he felt the beginning throb of an erection.

Sondra stepped out of the bedroom. She was dressed in black leather pants and the leather bomber jacket in which he had originally seen her. Her short blonde hair was combed straight back from her forehead, sleek, wet looking.

"Where were you?" Her grey eyes locked onto him.

Brisk shrugged. "Thinking."

She seemed about to say something, but turned away.

"Sondra . . ."

"We have to leave here," she said, turning back to him.

Brisk nodded, surprised. "Yes."

"But I have to finish my business with Michael Smith."

He had expected this. He frowned. "There are people looking for you. By now they're probably looking for the both of us."

One of her eyebrows arched. "Then you should have been acting, rather than thinking," she said.

Brisk sighed. "I think we should leave right now. Forget about Smith. He's with Elizabeth Turner. Forget him."

Now she laughed. Brisk didn't like the sound of it. "Bob, don't be silly." She stepped closer to him until her face was less than an inch away from his own. Her tongue flicked out and licked his lips, drawing a wet line from one corner of his mouth to the other. "It won't take long," she said softly, and kissed him. "But I need some kind of leverage to deal with him."

Brisk backed away an inch. "Leverage?"

"An advantage," she said, and drew him closer again. This time, her tongue probed past his lips, and one of her hands cupped the hardness between his legs. Brisk groaned.

"What kind of advantage?" he said hoarsely.

"Phone him. Get him away from the woman and the boy."

Brisk stopped breathing. Again he backed away. He found himself held by her grey eyes. "Leave Elizabeth and Tommy out of this."

She smiled and pulled him closer again. She kissed him hard, sucking his lips and tongue. "I'm not going to hurt them," she whispered. "I just want Michael Smith."

"You hurt her already," Brisk managed to say. "You visited her at the store."

Sondra's tongue, halfway into Brisk's mouth, froze. In a moment it moved again, darting across his teeth. "That wasn't *hurt*," she said. Her voice was very flat. "Please, do it," she said.

Brisk did not move. In his mind, the past three weeks ran through his head like a movie, a collage of pornographic images. What had happened to him? How had he fallen so far, so quickly?

But Sondra's lips worked upon him, kissing along the edge of his mouth, down his chin. "After today, darling, it will be just you and me. And I'll make you the same as me," she nipped his neck with her teeth and Brisk gasped. "We'll be able to do anything we want, darling. *Anything*. To anybody."

Brisk pushed himself away. He breathed deeply. He looked at Sondra, focusing on her lips rather than her eyes. The eyes scared him.

"You're going to kill Michael Smith, aren't you?"

She sighed. "Something like that," she said.

Brisk took another deep breath. He turned from Sondra, escaping momentarily from her gaze. He quickly ran through his head ten good reasons for walking out that door and turning himself in to Sally. He ran through them again.

Then he picked up the phone and dialed Elizabeth's number.

CHAPTER TWENTY-THREE

Sally Warner sat in her cruiser car outside Chuck's Grill, smoking a cigarette and sipping from a white styrafoam cup of Chuck Patterson's chicory-laced coffee. Neither the cigarette nor the coffee did much to cut through the blanket of cold that seemed to be pushing at her edges, seeping into her pores. And the anger poking at her from the inside was as icy as an arctic night.

For almost six hours she'd been checking the abandoned cabins in the north allotments, spending most of her time outside of the car. With each passing hour she had felt the anger within her growing, intensifying, easily matching nature's frigid assault. Twice she had checked in with Bob Brisk, both times bemoaning the futility of the search she was conducting, but he had been adamant. "Keep looking, Sal. Doesn't matter if you find anything. At least our butts will be covered."

So why did she get the feeling that Brisk was sitting in the warmth of his car, chain-smoking, and never setting a foot in the snow?

She flicked the smoking remains of her cigarette out the window and into the street, then immediately lit another. She sipped her coffee, swallowed, then took another sip.

She had not radioed Brisk to tell him she was taking a break, and she felt mildly guilty about the small deception. But the feeling had been strong that if she had done so, he would have ordered her to stay where she was in the north allotments. Even thinking about it made her cringe. *The bastard*.

What had happened to Bob Brisk over this past month?

During the six years she had been part of the two-person New York police force, she had come to know Bob Brisk very well. At first he had been aloof, condescending toward her. His attitude to women was archaic, and his opinion of female cops comically chauvinistic. But she'd worked hard to impress him, worked very hard. Bob Brisk may have been a stubborn, old-fashioned male chauvinist pig, but he was not stupid. Whether he liked it or not, he knew he'd latched onto a damned good partner. It did not take long for his attitude toward her to change. The aloofness soon turned into a grudging respect, the condescension into trust.

Their working relationship was one Sally was proud of. There were none of the arguments she heard about from the other townships, none of the petty squabbles that could make police work in small towns unbearable. She and Brisk were a team, a well-oiled machine. And the relationship had continued outside the structure of work. They had begun to see each other socially, had even occasionally slept together. It had been comfortable. It had worked. Until Michael Smith arrived in town.

The sudden jump in the murder rate was the least of the changes that had taken place in New York since Smith's arrival. If she thought about it, Sally had to admit that this kind of police work was exciting. A change from the weekend drunken brawls and the annual winter break-ins. In fact, she felt mildly grateful for the opportunity to work on such a case. More pronounced, however, and far more disturbing, was the change in Bob Brisk. He had become secretive, almost cagey. His attention to detail, and to procedure, had slipped. As often as not, Sally felt she was working by herself. She hardly saw Brisk at all during working hours, and never, since Michael Smith arrived, at night.

But worse than this change in his behavior was the change she sensed in the man himself. Bob Brisk's shortness of stature had been one of the mainstay jokes in New York, in a friendly sort of way. Anybody who met him knew that he could be a very imposing presence. It was easy to forget his height when you had the feeling he could whip the pants off you if he ever got the notion to do so.

The sudden memory of Brisk's confrontation with Big Bill Flahrety over in Vinning last summer came to her, and she smiled. Flahrety had been in the process of breaking chairs and tables at Foster's Lounge, having already knocked senseless two young rednecks who had antagonized him, when an off-duty Brisk and Sally had arrived. Flahrety had immediately turned on Brisk, claiming that if Brisk wasn't a cop he'd beat the tar out of him.

"Don't think of me as a cop," Brisk had said, removing his light summer jacket and sunglasses and handing them to Sally. "Think of me as Mohammad Ali."

Flahrety had blinked. He had retreated a step at Brisk's approach and had nodded humbly when Brisk suggested he walk down the road and turn himself in to Mac Henderson at the police station before anybody got really hurt. And that had been that. A potentially explosive situation defused by Bob Brisk, simply because of his presence. And that sort of thing was not unusual. He had a talent for being at the right place at the right time, always ready to step in when needed.

But now . . .

Something had happened to Bob Brisk. The inner structure of the man, the *presence* that seemed to tower over his physical body, had collapsed. He had shrunk in on himself, and he was still shrinking, as if he had been quashed by a better or submitted himself to some unforgivable degradation. She could not imagine Bill Flahrety backing away from this new version of Brisk.

Sally took a final drag on her cigarette and tossed it out the window. Her mood was bleak and it wasn't doing her any good. She finished the coffee in a gulp, then tossed the empty cup onto the floor on the passenger side. Bob Brisk's decline was somehow connected to Michael Smith and to the mystery woman they were looking for. The sooner it was all cleared up, the sooner Bob would return to normal.

She was about to head back to the north allotments when she heard the approach of the car from behind her. She glanced in the rearview mirror in time to see the flash of color, and then the car roared past. It did not slow as it roared through the arch of New York, and a cloud of loose snow rose from the road behind it. She did not need radar to tell it was over the speed limit by far more than the five mile-per-hour grace zone.

"Jesus Christ!" That had been Michael Smith's car.

She acted then on reflex. The only conscious decision she made was to leave Brisk out of it. He might tell her to stay where she was, and she could not bear that right now. She threw the car in gear, pulled out onto the blacktop, and followed.

Smith did not go far. About a mile along the road she saw his brake lights flash, and then the car turned into one of the cabin access roads. Sally slowed the cruiser and turned after him. In a moment she spotted the metallic blue paint of his car parked beside the cabin. This was 93 South. Terry and Fran Bollack's place. They usually opened up sometime in May, so the access road had not been cleared of snow all winter. It looked as if Smith's car was firmly stuck.

Sally parked the cruiser before the snow became too deep. She opened the door and stepped out, leaning against the roof of the car. Michael Smith was crouched low, moving around the perimeter of

278

the cabin, as if waiting for something terrible to happen. But why the furtiveness?

"Mr. Smith?"

He spun at the sound of his name, staring at her in shock. It was almost as if he did not recognize her.

"What are you doing here?" she asked.

Smith looked confused. He came tramping through the snow toward her. Warily, Sally placed her hand on the butt of her revolver. But Smith stopped about ten feet away, knee-deep in snow. His face was wild, his breathing ragged. He looked almost out of control. His jacket was half undone.

"Where's Brisk," he said. His voice was so hoarse she could hardly understand him.

"I don't know," she said. "What are you doing here?"

Again his eyes turned wild. He seemed to fight for control against some inner demon, and finally managed to focus on her again.

"Brisk phoned me," he said, running a hand through his hair. "He said he found . . . Sondra. He said he needed help, and for me to come here."

Sally opened her mouth to speak, then snapped it shut again.

"Where is he?" Smith said.

"I don't know," Sally said softly. *Why didn't Bob call me?*

"He said . . ." There was panic in Smith's voice now.

"Are you sure you have the right address?"

Smith frowned. "93 South. Bollack place. That's

what he said."

Sally nodded, confused. Why hadn't Bob called her for help? And why wasn't he here? A sudden shiver ran up her spine, feeling like the icy fingers of a dead man. "Where were you when he phoned you?"

Smith frowned. "I . . ." His eyes widened, and a pained expression passed across his face. "I was at Elizabeth Turner's cabin," he said.

"Is she alone there now?"

Smith shook his head. "With her boy."

For a moment their eyes locked, and a terrible understanding seemed to come upon both of them at once.

Sally said, "It looks like your car is stuck. Come on. We'll take mine. We better check on Elizabeth and Tommy."

A sound emerged from Michael Smith's mouth, but she was not sure it had been a word. It had sounded almost like a growl.

Elizabeth Turner studied the sky with a feeling of dread. It was going to storm. No doubt about it. They were going to be snowed in for days, just like last year. Already the front had swept out of Canada, over North Dakota, sealing both Fargo and Grand Forks in what the station in Fergus Falls was calling an "icy tomb." And that would be the icing on what was already a pretty awful afternoon.

She had been relieved, at first, when Michael had suggested they spend the day together. Somehow, his nearness calmed her. But the little episode this afternoon had cut through the thin blanket of security and exposed the bone of her fear. *There was something wrong with Michael!* And it was the same thing that this woman, this Sondra, who purportedly had killed 150 human beings, had wrong with her. The thought was not comforting at all.

Bob Brisk's phone call had been a shock. Michael, who had answered the phone, had turned pale. After he had hung up he had been nervous, hardly able to talk at all.

"Brisk found her," he whispered. "He *found* her!"

"Where?"

"Somewhere in the south allotments," Michael had said, picking up his coat. "He wants me to come and help. He's not sure he can handle her."

A chill had spread across Elizabeth's neck. "Michael, maybe you should wait for the others to get back."

Michael had shaken his head impatiently. "And take the chance she might get away again?" He breathed deeply. "This is a chance to end it. I have to help Brisk."

She had watched, dismayed, as he climbed into his car and drove away. In a small way she felt a surge of relief that he had gone. The sudden rise in the symptoms of his disease this afternoon had frightened her. But she immediately felt ashamed at the feeling. Michael was trying to help.

Now she lit a cigarette and sipped her coffee. In the living room Tommy was reading a book while the TV continued to fill the house with its static.

Somehow, that noise had taken on a comforting tone. *Life on the outside. We're not alone.*

It was Tommy who heard the noise first. He came through from the living room and looked at her nervously. "Car outside," he said.

Elizabeth rose and stepped over to the kitchen window. There was a car outside but it was not Michael's. It was a police cruiser. She caught a glimpse of Bob Brisk stepping beyond the corner of the house, and then the knock sounded on the door. For a moment she felt confused: *But you just called Michael.* And then a surge of relief: *It's over!*

"It's okay, honey," she said to Tommy. "It's just Bob Brisk."

Tommy made a sound of disgust and moved to answer the door. But the moment he did so he stumbled backward, dropping his book to the floor. His face was slack.

Bob Brisk stepped into the kitchen. Behind him came the woman who had crushed Elizabeth's wrist at the book store. Elizabeth gasped, holding her hand to her throat. Bob Brisk stepped fully into the kitchen, appraising the scene quickly. In his hand he held the Winchester. He popped the magazine and dropped it into his pocket.

"Found this on the porch," he said, looking at Elizabeth. "Yours?"

Elizabeth found herself nodding. She could not take her eyes off the woman behind Bob. Gone was the fur coat and cap, replaced by a sleek leather outfit.

"Sondra . . ." the name slipped from her mouth

282

as a whisper.

Sondra stepped past Bob, smiling. Her teeth gleamed behind red lips. Bob leaned the rifle in the corner, propped against the wall.

Stupid! Elizabeth thought. Why hadn't she brought it in? *Stupid* . . .

"Where's Michael?" Elizabeth said, her voice shaky.

Bob Brisk shrugged, smiling as if he were embarrassed. "Looking for me in the south allotments."

Sondra took a step toward Tommy, holding out her hand. But Tommy stepped quickly away. "Such a nice boy," Sondra said.

"Leave him alone!" Elizabeth said.

Sondra smiled. Bob Brisk shook his head. "It's okay, Liz. She's not going to hurt you or Tommy. She wants Michael."

Elizabeth felt the shock sinking into her system. She felt stunned, incapable of moving. Hardly capable of thinking at all. The entire scene playing out before her had the atmosphere of a dream. A nightmare. "You knew about her," she said at last, her tone accusing. "You're helping her."

Bob Brisk shrugged again.

"How could you?"

"You don't understand," he said. "I couldn't . . ."

"Couldn't what?" She was surprised at the anger in her voice, because she felt none of it inside. "Couldn't resist? What did she do for you, Bob?"

He coughed, looking down at the floor.

"We have no time for this," Sondra said, taking a step toward Tommy again.

"Wait," Bob Brisk said. "I thought . . ."

Sondra paused, turning toward him. "You do too much of that, Bob," she whispered. "It's time to *act*."

"You said you weren't going to hurt them," he said hoarsely.

Sondra looked at him for a long moment. Tommy edged over toward Elizabeth, and she held the boy tightly. "I'll do what I have to do."

"But . . ."

"If you want to be like me," she said, "then stand aside."

Bob Brisk looked very confused. His hands balled into fists, then relaxed, then balled into fists again. He looked back and forth between Elizabeth and Sondra.

"Bob, *what* did she promise you?" Elizabeth said, ignoring the savage glance from the other woman.

Bob blinked. "I . . ."

The sudden understanding of what might sway a man like Bob Brisk had come to Elizabeth so suddenly it left her reeling on her feet. "You can't be like her, Bob. Or like Michael. He told me."

Bob Brisk's mouth snapped shut and he stared at Elizabeth. For a moment his eyes were as sharp and wary as she remembered them. He turned to Sondra. "What does she mean?"

"The virus isn't contagious," Elizabeth said. "Michael told me. He was involved in research in Chicago. He said they never managed to infect lab rats with the virus, no matter what they tried."

Bob continued to stare at Sondra. "But you

said . . ."

Sondra smiled.

What happened next was so fast that Elizabeth could hardly follow it. It seemed, for an instant, that Sondra's pale face shrank in on itself. The glossy lips turned up in what appeared to be a grin, exposing the whiteness of her teeth. But it was too wide for a grin. Far too wide. The tendons of her neck were taut, pushing through the skin like cables. A faint sound, growing louder, emanated from her throat.

A cat purring.

Sondra's upright posture suddenly changed. Her shoulders leaned forward, her supple legs bent at the knees, her spine arched, and her long arms reached out as if she were ready to pounce.

Bob Brisk looked on in horrified wonder, his mouth hanging open in surprise. His right hand suddenly rose, fumbling with the toggle strap of his holster. For a second it looked as if he might free the weapon, it moved slightly, but the hammer caught on the strap. A faint wavering sound came from Brisk's mouth and his eyes darted fearfully toward Elizabeth and Tommy.

"Run, Liz!" he yelled. "Run . . ."

And then Sondra moved. One moment she was facing Brisk, the next she was a blur of white and black, moving through the air faster than anything Elizabeth had ever seen. Something glittered in the blur of movement. Something sharp. Bob Brisk might as well have been standing still. He hardly managed to raise his arm in protection before she

285

was upon him.

It was as if the policeman were caught in the middle of a whirlwind. His scream emerged from his mouth in a high waver, and was suddenly cut short. A sheet of red splashed out of the thrashing limbs, across the floor. Elizabeth screamed and crushed Tommy's face to her bosom so the boy would not see.

Brisk's scream changed to a coughing gurgle, and a high fountain of blood arched into the air and splashed across the wall. The flurry of motion ceased, and the form of Sondra seemed to solidify, stepping away from Brisk. The cop fell to his knees, eyes focused on Sondra. He keeled over on his side with a thud. Sondra jumped forward again, kneeling by him, and pressed her face to her ear.

"Say hello to death, darling." Her voice was a guttural whisper.

Brisk gurgled wetly, incapable of speech. Horrified, Elizabeth could not turn away, could not move a muscle. Sondra pressed her face into Bob Brisk's sliced throat, opening her mouth fully. She bit down and ripped out a chunk of flesh. More blood splashed across the floor. Brisk's body shuddered, then stopped moving.

The thing that had been Sondra stood slowly, regaining her original posture. She turned to Elizabeth. The lower part of her face was a mask of red, and a waterfall of blood cascaded down her black jacket. She smiled and spat out a chunk of meat. Her teeth gleamed in the red sea.

Elizabeth heard a soft moaning sound, an inartic-

286

ulate whimper that seemed to come from the walls themselves. It took her a moment to realize it was her own voice. "Oh, Bob . . ." she said.

A thought came to her then that almost made her collapse with dizziness, a thought that filled her with horror: *Michael is just like her. He might have done this.* . . .

As if she sensed Elizabeth's thoughts, Sondra nodded, and her smile brightened. Then the purring noise started again. And Sondra moved toward them.

CHAPTER TWENTY-FOUR

Michael Smith felt that his head was spinning and that he could not stop it. All the way back to Elizabeth's cabin he had sat with his cheek pressed against the cold glass of the passenger window, eyes focused to infinity against the blurred background. Sally had turned on the cruiser's siren and lights, but inside the car the sound was oddly muted, like the sirens that brought him out of sleep almost every Chicago morning. Michael tried to keep an image of Elizabeth and Tommy in front of him, but was horrified to discover that he could not. It was as if he had forgotten what they looked like.

The sudden deceleration knocked his head against the doorpost and he sat upright, looking forward as Sally turned into the access road for Elizabeth's cabin.

"Brisk's car isn't here," she said.

Michael's eyes took in everything quickly. There were looping tire tracks in the snow beside the cabin, as if somebody had hurriedly turned a car to drive away. Many more than his own car would have left behind.

He opened the door before Sally had stopped, stepping out as she swore in consternation.

"Slow down!" she said.

Michael ignored her. He moved toward the cabin, bent slightly forward as if he were trying to sneak up unnoticed. The rhythmic flashing of the cruiser's lights reflected off the snow and trees, giving the entire scene the eerie look of something out of a movie. Behind him, the cruiser's door ajar signal pinged annoyingly.

"Mr. Smith!" Sally came crunching through the snow toward him, and he paused until she caught up. She held out a hand and gripped his arm. "Don't go barging in there," she said.

Michael locked eyes with her a moment. His instinct was to break down the door, but the earnest expression in her eyes stayed him. He forced himself to take a deep breath and calm down. So far, there was no indication, other than the tracks, that anyone had been here except himself. Elizabeth and Tommy might, at this very moment, be watching him from one of the windows, wondering what lunatic thing he was up to.

"Okay," he said hoarsely. His voice did not sound like his own. The symptoms had reached a plateau level within him, one that he was intentionally ignoring without lowering.

Sally nodded. "Okay. One step at a time." She pulled her revolver from its holster and inclined her head toward the cabin. "I'll enter first."

The logic of this was unmistakable, of course. She was a police officer. He was a civilian. But . . . *those were his people in there.*

He nodded reluctantly. He allowed her to move ahead, and followed close behind.

He had fully intended on allowing Sally to enter the cabin first. But less than five yards from the front door the smell hit him with such force that he groaned audibly. Sally spun around. "What is it?"

Michael paused, crouching, hands buried past the wrist in snow. The odor was like a physical force, hammering at him. It easily unmoored the anchors of his control. He felt himself shaking, and he could tell from the expression on Sally's face that something not quite human had twisted his features.

"What is it?" Sally's voice had assumed an almost panicky note.

He sniffed the air, and said, "Blood."

"Blood?" Her hand opened and closed nervously around the butt of the revolver.

"I can smell it. A lot of it."

"Jesus . . ."

Michael stepped past her, still crouching, and ran toward the house.

"Smith!"

He paused at the door, leaning against the cold wood. The smell was stronger, thicker, like a mist. He felt his whole body responding to it, attracted to it. But his mind rebelled in horror. Whose blood was it? Dreading to, but not daring to wait longer, he twisted the door handle and stepped into the cabin.

Blood was everywhere.

It dripped from the ceiling in thick blobs. It spilled down the walls, as if the plaster itself was wounded flesh. It stretched across the floor like a sea. And in the middle of it lay the prone form of

Bob Brisk, arms flailed out in a position of supplication, one hand loosely holding his revolver. His face was blank, relaxed, blood-smeared, open mouthed. His sharp blue eyes now looked like marbles, lifeless, staring at the ceiling. *Counting the drops.*

But it was the throat that caught Michael's attention. It had been ripped apart like a wet paper bag. A flap of skin hung down across Brisk's shirt, exposing the ragged edges of the wound. A number of veins and arteries, like ropy tentacals, hung down to the floor. Something impossibly white glistened in the dark recesses of the bloody hole.

Michael turned away, stomach churning. His mouth watered freely, and he swallowed twice before he could talk.

"Elizabeth! Tommy!" The names fell flat and unanswered in the cabin.

He heard Sally stumble across the threshold, heard her sudden ragged intake of breath. But he did not turn around. He stepped into the master bedroom, then into Tommy's room, then into the living room.

Empty.

A mug of coffee rested on the kitchen table. He held it in his hand. Hot. Not warm, hot. He looked inside. Almost full. He could see that a drop of blood had somehow entered the cup, forming an oily film on the coffee and leaving a red line around the inside surface of the mug. He placed it carefully back on the table.

When he turned again, Sally was kneeling beside Bob Brisk, oblivious to the fact that her knee was immersed in a stray puddle of blood. She was bent over the dead cop, cradling his head in her hands. As he watched, a tear spilled off her cheek and washed a streak of blood from Brisk's face.

"They're gone," Michael said.

Sally carefully placed Brisk's head back on the ground. She did not close his eyes. When she stood, her face was livid. Tears brimmed in her eyes, but the anger behind them was unmistakable. She took a step toward Michael.

"This is your fault," she said softly.

Michael shook his head and sighed.

"If you hadn't come here . . ."

"I didn't do this," Michael said, indicating the bloody walls.

Sally did not look around. "*She* did it. The fucking bitch."

Michael nodded, glad to direct her anger elsewhere. "Sondra."

For a moment Sally stared at him as if she did not see him, then she lowered her eyes. "Bob must have followed her here. He must have burst in while . . ." she seemed to be trying to piece together the action logically, but it was not clicking.

"Brisk led her here," Michael said. "He was with her."

Sally turned away from him and her shoulders shook. Michael groaned. His stomach rumbled. Again the saliva flooded his mouth.

"She's taken Elizabeth and Tommy," Michael said, fighting to keep his voice normal. "They must have taken Brisk's car."

"They didn't pass us on the road," Sally said, still looking away from him. "Must have gone north."

"We have to go after them," Michael said.

Sally's shoulders straightened, and she turned to face him again. Though red rimmed, her eyes had cleared of tears. "I'll go after them."

"I'm coming with you."

"Mr. Smith . . ."

"Damn it!" She's got Elizabeth and Tommy!" His voice cracked, became almost unintelligible. He breathed deeply, relaxing his throat. "I'm the one she wants. This is what this whole game is for. I'm going with you."

Sally eyed him carefully, then nodded once.

From the corner by the door Michael picked up the Winchester rifle. The magazine was missing. He glanced around the room, but could not see it. On impulse he bent and inspected Brisk's coat pockets. In the right one he found the magazine. "You son of a bitch," he muttered. He pushed it back into the rifle.

In the car, Sally tried radioing the New York switchboard operator for an ambulance, but could not get through. She hung up the microphone and continued driving, looking thoughtful. Brisk must have done something to the base radio, Michael thought. Smart son of a bitch.

They had traveled about ten miles when they saw the cruiser car ahead, parked sloppily on the shoulder. Sally slowed to a stop directly behind it. Michael got out first and ran to the other car. The driver's window was wide open, and the smell of blood was thick. Sally came up behind and peered over his shoulder.

"At least two people."

"Huh?"

"There's blood on the passenger window, and on the dash, but none on the steering wheel. I bet Elizabeth Turner was driving."

A surge of relief washed through Michael. "But where have they gone?"

Sally nodded to the trees at the west side of the road. They started about six feet beyond the blacktop, inclining quickly into the hilly country that extended almost all the way to Fergus Falls. But in the snow before the tree line there were three sets of ski tracks that merged into one as they entered the forest.

Sondra must have taken his skis. He remembered leaning them against the porch wall at Elizabeth's, the boots hung around the bindings.

Three sets of tracks. *Tommy and Elizabeth are okay!*

"Now we'll have to wait," Sally said. She leaned against Brisk's car, pulled out her cigarettes and lit one. The horror of the past hour seemed to settle on her, and she looked small and fragile.

Michael shook his head. The anger and fear that had been working on him all day suddenly popped free of the restraints he had built around them. His body began to shake.

"What's up there," he hissed, his voice low, almost croaking.

Sally drew thoughtfully on her cigarette. "You could get to Black Lake Lodge, I guess. About ten miles." She hissed some smoke from her nose, took another drag. "Little place. Only used in the summer. For fishing, mostly."

Michael turned and stared at the ski tracks. "I'm

going after them."

Behind him he heard Sally push from the car. "Don't be stupid, Smith."

"This is what she wants," Michael said, and knew it was the truth. He stepped over to the car and retrieved the rifle, then moved back to the edge of the road.

"You don't have skis," Sally said calmly. "You could never follow. Besides, there's a storm coming." She looked up at the sluggish grey sky.

"I can't leave them alone with her."

"We'll go back to town. We'll get a chopper. Maybe the FBI will have some ideas."

Michael shook his head. "She wants me. Alone."

Sally took a deep breath. "You'll die up there," she said.

Michael grinned. "No, I won't."

He turned from Sally. There was only one way he was going to be able to do this, and it occurred to him that he had resigned himself to it some time ago. His duty now was to Elizabeth and Tommy. His own needs were secondary. His own life, if necessary, could be forfeit.

For three years he had been running from this. For three years it had hung over him like a shadow, a disease, a nightmare.

But now it was offering itself to him as his only hope.

And the only hope for Elizabeth and Tommy.

He forced himself to think about the blood in Elizabeth's cabin. He brought to mind the smell, the thick cloying mist. He imagined sinking his teeth into the bloody flesh, ripping, gulping . . .

The pain in his hip came first, sharper than he had ever felt it before. But miraculously it passed quickly, and a sudden truth came to him: fighting against the pain only increased it.

Submitting brought relief!

It was almost funny. Three years of fighting, of pain. When all he had to do was submit.

Like Sondra had done.

The sudden thought of her name released his anger fully. It surged within him until he thought he might explode. He could hardly breathe.

He squinted his eyes in pain at the brightness of the day. Needles poked to the back of his head, and he welcomed them. As with his hip, the pain quickly subsided when he accepted it. The shadows within the trees suddenly seemed to be illuminated. He saw the forest in almost hallucinogenic detail.

He heard his name called from somewhere behind him. "Smith?"

It was Sally. He knew her position. Could sense her fear. If he wanted, he could have her throat out before she could scream. Such easy prey.

But his prey was in the forest. Moving quickly away.

He muttered her name: "Sondra."

The name emerged as an inarticulate sound. Like a cat purring.

Then, with the rifle hugged across his body, he lunged forward, through the snow and into the forest.

CHAPTER TWENTY-FIVE

Franklin had driven like a maniac on the trip back from Hinton, but had expressed no opinion on the theory that Bob Brisk might be involved with the killer they were hunting. Browning had to admire the younger agent's poise, but he could not copy it. He fretted continuously, and ended up clutching the base of his seatbelt to keep his hands still. A strange mixture of panic and anger had grown inside him, making it almost impossible to think clearly.

Back in New York they had found the police station empty. It was Franklin who had the presence of mind to suggest visiting Elizabeth Turner's cabin. But they had been too late. When Franklin had turned onto the access road for the cabin they had been met by an ambulance and a police cruiser, both empty. Browning had leapt from the car and run to the open front door. The scene that had met him had almost made him collapse. In all his years at the Bureau he had never seen so much blood.

The young police woman, Sally Warner, approached him. She looked grim.

"What happened?"

She seemed to have difficulty speaking. "Brisk led the woman here. She killed him. She took Elizabeth Turner and her boy."

"Where's Smith?"

"He went after them."

"Jesus . . ." Browning said.

Franklin moved past him and into the doorway. The younger agent scanned the room impassively, though it looked like his jaw quivered momentarily. He stepped out again and leaned against the porch.

An older man came out of the bathroom with a small plastic bag dangling from his right hand. He was dressed in a knee-length green hooded parka, tattered and torn around its lower hem, and splattered and stained by God only knew what kind of substances. The bag was filled with something red, soft, and wet, and the man held it up to the light to peer at it closely. His face was gaunt, pale, waxy looking. His nose was a lump of burst capillaries.

"Who's that?" Browning eyed the other man suspiciously. He looked drunk.

"Doctor Unger," Sally said. "I called him."

Browning turned away from the abbatoir, leaned on the outside doorjamb, and let the cold air wash over him. Even outside, the blood smell was strong. A bubble of something had risen in his gullet and threatened to emerge, but he managed to keep it down with sheer force of will. He wished he had a cigarette. The smoke would do wonders to cut through the envelope surrounding him. From the corner of his eye he watched Doctor Unger at work in the kitchen.

Unger's cursory inspection of the corpse was callous, almost brutal. He poked at the throat wound with a sharp instrument, lifting the flaps of skin for a closer look. A cigarette hanging from his lips obscured his vision with a thin veil of smoke, and Browning was terrified that the finger of ash on the end of the cigarette would fall into the dead man's throat. But miraculously it held until Unger straightened, groaning, and stepped away from the body.

"Let's get away from here," Browning said. "Can Unger handle this?"

Sally frowned, then nodded. "I'll let him know."

She went back into the kitchen, carefully sidestepping the tributaries of blood. Unger nodded, then shrugged as she spoke to him. He spoke a few curt words back at her, and when she finally walked over to Browning again she was pale and shaky.

"Okay," she said.

"What'd he say?"

She took a deep breath. "He said Bob probably took a few minutes to die." Her voice shook. She stepped past him and moved toward the car.

Browning followed and Franklin left his leaning post at the porch and fell in step behind him. "Meet at the station?" Browning said.

Sally nodded, then ducked into the car.

In the Plymouth, Browning found that his hands were trembling. Franklin, who had noticed, pretended not to. He started the car and followed Sally Warner's cruiser. Browning kept quiet, afraid his voice might shake if he spoke.

By 4:00 P.M. Sheriff Willson and Deputy Harper had returned from Vinning and heard the news. It was a grim-faced group that congregated in the reception area of the New York police station. By default rather than by consensus Browning found himself in control. It was a situation he was familiar with, and one he adjusted to quickly.

He listened intently with the others while Sally told her story again.

"You don't think Smith could have done it himself?" Sheriff Willson drew lazily on his cigarette. Browning smiled at the question. He liked this rugged, windburned man, despite his suspicious nature.

Sally considered the suggestion seriously. Finally she shook her head. "No. I don't think so. He was very distraught when I saw him. I believed his story . . . that Brisk had called him."

Willson shrugged. "It seems possible to me that Smith could have planned this whole thing. I mean, maybe he had a fight going with Brisk. They both dated the Turner woman. Maybe there was a personal war going on there."

Sally guffawed and Browning kept his smile to himself. This girl wasn't taking shit from any of the men in the room.

"Smith wasn't the type to hold that kind of grudge. Not from what I saw of him. And if Bob was nursing one, he'd have more likely called Smith out and whipped him fair and square. It's all too elaborate."

Willson seemed ready to argue further, but Browning held up his hand.

"That's irrelevant right now," he said.

"We have a cop killer running loose." The note of almost playful skepticism in Willson's voice gave way to a hint of petulancy.

"Maybe so," Browning agreed, and looked squarely at Willson. "But our primary concern right now has to be Elizabeth Turner and her boy. They're the innocent parties."

Willson mulled this over then acquiesced. He nodded, a barely perceptible movement, and took a drag on his cigarette.

"What I'm interested in right now," Browning said, addressing himself to Sally, "is what happened to Smith. You say he changed?"

Sally frowned, and her eyes narrowed. "Something happened to him. He was very nervous, jumpy. He could hardly talk."

"That's it?"

She shrugged. "When he went after them, into the woods, he . . . well, he seemed to crouch down, almost as if he couldn't stand up straight. I couldn't see his face, but I had the impression he was grimacing. I know he was making some sort of growling noise. When he moved, his strides were long. Very quick. He almost seemed to *lope,* like some sort of animal. I've never seen a man move so quickly."

"You said he said something. What?"

Again, Sally frowned, remembering. "Something like . . . 'She wants me. Alone.' "

Browning shook his head. "You said there was a lodge up there?"

"Black Lake Lodge. Just a big shack, really. Locals use it for a hunting base or for fishing."

"Any way to access it by road?"

301

"Nope. Walk in only. Fly in, maybe, with a chopper, since the lake is frozen."

Browning turned to Willson. "Can you get a chopper in here from Fergus Falls?"

"I could. If we needed one."

Browning ignored the comment, turning again to Sally. "Can you get me the geological survey maps of the area?"

"Sure."

"I don't like the way this is sounding," Sheriff Willson said, looking back and forth between Sally and Browning. "Myself, I'd be tempted to leave them up there until they come down. They're gonna have to come down sometime."

Browning stood up, now angry. "If it was just this Sondra Palmer, and maybe even Michael Smith, I'd agree with you," he said. "But there's innocent people up there too. We can't leave them. I won't leave them."

Willson blushed, but said nothing more. Both Franklin and Harper had witnessed these proceedings with apparent calm, ready to act upon whatever decision their superiors made, not willing to offer support until a decision had been reached.

"Now," Browning said to Willson, "I want you to get a chopper out here. And as many men as you can spare." He did not wait for a response but turned to Sally. "And you can dig out the survey maps. Go over them with Franklin and Harper. I want that lodge isolated."

He waited until the others in the room flew into motion then sat down at Sally's desk. He called directory assistance in Chicago and got the number for

Dr. John Muir. The doctor's answering service at first refused to put the call through.

Browning took a deep breath, and when he spoke his voice was quiet and even. "My name is Ivan Browning," he said. "I am with the FBI. Dr. Muir knows me. This is an emergency." He waited for this to sink in, then continued. "I will wait on the line. You will phone him. When you tell him who it is, he will accept the call."

When at last the call was put through, Muir answered quickly. He sounded worried.

"Agent Browning? How can I help you?"

"Dr. Muir, I'm sorry to bother you at home, but I'm calling you long distance from Minnesota and we have an emergency here."

There was a brief pause. "I understand. Is Michael Smith involved?"

"Yes, sir, he is." Briefly he explained what had happened. When he finished Muir was silent. "Dr. Muir, are you still there?"

"Yes."

"You understand my predicament?"

"I do."

"I believe Smith's story. I know this Sondra is the one we're after. But . . ."

"Agent Browning, I understand your concern. And it is well founded." He drew a deep breath. "Michael Smith is my friend. My good friend. I don't want to see him hurt."

"I understand that, sir."

"But neither do I wish to see any more innocent people hurt."

"That's gratifying, sir."

"Sondra Palmer is a very dangerous woman. You have never met anyone — or any*thing* — like her."

Browning listened but said nothing.

"If Michael Smith has . . . succumbed to the virus, then he is as dangerous as she is. Perhaps more so. She, at least, will be predictable."

"What exactly will he be like?"

"I don't know. For a long time we believed the virus worked in a cycle, but I have my doubts. It's a very strange disease. It impregnates itself in the nervous system and virtually becomes part of the host. I don't believe it's the virus itself that causes the symptoms to appear. I believe it acts as a conduit for a mode of behavior buried deeply within all of us. Michael, and this Sondra Palmer, may simply be allowing a deep-rooted, sublimated bestial behavior pattern to control them. The problem is that this pattern is augmented by contemporary human intelligence. A deadly combination."

"But, Smith . . ."

"If he has succumbed, he is not human."

Browning sighed. "What about my people? Are they in any danger of contracting this virus?"

"Not that I know of. But I'd try and avoid being bitten, if I were you. My guess is that death would ensue before infection."

"Thanks a lot," Browning said unhappily.

"Do you understand me?" Muir said.

"Yes, I understand," Browning said.

"Shoot first. Ask questions later."

"I understand."

"Please, call me when it's over."

"I will." He hung up and leaned back in the seat.

Outside, fat flakes of snow, buffeted by a wind that had gained force in the past hour, brushed the glass door of the station house and congregated in a shallow drift at its foot.

Sally Warner stepped up to the desk and regarded him curiously. The sudden flurry of work had taken her mind off earlier events, and she appeared reasonably cool.

"Everything alright?" Browning asked.

She nodded. "We're working out a viable displacement plan. Chopper's on its way from Fergus. A Blackhawk, on loan from the Reserve base. Should be here in about five minutes. Four extra men on board."

Browning nodded. "That's good. Because we may have a nasty situation here."

Four men. He hoped it would be enough.

They had been skiing for almost two hours, and it had grown progressively darker until now the forest was an inky wall. The walking path they followed, smothered in snow, was only slightly less dark than its surroundings. Tommy, who was in the lead, slowed noticeably as the darkness intensified, until Elizabeth's skis were almost on top of the boy. She slowed, turning to look over her shoulder.

"It's too dark! We can't see!"

Sondra slowed to a halt. In the darkness she was a pale shape, ghostly. "Faster." The word emerged as a hiss.

"My son is getting tired," Elizabeth said. "We need to rest."

The slouched outline of Sondra straightened slightly. "How much farther to the lodge?"

"I don't know. Not much, I don't think."

"Then move."

"But Tommy . . ."

"Mom, I'm okay."

Elizabeth spun at Tommy's voice. He was looking back at her, and even in the darkness she could see the glint of his eyes. Angry. *He's not frightened.* She did not know whether to be relieved or even more frightened at this realization. Since Sondra had attacked Bob Brisk, Tommy had been silent. She had feared he was entering some kind of shock state. No eleven-year-old should have witnessed that scene.

She turned again to Sondra. "We need a rest."

For a moment she thought she saw flash of white. *Teeth?*

"Move, or I will kill the boy."

"You can't get away with this!" She spoke in a sudden rush of anger. "They'll find the car. They'll follow."

"We'll be gone by then."

"We can't keep skiing forever."

Sondra laughed, a sound immediately swallowed by the snow and trees. "Not you. Michael and I."

"Michael's not that stupid. He won't come after you."

"He'll come for you and the boy."

Elizabeth sighed, weak with fatigue. The brief stop had allowed her legs to begin aching. They felt like lumps of rock beneath her.

"Move," Sondra said.

Tommy began moving again. For a moment Elizabeth did not follow. She turned and looked at Sondra. Desperately, voice weak and trembling, she said, "Please don't kill my son."

It sounded like Sondra chuckled, but Elizabeth was not sure. "I won't kill you," Sondra whispered. And what she said next drove a spear of terror into Elizabeth's heart; "Michael's going to do that."

Elizabeth felt herself stiffen, a chill spreading through her body. "Michael won't follow," she said stubbornly, voice hardly audible.

But Sondra looked back along their trail, into the darkness. When she turned she was smiling. "He's coming now," she said softly.

CHAPTER TWENTY-SIX

He had been in the forest less than an hour when the dusk began to turn slowly into night. The part of him that was Michael Smith, holding grimly to the helm, recognized the fall of night with a sudden pang of fear. But the other part of him, the larger part, welcomed the darkness. The forest glowed with a light of its own, a candle-lit cathedral, deep, endless.

The small remnant of pain had disappeared quickly as he fell into the spirit of the hunt. The exertion of moving through knee-deep snow took all his attention. Although the passage of three sets of skis had packed the snow to some extent, he still sank to midshin at every step. His prey's lead might increase, but he would eventually close the gap. They would have to stop.

His own body heat rose so quickly that soon it became necessary to remove his coat. He did so as he moved, holding the rifle in one hand while he shucked the opposite coat sleeve. He tossed the coat into the trees. The cold night air rushed across his torso, cooling him.

With every step he felt his control slipping. The thing he had become, the thing he had never given into before, was consuming him. Yet there was very little fear. Every part of him, both man and beast, was concentrating on the hunt.

Even without the ski tracks to follow, there would have been no problem. The smell of blood still clung to his prey, had followed them into the forest, a trail in the darkness that his senses could not miss. Inside the almost overpowering blood track, there were others. Elizabeth: faint trace of tobacco, sweat, mild perfume. Tommy: boy smell, sweat. A mingling odor from the two of them, very similar. It took him a while to recognize it as fear. It tainted their sweat like a dye. Unmistakable.

And the other.

It came from his prey.

A thick, pungent underodor that seemed to cut through even the blood mist. He had sensed it before, obscured by blood, at the cabin. But it had never reached him fully. It called to him now in a way he had never before experienced, in a way he could not understand. The small corner of his mind that had remained under control became smaller, pushed back. The creature that he now was, this mass of instinct and mindless reflex, surged in strength.

The blood hunger rose within him, a rising tide he could not deny.

But even stronger was the other hunger.

Newly awakened but somehow familiar. Focused on Sondra.

She was still ahead of him. But not for long.

He rushed headlong, eagerly, into the glow of the forest.

The Sikorsky H60 Blackhawk's landing gear rested on the shoulder of the highway. Its blades twirled almost lazily above the blacktop, creating its own minor blizzard in the midst of the approaching storm. Browning crouched low as he approached the chopper, painfully aware of the proximity of the blades above his head. *Not as close as you think.* The steady *thwup thwup thwup thwup thwup* sounded like distant thunder.

He leaned inside the open door, shielding his eyes against the snow tornado. There were eight passengers aboard the craft, pushed back against the dark walls, seated on the thin metal rail that ran around the perimeter of the cabin. The four deputies from Fergus Falls sat together against the rear wall, M-16's held tightly against their chests. They looked mean, angry. Browning had the impression their anger was directed at him for hauling them out on a night like this. Against the forward wall were Franklin, Sally Warner, Deputy Harper, and Sheriff Willson. Willson reached out a hand and helped Browning into the compartment.

"Everything ready?" He shouted above the roar of the engine.

Sally nodded.

Browning looked from one person to the next in the small compartment, making eye contact with each. "I want one thing understood," he said at last.

"This is not meant to be a surprise attack. This is a containment exercise. Miss Warner has gone over everything with you, and I want her instructions followed to the letter. Sheriff Willson and I will be dropped off in the clearing east of the lodge. The rest of you will land south, on the lake. Flank out as per Miss Warner's instructions. Do not, I repeat *do not* move in until I launch the flare."

There were nods of understanding, a few grunts.

"And no indiscriminate firing. Please. There are a mother and her son up there, and I don't want them hurt."

Deputy Harper asked: "What about the other two?"

Browning paused before answering, looking down at his hands, remembering John Muir's words. When he looked back up his face was stiff, emotionless. "You have the description of the man and woman. Shoot on sight. Shoot to kill."

Harper nodded, then looked away.

Sally Warner handed Browning a pair of molded fiberglass snowshoes, each in the shape of a figure eight about a foot long. Browning took the things and looked at them distastefully. Everybody else in the compartment was wearing a set.

"Deep snow," Sally explained. "You won't be able to move otherwise."

Browning nodded. "Everybody ready?"

Eight heads nodded in unison. Browning reached forward and stuck his head into the cockpit. The Blackhawk was designed for a flight crew of three in wartime, but now, with no armaments to control, the single pilot looked lonely and inadequate. Browning tapped him on the arm, and made an upward gesture with his thumb.

The pitch of the motor increased, the beat of the blades merging into a constant roar. The chopper lifted in an explosion of snow. Two searchlights speared down into the darkness, passing briefly over Bob Brisk's abandoned cruiser, visible for a moment in the artificial snow storm as swirling pillars of light and then as a brilliant patch on the highway.

Browning's stomach rumbled restlessly and his mouth swam with the taste of foul coffee, but he hung on to the bench beside Willson and held his breath. The Blackhawk moved out over the forest, and the darkness opened like a wound before the searchlights.

They came upon Black Lake Lodge suddenly. One moment they were skiing through the cathedral of trees, the next minute they had emerged into the stadium bowl of Black Lake; one moment surrounded in the silence of the forest, the next swept by a howling wind in the clearing. The change in light quality was profound; without the tree cover the night seemed almost bright.

Sondra skied ahead, passing both Elizabeth and Tommy easily, and approached the leaning bulk of the shack. It squatted on the edge of the lake like a piece of debris. Snow had drifted high along its northwest side, obscuring most of the rough-hewn logs. Half of a dark window was visible above the snow line. But the wind had kept the other sides relatively clear. It took Sondra only a moment, leaning into the door, to shatter the fragile lock and gain entry.

Inside, the cabin reeked of sawdust and mildew. Elizabeth and Tommy stood at the doorway, shivering, as Sondra entered the darkness. She returned in a moment with a rusty looking kerosene lamp. When she shook it, a small amount of liquid sloshed noisily in the tank. With Elizabeth's lighter, and using a strip of Tommy's plaid shirt, they got the lamp going. The light was feeble, sputtering, but good enough to navigate about the small shack.

There were two small beds, one in each back corner. One had a mattress, the other a covering of torn cardboard boxes. The cardboard was dark with frozen water. On the other bed they found a blanket, and Elizabeth and Tommy covered themselves, huddling in the corner, trying to stop their shivering. They were soaked with sweat, and now that the heat of exertion was dissipating, the cold was reaching icy fingers into their bodies. Elizabeth held Tommy's face crushed to her bosom, the blanket over his ears. The boy suffered silently.

Elizabeth watched Sondra, overcome with a combination of awe and revulsion. The other woman paced back and forth across the cabin, shoulders hunched, breathing deep and slow. Even in the darkness the shape of her body was clear: long, supple. *Beautiful, but terrible.*

Piece by piece, as she paced, she stripped the meager clothing from her body. First the leather jacket, flinging it into a dark corner. Naked from the waist up, her skin glistened with sweat. Her breasts, high and pointed, jutted proudly in the flickering light.

Next the leather pants, stripped with a cry of impatience or anger, thrown wildly after the jacket. Now, fully exposed to the cold air, she stalked back and forth.

Like a tiger, Elizabeth thought.

Her legs were bent strangely at the knee, giving her a crouched posture. As if she were ready to pounce. The slouch of her shoulders pushed her forearms forward, reaching. Every one of her tendons and muscles seemed taut, stretching the skin, rippling. And as she moved, she emitted a faint growl from her throat. Constant, thick. The flickering light from the kerosene lamp made her appear warm and inviting, but Elizabeth imagined the touch of that skin would be cold beyond imagining.

Periodically she would spin, eyes burning, and stare at the huddled form of Elizabeth and Tommy. At those moments, Elizabeth would hold her breath, clutching the blanket, squeezing Tommy more tightly. Sondra's eyes seemed to glow in the darkness, furious, mad. Her pale skin appeared almost translucent. Once she paused, leaned against the doorway, and rubbed her behind against the rough wood. The growl from her throat deepened, became almost a sound of pleasure. Her mouth opened in a languorous yawn of erotic invitation.

Bob Brisk didn't have a chance.

No man could resist that, she thought.

It was Sondra who broke the silence. Pausing in her relentless pacing, she turned to face Elizabeth. In the flickering light her lips seemed to quiver, but they had only curled in a smile. It was not a pleasurable smile.

"I don't know what he saw in you," she said. Her voice was heavy, almost hoarse. Elizabeth had seen a documentary a few months ago about the prevalence of phone sex lines, and she remembered now the taped voices they had played on the air. Sondra sounded like that. Controlled, erotic, hinting at God only knew what kind of sexual experiences.

"Michael's not like you," Elizabeth said defensively, and was surprised to hear that her voice was not trembling.

Sondra laughed. "We are the same kind."

"He doesn't *want* to be like you."

Sondra stepped closer, crouching to face Elizabeth at eye level. She inclined her head at an odd angle, as if she were seeing Elizabeth for the first time. Elizabeth tensed, tightened her grip on Tommy.

"Michael," Sondra said, "has been fighting himself."

Realizing that it might be a mistake, but with no other option available except submission, Elizabeth shook her head. "He's been fighting the virus. It's a disease. At least he has the courage to fight it."

Sondra's face tensed. "That's cowardice. If he had been courageous, he would have come with me three years ago."

"And become a monster."

Sondra laughed. It sounded like glass breaking. "A monster? In your eyes, perhaps." She smiled thoughtfully. "To its prey, the puma is a monster." Her eyes brightened. "Sleek black killer. To the deer, the wolf is a monster. Howling death."

Elizabeth shivered, willing herself not to understand what Sondra was saying.

"To any creature, the thing that walks among its numbers and kills is a monster. But even you . . . ," she reached out a long finger and touched Elizabeth's cheek. Elizabeth tensed, but did not pull away. "Even you can appreciate the beauty of the tiger, can you not?"

"But Michael is a man," Elizabeth protested.

Sondra stood upright, knees creaking, and looked scornfully down upon Elizabeth. "Michael was once a man. As I was once a woman." She began to pace again. "But we received a gift."

"You became infected with a mutant virus."

Sondra laughed. "Some gifts come in strange packages." She paused, turned to stare at Elizabeth. "And some gifts cannot be refused."

"You convinced yourself of that very easily, didn't you?" Elizabeth said. "Michael told me about you. You didn't have much fight in you."

Sondra spun, teeth bared. "Michael is a fool," she said.

Elizabeth knew she was treading on dangerous ground. But her fear had been tempered by a strain of anger. "So why did you wait three years to come after Michael? Why now?"

Sondra looked shocked, and then she smiled. "Michael didn't tell you?"

"Michael knows nothing," Elizabeth said. "He's been trying to forget you."

Now Sondra chuckled. "Poor Michael. He's been fighting himself for so long he doesn't know how to read the signs from his own body."

"What signs?"

"I knew it would not be easy. I knew he would

fight me. Even now, the only way he will give in to the virus is to save you. A bad reason, but the end result will be the same."

"What are you talking about?" Elizabeth felt a surge of panic building within her, panic that she was about to learn something she had no wish to know.

"Michael," Sondra said, almost sadly, shaking her head, "has no idea of the depth of changes wrought in us by the virus. Even I am at its mercy in this."

"In what?" Elizabeth's fear was now reflected in her voice.

"It appears the cycle will be about three years," Sondra said flatly. "I'm in heat. It's time to mate."

Elizabeth could not speak. The depth of her horror was unfathomable, her revulsion complete.

Sondra smiled, then suddenly cocked her head as if she had heard a faint sound. She sniffed the air, nose wrinkled. Then she looked down upon Elizabeth.

"He's here," she said.

CHAPTER TWENTY-SEVEN

He stood less than ten yards from the lodge, crouched low, elbows buried in snow as his hands clutched the rifle to his chest. The smells were strong. The ski tracks led to the door and ended. Through the partially obscured window on the northwest wall he could see flickering light, orange glow. Faintly, voices. Perhaps arguing.

But he did not advance. Not yet. He allowed the cold to surround him, cooling him after the journey. Falling flakes of snow tingled on his skin, melting instantly, trickling down his torso in cool lines. His breath billowed around his head in a cloud, then was swept away by the wind.

Michael Smith, backed into a far corner of his mind, experienced his surroundings with little contemplation. He was there; observing, but he was not in control. Not a part of him that he recognized, at least. The hunger was driving him, a hunger that seemed to be a mixture of desires. The blood trail still excited him, filled his mouth with saliva when he thought about it. Even now he drooled. But the other hunger was growing in strength, almost to the point where it encompassed the first. He could not distinguish between the two, and he was not sure he would have been able to identify them if he had.

The purpose of his journey was beginning to elude him, had begun to do so as soon as night had come. In the darkness the other part of him had grown stronger, it's desires and needs building within him. He recognized the odors of Elizabeth and Tommy in the air, sensed their terrible fear, and knew on some level that it was because of them he had come this far. But their plight had lost its meaning for him.

He focused, instead, on Sondra.

More than the other two, she was the reason he was here.

His breath quickened as he thought of her. His emotions boiled, confused. Anger. Desire. Hatred. Want. He could not sort them out.

He needed to move. His course would unfold before him naturally if he did so. Standing still only caused confusion.

He lifted one foot and stepped forward, but stopped in midstride. He held his breath, listening. The wind howled from the trees, tugging at his hair and ears. But above that sound, fading in and out, was another. He frowned as the sound intensified. Suddenly light exploded above the trees, lancing down into the clearing like sunlight. Michael cringed, holding up a hand to protect his hypersensitive eyes. The chopper roared over head, and for a moment he was surrounded in a funnel of snow. For an instant the light pinned him, then passed. The chopper moved out over the lake and began to swing around for another pass.

He did not wait for it to return. His legs exploded into activity and he lunged forward toward the cabin, a roar growing inside him until it erupted from his throat.

He hit the door with his shoulder at full stride, splintering the already damaged wood. It collapsed under his assault, swinging on its hinges to smash against the inside wall. The blow reduced his momentum sufficiently, and he stumbled to a halt just inside the threshold.

When the door crashed in Elizabeth screamed. Beneath the blanket, holding tightly to her, Tommy stiffened in surprise.

The roar of the helicopter overhead had given her a momentary surge of hope. Sondra had glanced upward, face twisted in anger. But when the thing that was Michael Smith stumbled to a halt in the middle of the shack all hope departed.

Like Sondra, he was bent at the knees, almost crouching, stooped at the waist. He held his arms before him, clutching her rifle, ready to pounce. The meager clothes he wore, a shirt and pants, were torn badly and completely soaked. The shirt, open to the waist, revealed his heaving chest and torso. Beneath his glistening skin muscles rippled and twitched. But it was his face that caught her and would not let her go.

The fine features that had so attracted her at first were now twisted out of all recognition. His lips trembled, pulled back from teeth that chattered unceasingly. Tendons in his neck formed high ridges in his flesh, pulling skin taut and shining. Gone was any hint of vulnerability. His eyes, glittering like ice in the paleness of his flesh, passed over her. They seemed to catalog her position, but did not otherwise acknowledge her existence. There was no recognition there.

"Oh, Michael," she said.

Both Sondra and Michael twisted their heads at her words. Michael merely responding to a sound, Sondra with glaring eyes. But in a moment, their attention was fixed firmly on each other.

Standing less than a yard apart, the two creatures began to circle each other warily. Sondra took small sideways steps, appearing almost fluid in motion, while Michael moved jerkily, like a poorly animated dinosaur from a sixties special effects movie, each step convulsive in appearance. The shack reverberated with the low growls that issued from their throats.

When Sondra finally spoke, Elizabeth held her breath in fear. The voice was low, hoarse, hardly intelligible. "Michael," she said. "Now you see how really different we are."

Michael, who had been in midstep, paused. He inclined his head toward her, as if he were striving to understand. His mouth moved spasmodically; inarticulate sounds emerged. Again he inclined his head, as if surprised at what he had done. His growl returned, but its intensity had changed. It sounded like a moan.

A moan of despair.

Sondra moved again, hands held out before her like claws, teeth bared. Her neck was still red with

321

Bob Brisk's blood.

"Don't worry," she said, "you are not yet familiar with your body, or what it can do."

Michael growled louder in response. Outside, the roar of the chopper passed again, and a saber of light slashed across the floor. Both creatures in the center of the room ignored it, focused only on each other.

Sondra smiled. "It will not take long. Soon you will be like me. Control will come. And with it, greater power." She tilted her head back, and what might have been a laugh erupted from her mouth. "You have denied yourself too long."

Elizabeth could not believe what she was seeing. How could this be the man who had been in her cabin only a few short hours ago?

I made love to this creature.

She closed her eyes and shook her head.

It's only a dream. It's a nightmare. It will be over soon.

A sudden roar from Michael caused her to open her eyes. He was staring at her, but still there was no recognition there. Elizabeth sobbed and hugged Tommy tightly. Beneath the blanket, the boy was unusually quiet.

Both Michael and Sondra had stopped circling and were now facing each other, motionless. Sondra stepped closer to him. Michael's nose wrinkled and his growled deepened.

"Yes, we are alike," Sondra said. "There are no others like us. We must be with each other."

Up to this point Michael had been holding the rifle in his hands, held out before him, as if he did not

322

know what it was for. Now he flung it away, and it clattered by the door. Elizabeth's eyes widened as she followed the weapon.

I could never reach it. They would tear me apart.

Close now, Michael reached out and touched Sondra's breast. His hand lingered on the pale flesh, squeezing it roughly. Sondra's mouth opened, her growl changing to a purr of pleasure. She took another step closer, encircling Michael with her arms. She began to move slowly, rubbing against him. Her pelvis moved in small circles, pressed against his thigh. Although their faces were close, they did not touch. Sondra's lips quivered, open, pink tongue pushing past her teeth.

Michael scrambled to hold her, thrusting his pelvis wildly. But she backed smoothly away, her growl almost a laugh.

"There is no time now," she said. "We must leave here."

For a moment it appeared that Michael would pay her no heed. He advanced on her, reaching eagerly. But Sondra hissed angrily and he paused.

"We will mate, my lover," she said. Michael's growl deepened. "But first you must come over completely. There can be no going back this time. No running."

Michael inclined his head, pricking his ears at every word.

"There must be no others," Sondra said, and nodded her head toward Elizabeth and Tommy.

Elizabeth cringed, holding her breath. Terror bubbled up within her, and she heard a soft moan escaping from her mouth. Michael turned to follow Sondra's gaze, and his eyes locked onto hers. "Michael . . ."

"Come over completely," Sondra said.

Again the growl in Michael's throat deepened, became almost a purring sound. His teeth clattered together and drops of spittle flew from his mouth. Elizabeth moaned in terror. Beneath the blanket, Tommy stirred. She had wanted to protect him from all this, save him from seeing any of it. But his hand pulled away the blanket, and his face came away from the protection of her bosom.

"Oh, God," Elizabeth whispered. "Please, no."

What might have been a grin exposed Michael's teeth fully. They gleamed in the flickering orange light of the kerosene lamp. If he had been a human once, he was not one now.

He growled loudly, sending a long string of saliva to the floor, then reached for her.

Browning felt sick.

The ride in the helicopter, the trees rushing by below, the cold wind whipping through the compartment, had done the initial job of loosening his innards. But it was the sight that had greeted them after the abrupt end of the trees, in the clearing by the lodge, that had started the rumbling deep in his gut.

The searchlights had passed over the crouching form of a man in the snow, a man dressed only in a torn shirt and pants.

"That's Smith!" Sally Warner had yelled.

Browning grunted, looking down. Smith had looked up, and Browning had caught his breath in surprise. He did not know what he had expected, but it had not been this. Smith's face was twisted out of all recognition, looking in the harsh light like a lump of melted wax. There were ridges where the skin should have been smooth, hollows where there should have been curves. And the lips were pulled back in what must have been a snarl.

"Christ!"

The searchlight passed over the crouched form, but even in the sudden darkness Browning saw the explosive movement of the man. Snow erupted in a cloud behind him as he lunged at the cabin. Then they were past, swinging out over the lake.

"What now?" Sally shouted.

"We stick to our plan," Browning said.

The chopper swung around for another look verifying the layout of the land as presented in the survey maps. The lodge was further from the trees than Browning had expected, looking very small against the white expanse of the lake. For a moment the searchlights passed over the roof of the lodge, bringing it into stark relief, and then swung out across the clearing and into the trees.

Browning forced his insides to calm down, then stood and leaned into the cockpit.

He shouted at the pilot. "What do you think?"

The narrow face turned toward him, orange and green in the glow of the instruments.

"I don't want to touch down on the ice, but I could hover. Your men could make the jump."

Browning nodded. "What about the clearing?"

"That's okay. But do you really want to be dropped that close?" The pilot returned his attention to the instrument panel. "Did you get a good look at that guy?"

Browning grunted. "We don't have a choice." He pulled himself back into the passenger compartment.

Sheriff Willson shouted across the compartment. "How does it look?"

Browning shrugged. "It'll have to do."

The chopper banked, and in the doorway the tops of the trees rushed by in a blur. They passed over the clearing, losing altitude, and finally skimmed across the surface of the lake. The chopper's forward motion slowly, finally stopped, and it dropped lower. It was like being in the eye of a hurricane. Immediately outside the compartment the air was still, but a few feet away the twirling blades whipped the snow into a blinding storm.

Browning nodded to the four men against the opposite wall. Sally stood, moved to the doorway, shielding her eyes from stray particles of ice and snow. Browning held out a hand to touch her elbow.

"Once Willson and I are in the clearing, we'll give you three minutes. That should be enough time to assume your positions."

Sally nodded. She looked dangerous.

To the whole cabin Browning said: "Wait for the flare. It's too dark to see anything otherwise. The second it goes up, move in." He looked from face to face. "Remember, nothing gets out of there."

For a second it looked like Sally smiled, then she leaned forward and disappeared into the whirling snow. Harper followed, clutching a rifle across his chest. Franklin nodded once to Browning, then jumped. Then, one by one, the four deputies from

326

Fergus Falls made the jump, until only Browning and Willson remained in the compartment. Browning leaned into the cockpit and gave the thumbs up signal. The chopper engine roared, and the craft lifted out of its own storm. Down below, Browning had a glimpse of the dark shapes scattering, moving with obvious purpose.

Then the Blackhawk swung down into the clearing, throwing snow into another tornado. For a moment it hovered, and then touched down with a thud. Browning turned to Willson.

"Let's do it, Sheriff."

Willson grunted, then grinned.

The two men jumped down into the darkness.

CHAPTER TWENTY-EIGHT

Michael Smith was not quite sure what had made him pause.

He had been in the process of reaching for the shuddering mass of fear beneath the blanket, his entire attention focused on satisfying the part of his hunger that these two could meet, when a small hand had emerged from the fabric and tugged it lower.

The face thus revealed was small, pinched in terror, glistening with sweat and tears. The brown eyes that pinned him with their gaze were wide with disbelief. But the smell of fear emanating from the two bodies beneath the blanket was not pure. Within the acrid stench of terror, almost smothered, there coiled another emotion.

Behind him, Sondra growled. "Take them!"

He turned his head to regard her, feeling the surge of the other hunger within him, the newly risen force that was sweeping him away. He turned back to his quarry.

"Mike?"

The sound of his name, coming from the boy,

struck a chord within him, and for the first time since the coming of the darkness, Michael Smith felt a small resurgence of the control he had lost. Hands reaching out to claw, he paused. He shuddered, then cocked his head to study the boy.

"Tommy . . ." His voice was so warped that the name emerged as grunt.

But the boy recognized it, and responded. His free hand reached out toward Michael. "Hey, Mike."

This creature, within which his soul struggled for a foothold amid the roiling power of instinct and half-understood hungers, seemed to cringe in pain at the sound of his name. With great difficulty, Michael regarded the woman and boy huddled before him. He tried to focus on the impurity of emotion he sensed coming from them. He separated the fear, and ignored it.

What remained was also pure. And he could hardly believe or understand its presence. *Love.*

And from it he gained the small advantage he needed to secure his control. Dimly, a memory played out in his mind. In it he held the woman, while across the room the boy regarded him. He focused on those eyes and sensed, in the memory, *something* pass between himself and the boy. *A promise.* He had nodded. Given his assent.

But to what?

It had never been clear to him before, but it became so now.

That night that seemed so long ago and was not, his silent nod had spoken volumes: *Don't worry. Whatever happens, I won't hurt you. I'll protect you.*

Now the force of that promise, rooted within his

trapped soul, bloomed fully. His shuddering intensified. For the first time he saw them clearly, huddled
before him, cowering before his assault. Elizabeth's
face was pressed to Tommy's head, her eyes closed,
waiting. While Tommy watched him, knowing what
was about to happen, *forgiving* him for it.

Michael shuddered, fighting for control of his
muscles. He lowered his outstretched hands. "I'm
. . . sorry," he said, voice weak.

Behind him, Sondra's low growl turned into a
snarl. "Kill them!"

Michael spun around to face her. "No."

For a moment Sondra appeared shocked, an emotion that even managed to show itself on the savage
twisting of her features. Then she arched her neck
and laughed. "Michael, you fool. Don't you realize
you can never go back to what you were?"

Michael growled. "It doesn't matter. I can't become like you, either."

"You are close, lover, very close." She took a tentative step toward him, head held forward, bent at the
waist. The energy potential in her stance was frightening.

"I'm caught between," Michael said.

Sondra stepped sideways, and Michael moved to
block her advance against Elizabeth and Tommy. She
smiled.

"You've hardly tasted the power that can be
yours," she said. "Think, Michael! To walk among
these inferiors, doing as you please, taking what you
like."

"At your side," Michael said softly.

"Yes." The word emerged as a hiss.

330

Michael shook his head. "I'd rather be like them than like you."

Sondra paused. Her arms hung low, knuckles scraping the sagging wooden floor. Her breasts, dripping sweat, rose and fell to the rhythm of her breathing. Her fingers curled, uncurled, nails like talons poking the flesh of her palm. Her eyes locked onto his and a soft purring noise came from her throat.

"Feel your hunger, Michael," she said. "Feel your hunger for me."

She stepped toward him, but he did not move.

"No other woman can satisfy your need."

As she spoke, Michael again became aware of the strong odor emanating from her. The air was rich with her pheromones, and perhaps his own, plugging into his receptors, fogging his mind to all else but the hunger. The coals in his loins began, again, to glow.

"Have me, Michael," she said.

His lust rose within him like a wave, pushing him, crashing over him. It a moment he would succumb to it again.

He screamed his protest. "NO!" Knowing that if he did not direct his energy into action he would be hers again, he launched himself toward her.

She was not expecting the attack, and his shoulder caught her just above her breasts. She toppled backward, crashing into the cardboard covered bed frame. Michael collapsed on top of her.

Beneath him she screamed in anger and returned his attack. Her teeth snapped at his throat, but he held her down. Hands free, she raked her talons down his torso. Michael screamed in agony, the skin of his chest shredded and bleeding, and jumped away from her.

Sondra scrambled to her feet. In the middle of the room, Michael gingerly touched the wounds on his chest. His fingers came away dripping blood. Mingled with sweat, it dripped down his stomach and to the floor.

"You fool!" she said.

Michael growled, tensing himself to attack again. But Sondra acted first. Her legs straightened and she pounced. Michael held up his arms to ward her off, but her momentum was so great that he was knocked backward. He crashed into the door and it exploded outward. With Sondra pinned to his chest, reaching to rip his throat out, he spilled out of the lodge and into the snow. The force of landing separated them.

The coolness of the snow momentarily numbed the stinging pain in his chest. He clambered to his feet at the same instant as Sondra, and crouched to face her.

The creature before him looked less like a human being than she ever had before. Her face writhed, out of control, lips curled back from gleaming teeth that snapped reflexively. His blood trickled down from her fingers, creating small rivers along her arms.

"I should have realized you were too weak to come over," she said. As she spoke she began to circle him, and Michael turned warily to face her. "You have been fighting this thing too long. You have forsaken the gift that would have made you a god!"

Michael shook sweat from his head. "Not a god. A devil."

Sondra laughed. "I could never mate with you. You pitiful creature."

Michael said nothing, tensing for her attack.

332

"First," Sondra said, "I'm going to kill you." She grinned, and saliva dripped from her teeth, down her chin, and across her breasts. "Then I'm going to rip out the boy's throat as his mother watches. And then I'm going to kill *her*."

Michael froze. Her words stabbed into him like daggers. Inside of him the fires of instinct and of beastly hunger were instantly quelled. It felt as if his blood had turned to ice water. A shudder passed through him, and a blade of anger, razor-sharp and needle-pointed, rose from his gut and cut through him. He had been in the process of moving, turning to face Sondra, and now he stopped. His eyes focused on her, and he heaved in a shuddering breath.

"You fucking bitch," he said. His voice was cold, inhuman, and as he spoke his lips turned up into a tight smile.

Sondra immediately realized she had made a mistake. She stepped warily backward, and for the first time Michael detected a trace of fear in her face. Her eyes darted from side to side, seeking an escape route, anything to help her with this new creature she had inadvertently wakened. Michael smiled and pounced.

Sondra fell under his attack, screaming, teeth snapping. His strength was greater than it had ever been before, and he moved with a deadly precision impossible under pure instinct. Now, although the viral symptoms were still peaking, he was in complete control. He was a man, with a monster's strength and speed. His fist smashed into her nose, sending her toppling backward, arms windmilling. She collapsed into the snow, gasping for breath. The fear in her eyes was mixed with a look of absolute, utter hatred.

Michael pounced again, slamming his elbows into her ribcage. Her growl was cut short, the air expelled from her lungs in a gasp. He stooped over her and circled her throat with his hands.

For a moment their eyes locked, and the hatred fled from Sondra's. Now there was only fear, leaving no room for anything else. Absolute. All encompassing. Her lips strained to close over her teeth, to stop the snapping reflex, an act of submission. Her breath came quickly, in gasps, strained by his squeezing hands.

He could rip her throat out now, just by curling his fingers sharply. Tear her life out. Destroy her completely.

But he paused.

Beneath him, throat arched in submission, Sondra Palmer looked defeated. She looked fragile, human. Like a child. Her eyes were wild with fear, pleading with him.

Michael growled in dismay. Part of him wanted to destroy this creature. But another part, the part now in control, could not. He released her and stood. Suddenly the cold seemed deeper, the wind slightly sharper. He shivered.

"I can't kill you." His voice was hoarse.

Sondra clambered quickly to her feet, rubbing her throat. Her eyes flashed. She breathed deeply, watching him carefully.

"You weakling," she said. "You had me."

Michael hung his head, now feeling the pang of defeat himself. *If I kill her, I'm just like her.* Sondra began to growl again.

"I know I can beat you now," she said, stepping toward him. "You can't kill me!" Her face glowed, eyes widening in triumph. But suddenly the victor's glee vanished.

Sensing something, another presence, both Michael and Sondra looked up toward the lodge. Elizabeth and Tommy had emerged.

Elizabeth was holding the rifle. She pulled the finger lever, the sudden *click-click* of metal upon metal cutting the night, and a shell moved into the chamber. She raised the weapon, pressing the stock into her shoulder, and aimed it levelly at Sondra.

"He can't kill you," she said evenly. "But I can."

Browning watched the scene unfolding in the clearing with a mixture of horror and wonder.

Flickering orange light, cutting out of the shattered lodge doorway in a widening swath, provided hellish illumination for the two battling creatures. Beside him, crouched in the snow, Sheriff Willson groaned in disbelief.

"My God," Willson muttered.

Browning held up a hand to silence the other man. There was another minute before he would launch the flare. Perhaps in that time the two creatures would have killed each other. He fervently hoped so. He had no wish to face either of them.

But what of Elizabeth Turner and her boy? Were they in the cabin? Were they alright?

Instinct told him they were. *That's why these two are fighting.*

It appeared that Michael Smith was getting the

upper hand, and Browning was relieved.

Kill the bitch.

But when Smith finally stood, hanging his head in defeat, Browning gasped. What was going on? He had her! He had her down! Now he was letting her regain her footing.

Then Elizabeth Turner and the boy emerged from the cabin. The Turner woman was holding a rifle and she said something. Distance made it impossible to understand her words, but he saw clearly that the two creatures stiffened, turning toward her.

"Jesus . . ," he muttered.

Suddenly the night was shattered by a scream. It was the Sondra Palmer creature. She crouched, and then in an explosion of motion, limbs churning the snow into a cloud, she bounded toward Elizabeth Turner.

Browning raised his flare gun. It was still too early, but there was no other choice.

He shouted, "Now! Now!", and pulled the trigger.

The flare arched into the sky, a brilliant star, filling the darkness with light.

CHAPTER TWENTY-NINE

Elizabeth held her sight steadily on Sondra, finger squeezing the trigger almost to its fire point. Tommy stood slightly behind her, watching in silence. The cold and the wind seemed like distant things, hardly impinging upon her senses at all.

The two once human creatures regarded her in simple stupid surprise.

When Sondra screamed, her mask of disbelief twisting into one of rage, Elizabeth stiffened and her breath caught in her throat. For half a second the rifle wavered from its target, and she drew it back immediately. But it was too late. Sondra was moving.

Elizabeth gasped, realizing in horror that the creature was coming right for her. Tommy yelped, stumbling backward. She tried to steady the rifle, tried to bring Sondra's body back into the line of sight, but it was no good. The creature was a blur of motion, moving intentionally erratically to avoid being shot. One instant the savage face passed across the sight, and then was gone, the next instant an arm, then gone.

Shoot! Or you're dead!

She leveled the rifle at the advancing storm of churning limbs. She started to squeeze down on the trigger.

And that's when all hell broke loose.

Daylight exploded above the lake. A miniature sun was born, and immediately began to sink. At the same instant, she heard a man's voice, screaming, and suddenly there was motion everywhere.

But it was the light . . .

The scene that had been, only an instant earlier, playing itself out in the flickering glow of a single kerosene lamp, now found itself displayed in brilliant clarity. It took Elizabeth only a moment to realize what the thing was. A flare!

Shadows were born in a second, moving eerily across the snow as the flare descended.

Sondra stumbled to a halt, hand raised to protect her eyes from the blinding light.

A memory flashed through Elizabeth's mind, of Michael squinting in pain in the afternoon's sunlight. Now, experiencing the hypersensitivity the virus produced, Sondra was doing the same thing.

Sondra was immobile, cringing in agony, in Elizabeth's sights.

Elizabeth did not hesitate. She squeezed the trigger.

A dark keyhole appeared in the back of Sondra's raised hand, her head jerked as if she'd been punched, and then a spray of blood and tissue erupted from the side of her face. The sound of the shot echoed across the lake. Sondra stumbled forward. Part of her skull above her left eye was missing, a ragged hole spilling blood. She blinked, staring

338

at Elizabeth in disbelief.

Grey eyes, filled with hatred, locked onto Elizabeth's. Her breasts now dripped with her own blood, heaving ragged breath after ragged breath. She stood on wobbly legs, hands held out before her like claws. She began to move forward again, now slowly, barely keeping her balance.

Elizabeth heard herself moaning, heard the moan quickly change pitch into something out of control.

She pulled the lever, ejecting the spent cartridge and loading another into the chamber. Sondra was less than ten feet away, lips pulled back in a snarl, teeth snapping.

Behind her, Tommy whimpered. "Mom?"

Elizabeth steaded the rifle and fired again.

This time the bullet caught Sondra in the neck. A chunk of flesh disapeared in a bright red explosion, and the cry emerging from Sondra's lips was silenced. Another gush of blood splashed across her breasts.

And still she came.

Elizabeth stepped backwards, not wanting to believe the nightmare being enacted before her. She pulled the lever, loading another shell. She steadied the stock against her shoulder and aimed carefully. She exhaled, then squeezed the trigger. Her shoulder was already numb from the previous two shots, and this one sent her stumbling backward. The bullet slapped into Sondra's forehead. A spray of brain and bone belched from the back of her skull, filling the air with a fine pink mist. Her grey eyes widened, and her forward motion changed into a precarious stumble.

But she continued onward.

Elizabeth shook her head in disbelief, letting the rifle swing from her hand by the barrel. She heard the cry emerging from her lips, a scream rising from the pit of her mind, filled with all her horror and anger and hatred.

Die, damn you! Die!

She ran at Sondra, galvanized by her own scream, lifting the weapon over her shoulder. With the magazine almost full, it weighed over eight pounds. As she approached the other woman she swung the rifle like a baseball bat. But the stock thudded into Sondra's suddenly lifted hand. It felt, to Elizabeth, like she had hit a tree, and she dropped the rifle to the ground.

Sondra's grey eyes locked onto her's, and a faint sound emerged from her shattered throat. The claw that had stopped the swing of the rifle, dripping a mixture of her own and Michael's blood, reached out. Elizabeth cried and stepped back.

And then the life departed Sondra's eyes.

Carried by her own forward momentum, she fell face first to the snow. For a moment her fingers clawed at the white powder, digging themselves deeper, and then she was still.

Elizabeth's breath hissed out in a whimper.

For the first time she had a good look at what was happening in the clearing. There seemed to be an army descending upon them from all directions. Two men, running from the forest, were shouting something that she could not understand.

That's when Michael drew her attention. His head was raised back, the tendons of his throat pushing at his skin like steel cables. A howl emerged from his mouth. He faced her, but she could not read his twisted expression. With a cry, he bounded toward her.

She knew only one thing: *He would get to her before any of the others.*

Acting on relfex, she picked up the rifle, jacked another shell into the chamber, and aimed.

After the darkness of the night, the light was agony. But by squinting his eyes to slits the pain was bearable. Everything had happened so quickly, in such a blur of motion, light, and sound, that he felt it had all been a dream. But the crack of the gun had been real.

It was not seeing Sondra collapse that made him scream, but the sudden feeling of horror that had come upon him, the realization that it had all come to *this:* this mindless play of terror and violence.

When he moved forward, it was not so much that he had a plan of action as simply a need to move. Standing there, the weight of everything had been pressing down on him. A cold hard reality that he could not bear.

He watched Elizabeth raise the rifle, feeling nothing but the detachment of one who has accepted, long ago, that they are doomed. He moved steadily, smoothly, so as not to disrupt her aim.

Shoot! End it! Kill me, please!

He focused on the dark hole of the rifle's barrel, waiting for the sudden flash of fire, the impact of the bullet.

But it did not come.

When he reached Sondra's body he paused, looking down at her.

She smelled dead. He imagined she had smelled dead for a long, long time. The way he himself must smell.

He reached out and turned her body over. Her grey eyes were still open, but now flat and lifeless. In death she looked defeated. Worse, she looked *cheated*. The eyes seemed to focus on him, accusing him.

Her muscles had relaxed in death, slackening, falling back into their old contours.

Just a woman.

He shook his head sadly. Not even that. *Just a girl.*

Her body looked small, wasted. Destroyed. And with her, the virus within. He directed his anger at the virus.

You couldn't keep her alive, damn you!

He stood, turning his attention again to Elizabeth. She was shaking and her face was wet with tears. He stepped toward her, arm held out.

"Michael, don't."

He tried to smile, but his lips were already pulled too far back from his teeth. One more step, and the barrel of the gun pressed into his chest. He circled the cold metal with his hand, holding it steady.

"Shoot," he said. The word emerged as a bark, but Elizabeth must have understood.

She shook her head.

"Please," Michael said. "End it for me."

"No. I won't."

He moaned. "You don't understand. I'm just like her. I can't fight it any more."

Again she shook her head. Looking at her, he felt a tide of sorrow rising within him for all that he had become and all that he had lost. Elizabeth seemed to sense this, and more tears spilled from her eyes.

"Michael, you're *not* like her."

He started to respond, when he heard his name shouted.

"Smith! Get away from them!"

He released the rifle and spun around. Less than ten yards away stood Browning and Sheriff Willson. Michael crouched, regarding them speculatively. From the lake, and from behind the cabin, other shapes began to emerge, moving quickly, crouched low.

If he had followed Sondra, this group would have been easy to escape. *Like gods.* The thought rose, and he qaushed it instantly.

"Move away, Smith!" Browning was holding out a revolver, pointed in his general direction. Beside him, Sheriff Browning was aiming a nasty looking M-16.

One sudden move, and they'll shoot me. The thought was comforting.

The other figures moved in quickly. He recognized Sally Warner, Franklin, and Deputy Harper. The others he did not know. All of them brought their weapons to bear upon him.

One sudden move.

He crouched, ready to pounce.

"No!" Tommy Turner ran from behind the protection of his mother and stood in front of Michael. The boy reached out a hand toward him.

Michael blinked in shock. "Tommy, move," he grunted.

Tommy shook his head. His brown eyes locked onto Michael's, and for a moment the man and boy experienced the silent communication of their earlier promise. Tommy turned away, facing Browning.

"He helped us!"

"Move out of the way, son."

But as the FBI man spoke, Elizabeth too stepped closer to Michael. She reached out and touched his arm. When he faced her, he found himself looking directly into her brown eyes. Before he could move, she had encircled him with her arms, drawing herself closer to him. Her head nestled on his shoulder, and he felt her warm breath on his neck. She spoke softly, but even muffled against his skin he understood her.

"Michael, we love you."

It seemed, then, that all his energy left him. The strength he had been drawing from the viral symptoms disappeared, swept away as if by a broom. His chest throbbed painfully, and every muscle in his body felt as if it were burning up. Beneath him his legs trembled.

In a voice hardly more than a whisper he said, "I'm sorry."

Then he collapsed into darkness, and silence.

Browning launched the second flare, a red one, signaling the chopper to move in, and supervised the cleanup operation. Despite the fact that he was unconscious, and in spite of Elizabeth Turner's protestations, Michael Smith was restrained with handcuffs. Browning had seen what the man was capable of and had no wish to find out more in the confines of the chopper.

Largely because there was not enough room on board, but also by popular demand, the body of Sondra Palmer was left behind for a second trip. Browning stood over the crumpled corpse, looking down in sorrow.

Just a girl, changed by a disease she did not understand. How would she have turned out if things had been different?

Sally Warner came up beside him. With the tip of her snowshoe she nudged the dead girl's arm.

"I can't believe that Bob Brisk was manipulated by *this*."

Browning shook his head. "Nobody is impressive when they're dead."

Sally shrugged, then sighed.

Browning sensed that something was bothering her, and he had a pretty good idea what it was. "I wouldn't be too hard on your ex-partner, if I were you."

She turned to him sharply. "Why's that? He conspired with a monster. He might be partially responsible for three murders."

"But he was just a man," Browning said quietly. "I'd hate to find out what I would have done in his position. Everybody has their weaknesses."

For a long minute he thought Sally Warner was going to burst into tears, but finally she looked away from the corpse on the ground and into Browning's face. She sighed deeply.

"Bob Brisk was a damned good cop," and now her eyes did brim. "I guess it will take me a while to forgive him."

"I expect it will," Browning said.

He put his arm around her shoulder and guided her back toward the helicopter. In the glow of the searchlights reflecting off snow, her face looked sculpted, clean and pure.

Be pretty if she'd smile, he thought wistfully.

"How about when we get back I take you out for a good hot meal and a couple of drinks?"

She turned to him, eyes narrowed. Then her face relaxed. And, miracle of miracles, her lips curled into a bright smile.

Damned if I wasn't right!

"You got a date, Fed," she said.

EPILOGUE

Michael Smith studied the sky through the room's small window. Patches of blue were showing through the grey, and the easy movement of the clouds was lulling him, pushing him back into sleep.

He had woken, groggy, about two hours ago. The nurse, who informed him he was in the Fergus Falls Hospital and had been here, sleeping, for three days, force-fed him a bowl of hot soup. He had accepted eagerly.

The events he remembered were swathed in darkness, dreamlike. He remembered Sondra stumbling onward into the rain of bullets, finally collapsing into the snow. Dead. And Brisk. He remembered Brisk's body, surrounded in blood, blood everywhere. But somehow he could not work up any concern over the images. He could not grieve for the people involved.

Sondra was dead. The nightmare was over. After all these years, it was finally over. From the fog, it was the only thing he grasped firmly.

But some memories stuck out with sharp clarity. Like Tommy Turner's eyes. Like the words Elizabeth

347

had spoken, face pressed to his neck.

He thought of these things as he studied the sky.

But his reverie was interrupted by the young nurse who stuck her head in the door, smiling. "You have visitors, Mr. Smith."

The door opened wider, and Elizabeth and Tommy came into the room. Tommy stepped over to the bed, and peered closely at Michael's face.

"Hi, Tom," Michael said.

Tommy nodded, smiling, then walked back out of the room without another word.

Elizabeth took the seat by the bedside. "You'll see him later," she said. "I told him just a quick look, then I wanted to see you alone."

Michael arched his eyebrows. "Oh?"

Elizabeth smiled, and shook her head. "You're not well enough for that yet."

Michael pouted in mock disappointment. "How long will I be in here?"

Elizabeth reached out a hand and squeezed his. Her skin was warm, smooth. Michael squeezed back.

"That's what I want to talk about," she said. "I've been talking to Agent Browning. He said he called your doctor in Chicago. John Muir?"

Michael nodded.

"He's arranged to fly you down to Chicago tonight. Muir is expecting you."

Again Michael nodded.

"And I've been thinking about what you said earlier," she paused, eyes questioning his. "About coming to Chicago with you."

"Ah."

"Is the invitation still open?"

Michael curled his lips thoughtfully and then turned serious. "When I get back, I'm submitting myself to a thorough research program," he said. "This is something I talked about with John Muir."

"I know."

"I'm going to become the focus of a lot of attention," Michael said. "It won't be fun. They're going to be calling me a monster. That'll probably be the least of it."

"Yes, but you'll be *my* monster." She smiled.

Michael did not smile back. He held her hand tightly. "There may not be a cure."

Elizabeth shook her head. "There will be."

Michael opened his mouth to argue, but Elizabeth leaned forward and kissed him on the lips. When he tried to speak, she kissed harder.

"There will be a cure," she said when they parted.

"What about your life here?"

She shrugged. "We want to be with you. For now, that means Chicago."

"We could come back here eventually," Michael said.

"Eventually," she said, nodded. She released his hand, touched the bandages on his chest. "How are your wounds?"

Michael shrugged. In fact, they did not hurt at all. "That's one thing about this virus. It cuts the time of cell regeneration by about fifty percent."

"Good."

"John Muir also told me one of the beneficial side effects will likely be an increased life span. I could live to be a hundred."

Elizabeth smiled, reached over and kissed him.

"That's fine, darling. Longevity runs in my family too."

With that, she kissed him again and left the room. For a short while Michael watched the clouds outside his window. Soon, he slept.

TERROR LIVES!

THE SHADOW MAN   (1946, $3.95)
by Stephen Gresham
The Shadow Man could hide anywhere — under the bed, in
the closet, behind the mirror . . . even in the sophisticated
circuitry of little Joey's computer. And the Shadow Man
could make Joey do things that no little boy should ever do!

SIGHT UNSEEN   (2038, $3.95)
by Andrew Neiderman
David was always right. Always. But now that he was growing up, his gift was turning into a power. The power to know
things — terrible things — that he didn't want to know. Like
who would live . . . and who would die!

MIDNIGHT BOY   (2065, $3.95)
by Stephen Gresham
Something horrible is stalking the town's children. For one
of its most trusted citizens possesses the twisted need and
cunning of a psychopathic killer. Now Town Creek's only
hope lies in the horrific, blood-soaked visions of the MID-
NIGHT BOY!

TEACHER'S PET   (1927, $3.95)
by Andrew Neiderman
All the children loved their teacher Mr. Lucy. It was aston-
ishing to see how they all seemed to begin to resemble Mr.
Lucy. And act like Mr. Lucy. And kill like Mr. Lucy!

*Available wherever paperbacks are sold, or order direct from the
Publisher. Send cover price plus 50¢ per copy for mailing and handling to Zebra Books, Dept. 2682, 475 Park Avenue South, New
York, N.Y. 10016. Residents of New York, New Jersey and Pennsylvania must include sales tax. DO NOT SEND CASH.*

THE FINEST IN SUSPENSE!

THE URSA ULTIMATUM   (2130, $3.95)
by Terry Baxter

In the dead of night, twelve nuclear warheads are smuggled north across the Mexican border to be detonated simultaneously in major cities throughout the U.S. And only a small-town desert lawman stands between a face-less Russian superspy and World War Three!

THE LAST ASSASSIN   (1989, $3.95)
by Daniel Easterman

From New York City to the Middle East, the devastating flames of revolution and terrorism sweep across a world gone mad . . . as the most terrifying conspiracy in the history of mankind is born!

FLOWERS FROM BERLIN   (2060, $4.50)
by Noel Hynd

With the Earth on the brink of World War Two, the Third Reich's deadliest professional killer is dispatched on the most heinous assignment of his murderous career: the assassination of Franklin Delano Roosevelt!

THE BIG NEEDLE   (1921, $2.95)
by Ken Follett

All across Europe, innocent people are being terrorized, homes are destroyed, and dead bodies have become an unnervingly common sight. And the horrors will continue until the most powerful organization on Earth finds Chadwell Carstairs—and kills him!

DOMINATOR   (2118, $3.95)
by James Follett

Two extraordinary men, each driven by dangerously ambiguous loyalties, play out the ultimate nuclear endgame miles above the helpless planet—aboard a hijacked space shuttle called DOMINATOR!

Available wherever paperbacks are sold, or order direct from the Publisher. Send cover price plus 50¢ per copy for mailing and handling to Zebra Books, Dept. 2682, 475 Park Avenue South, New York, N.Y. 10016. Residents of New York, New Jersey and Pennsylvania must include sales tax. DO NOT SEND CASH.